HEAVY RAIN BEGAN AGAIN AND WE FOUGHT TO PUT UP THE TENT. I TIED SOME OF THE ROPES AROUND TREES AND KEPT THE REST ANCHORED WITH BIG STONES. WE CRAWLED INSIDE WITH ALL WE HAD MANAGED TO SAVE FROM THE BEACH, AND SAT, BREATHING THE FOUL SCORCHED SCENT OF EACH OTHER'S SKIN.

Breakfast was flying about in the sea and wind outside, and I wasn't eager to risk hunting it. The cabin bread didn't look like breakfast. It looked like thick dry slabs of cardboard and tasted like a sample left behind by Captain Cook. But it staved off hunger, and we sucked limes that Matthew had stuffed into his rucksack in the flight from the tent.

As the day wore on the sun emerged, the sea grew calmer, and the wind died down. We went out. The island looked littered and wrecked, like a dustbin overturned by stray dogs.

Tomorrow we would build a shelter . . .

£1.00
D0727602

TONY WILLIAMS

ISLAND OF DREAMS

A SIGNET BOOK

SIGNET

Published by the Penguin Group
Penguin Books Ltd, 27 Wrights Lane, London w8 5tz, England
Penguin Books USA Inc., 375 Hudson Street, New York, New York 10014, USA
Penguin Books Australia Ltd, Ringwood, Victoria, Australia
Penguin Books Canada Ltd, 10 Alcorn Avenue, Toronto, Ontario, Canada m4v 3b2
Penguin Books (NZ) Ltd, 182–190 Wairau Road, Auckland 10, New Zealand

Penguin Books Ltd, Registered Offices: Harmondsworth, Middlesex, England

First published 1994
1 3 5 7 9 10 8 6 4 2

Copyright © Tony Williams, 1994
All rights reserved

The moral right of the author has been asserted

Filmset by Datix International Limited, Bungay, Suffolk
Printed in England by Clays Ltd, St Ives plc
Set in 10/13 pt Plantin

Except in the United States of America, this book is sold subject
to the condition that it shall not, by way of trade or otherwise, be lent,
re-sold, hired out, or otherwise circulated without the publisher's
prior consent in any form of binding or cover other than that in
which it is published and without a similar condition including this
condition being imposed on the subsequent purchaser

For Cath, Craig, Matthew and Stacey

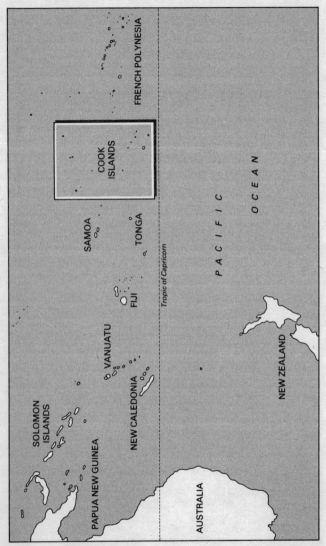

The South Pacific: the Cook Islands

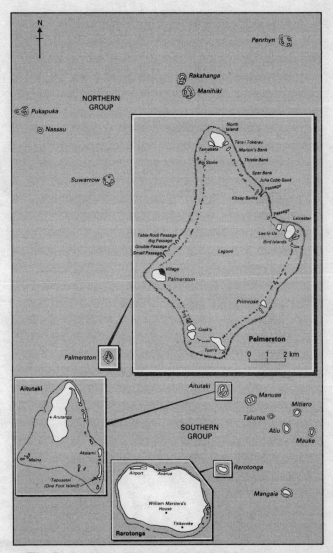

The Cook Islands: Rarotonga, Aitutaki and Palmerston

ACKNOWLEDGEMENTS

My thanks are due to William Richard and Tepu on Rarotonga for welcoming us into their family; to Richard Marsters, Palmer and Teré on Aitutaki, for all their help; to John James Marsters and the people of Palmerston for permission to use one of their beautiful islands; and to Kauraka Kauraka for all the cultural understanding he gave us. Cath's mother and father, Arthur and Brenda, provided support without which Cath would not have been able to join me on my first venture to the South Seas. My thanks are also due to Hannah Renier, without whom the book would not have been completed, to Harry Page and the *Daily Mirror* for the use of photographs, and to my agent Jeffrey Simmons, whose invaluable guidance led to its being published.

'This is my caretaker, Tony Williams,' the Headmaster said. As in This is My Employee, which was strange, because West Glamorgan County Council paid my wages, not him. I was an embarrassment, and he looked a bit cross about me being there at all. If I hadn't gone on about getting rehoused, the officials wouldn't have turned up in the first place.

After they had grunted a response to this introduction they fell quiet. They stood shoulder to shoulder like penguins at the zoo, peering. Four from Education and two from Housing and the Headmaster, all squashed into our living-room. They huddled together right inside the front door.

'Well, you'll want to look round, then.'

I was facing them with my back pressed up against a big bubble in the wallpaper. I had stuck that paper back about fourteen times; I tried Superglue, everything. They trooped upstairs past me, smirking apologetically at Cath, who was sitting on the settee with her pregnancy bump high in front of her. We sat there every night, watching television till the children needed to sleep, then we pushed the settee back and heaved the mattress on to the floor.

They all shuffled into the front room upstairs, with its damp mattress on an old bedstead, and its view down the hill past the houses and over Swansea Bay. They just stood there, staring, ignoring me as I sidled round to the front of the crowd. Some of them shifted their briefcases from hand to hand. One of the men from Housing stared upwards. He looked aghast. The ceiling bellied out brown and black and the wall above the picture rail was covered in swart mould. I was glad he'd noticed.

'This is the front bedroom, is it?' asked a man from Education, conversationally. Perceptive or what. I said, 'It would be if we could use it. Look under the bed here, it's all rotten and you can smell the mice.'

The front row inclined with polite interest to look at the floor under the lino where it was all chewed away. The Housing fellow nodded and backed out of the room towards the other bedroom.

I was last to get in this time, and I saw him running a finger down the wall where the wallpaper hung off in strips. There were drops of water running down it still, from the rain earlier. I suppose he couldn't believe his eyes. He wanted to check that it was really wet.

'That's condensation,' announced the Education official. 'Comes of keeping the windows shut. If he puts some radiators on for a month and leaves the windows open, it'll be fine.'

What radiators? I thought. Nobody was taking any notice of me. I piped up, 'What radiators?'

'Well, that's a matter for us to consider,' said the Housing man, looking shiftily at the Headmaster. He turned his gaze on me at last, as though mildly surprised that a lower form of life could talk. 'Would you show us the ground floor, Mr Williams?'

They clumped after me down the stairs and into the

kitchen. Cath was standing at the sink, clutching her back with the heel of her hand inwards, the way women do when the burden in front gives them an aching back.

'That one's about ready to be born, isn't it?' asked a cheery councillor with a chunky piggy face and an Aran-knit cardie under his suit.

'I'm going in this afternoon. They're going to induce me.' Cath was very nice to these council people. I was afraid she'd be offering them cups of tea next. As it was, she went back into the living-room. It broke the ice, her going, because there wasn't room for her to get past Aran-knit's stomach and they both giggled.

When I stood in the kitchen to show them where I once saw a rat crawl under the lavatory door, some of the crowd were peering over the shoulders of the others.

'The mice come in here, see, and we get hundreds of wood-lice under the lino. I've put new paper up twice and it just rolls off. This morning there was a Niagara coming down these walls in here. You see that mattress?' They all craned over each other's shoulders to see the mattress propped against the wall in the living-room. 'The four of us have to sleep on that because the upstairs is too wet. This time tomorrow there'll be five of us. My family should be at the top of the housing list.'

There was an awkward silence. Then the Headmaster said, 'Perhaps we should go and discuss this outside.'

They all made a grunting noise again and clattered

through the front door, with me following. You could see when they got out on to the playground they all breathed deeply. If they hadn't been buttoned up against the world, they'd have stretched and rolled in the school sandpit like dogs, in sheer relief. It was a horrible house we lived in. The previous caretakers of Plasmarl Primary School had been nice and snug there, because they'd all been able to keep fires going in every room. There had been an endless supply of coal from the school boiler-room, in the old days. The school was on gas now, and the chimneys in the care-taker's house blew icy draughts in winter and wept with the summer rain.

'Well, as we've seen, it's condensation. So we come back to the question of central heating,' said Education, opening his briefcase.

'Not necessarily,' said Aran-knit. 'Maybe there's no point in spending the money.'

The prospect of a conflict reminded them that they should be taking notes. They all opened their brief-cases. The ones who could, put them on the ground and bent over to flick through the contents; the fat ones balanced them against their stomachs and tugged papers out, like kangaroos rummaging through their pouches for babies. (I watched a lot of wildlife pro-grammes in those days. They were the only things on TV early enough for us to watch before we had to put the lights out for the children's sake.)

It was a breezy morning, a cool May wind coming up from the bay. The school's side door was only forty yards away, and a sweaty smell of dinner mince came across on the breeze. A desiccated councillor struggled to

4

hold down the wisps of hair pasted across his head from ear to ear. He said timidly, 'I do have some sympathy with the Headmaster's position on this. I can see that security is much better served by having a school caretaker on the premises.'

'That house wants condemning,' I said.

'It wants heating,' said the Headmaster. 'I haven't got the funds to install central heating. It is the council's responsibility.'

There was a general murmur of doubt and a looking-up from clipboards. 'It'll have to go to committee.'

'Right.' The Housing man was thinking of his dinner. 'Mr Williams, thank you for showing us the house. Over the next few weeks a report will go in. Now, it is possible that we may get the works sanctioned, or it is possible that the committee's views will go against the Headmaster here.'

'Yes, but in the meantime we've got to live here.'

'Indeed, Tony, but the house is perfectly adequate in the summer,' said the Headmaster.

I couldn't say anything to him.

'Would you expect your family to live in it?' asked Aran-knit unexpectedly.

The Headmaster pulled a face. 'I suppose you've got a point there.' He scratched his nose.

The man from Education said, 'With central heating and the windows left open, however –'

'He'll have a big bill, won't he?' said Aran-knit.

They stood and looked at each other. You could see they were annoyed because they had started arguing in front of me. I knew there was a problem over who was going to pay for the improvements, but they liked to think I didn't know. Whatever their views, their main objective was to preserve a united front against the lower orders.

My brother picked Cath and the children up after school and took them over to her mam's. After tea he was going to take her to the hospital. The baby would be induced first thing tomorrow morning for the convenience of the doctors and nurses who liked to work nine to five.

By about six they'd all gone and I'd finished my second shift at the school. Everything was locked away and tidy for tomorrow. I trudged across the sloping asphalt playground, checked the school gate and went back into our house. It was great having a place with a walled, locked schoolyard around it for Craig and Matthew to play in.

The smell of damp hit me as I came through the door. I put the television on for company. There was a programme celebrating this month of May 1988 as the ninth anniversary of Thatcher's triumphant government. Then I went upstairs to open some windows and dry the place out a bit.

The back bedroom looked on to the terraced houses down Britannia Road. In one of them lived three old ladies, two sisters in their seventies and their mother, who was ninety. All their lives they had been cleaners at the school and the old one said Fridays hadn't been the same since she retired. Friday had been the highlight of her week because that was the day she collected a big bag of cinders from the boiler-room, enough to keep them warm the whole weekend. Every Friday night, the same little treat, for fifty or sixty years.

I looked around me at the obscene black walls and opened the windows. Then I stepped into the front bedroom and looked out over the school wall and the huddled rooftops and down to the bay. I opened the window and leaned on the sill and stared out at the sky. You get lovely skies round Swansea, crimson and grey, with thousands of lights in Port Talbot, on the black distant shore, promising excitement that the town can't deliver. Port Talbot is just a machine that exhales great gobs of industrial gases, white and grey and black, into the sky over Mumbles Bay and you can't tell where the smoke ends and the clouds begin. Now there was a vast billowing black heap against the peachy colours of evening. It rose from the horizon in rolling folds that plunged against towering cliffs of cloud; contemplating their immensity made me feel giddy. You could see rivers in that enormous black cloud, rivers and forests and terrifying canyons.

I saw an island. Of course, I saw an island. Not a day went past but I talked about an island. I thought all the time about getting away to a place of warm sand, blue skies and coconuts dropping softly from the trees to the sound of twanging guitars. I was convinced that if I could only live in such a place, with no cars and phones and bills and rain, I would be a happy man.

It was very frustrating when you asked so-called educated people about Captain Bligh and *The Mutiny*

7

on the Bounty and whether there were still any desert islands in the world, and nobody ever gave you a straight answer. Maybe they thought I ought to know. They had no idea how little I knew of life outside Swansea and the daily paper, and how it had come about that we now lived in this noisy, polluted twentieth century. They usually said what did I want to know for, and when I said I wanted to take Cath and the children and live on one, they laughed. Some of them got right into it, encouraging me. They thought it was fantasy. They thought I was mad.

Sometimes you can watch the clouds racing by over the bay. They go very fast and you can see your whole life in them: getting a wife, and a baby being born, and a job, and there's the television in the corner and another baby, and you're working and sleeping and eating, and there's another baby, and more television, and the children are at school, and your wife's growing older, and your life hasn't changed and soon you'll be like old Owen. Owen was the first caretaker I worked with. He was dead now after a lifetime in the same job, and forgotten.

I had been talking about finding a desert island when I met Cath, and ten years had passed since then. Now I was twenty-seven and I still hadn't really done much more than talk. I had children; I had a job to worry about; I had accommodation to organize. But I was always going to have these problems.

I looked at the bottom of the towering heap of clouds, at the long terrifying climb from the horizon to the stars, and I saw a way to reach the island. I just had to keep it in sight. I had to ignore defeat and keep going.

So that summer I made a start. We did something radically different. We went to Butlin's at Minehead for a week.

I took Cath and her sister, who was twenty-five then, and her mam and dad and all three of our children, that is to say, Stacey, the new baby, darker haired than the boys, and Matthew aged four and Craig just eight. None of the women had ever been out of Wales before. I had spent six weeks in London once, but that was something I didn't talk to my in-laws about.

It seemed that no sooner had we gone than we were back at Plasmarl. And then the autumn term started, with the first dark afternoons and the wet windy play-ground to cross before the cleaners arrived at seven in the morning. It was my job to unlock everything, and to make sure things were clean and tidy and safe and warm before the Headmaster and the teachers arrived after eight. Then, when they'd finished assembly, I had time off until the school emptied at going-home time. The Headmaster was always the last to leave. While the cleaners saw to the classrooms, I hoovered his office personally.

Some nights we had Lettings: people who hired the school hall. I had to be on call until they left around ten at night. Old Owen, the fellow I'd been relief caretaker for when I was eighteen, had saved up all his overtime from Lettings for nearly forty years. He used to sit in the boiler-room – it was coal then, and the boiler was a mystery, it was like running a power-station – and he'd talk about his nest-egg and what he was going to do when he retired. He would sail down the Rhine with his wife, he said. He showed me the brochures; it looked very nice. But he'd only been retired ten months when he dropped dead of a heart attack, and he still hadn't been down the Rhine. All that dreaming and nothing to show for it.

That autumn term we were still in the caretaker's house in the Plasmarl schoolyard, sleeping like sardines and waking in a warm fug. At last a letter came from the Housing Department at Guildhall, to say that we would be allocated a council house at West Cross. The Headmaster was not particularly pleased with me because I had made waves, and thanks to me the old house was scheduled for demolition and future caretakers would have to live out.

I started looking for another school to work at. I said to my brother Alun, 'D'you think I'll find another school, Alun? D'you think so?' I always asked him questions like this as we walked around the city centre together; I'd done it when we were kids and selling papers in the pubs. Now on Saturday mornings he gave me a lift in to the big Tesco's sometimes, with a list from Cath. This morning we'd done our shopping and we were having a look round – just ambling round the streets as usual, in the old Victorian part of the city. My brother is taller than me, eighteen months older and more heavy-set. If I ask him a question, I know he'll take a while answering; he thinks before he speaks. He said, 'You'll have no problem.'

That was comforting. I side-stepped an old woman

wheeling a shopper and stopped to look in a second-hand bookshop. It's one of those places where you buy books and when you've read them you take them back and get another one. Some of the covers are quite embarrassing. Idly, I looked in the window, scanning the titles. At the back of my mind I knew that I was looking for information about islands, as usual. It was an obsession with me.

'Hold on a minute, I'm just going in here,' I said, and I slipped through the door. On a trestle-table in front of me, on top of a pile, was a paperback called *An Island to Oneself*. The cover showed a photograph of a man under a palm tree on a desert island. I picked it up eagerly and turned it over. Tom Neale had lived on a desert island in the South Seas in the 1950s and 1960s, I read in disbelief. I felt like a prospector who has found gold. If this Tom Neale could do it only thirty years ago, I could do it now.

'You'll be leaving us soon to sit under a palm tree, I hear,' said Mrs Carpenter, lighting a cigarette.

When the children had gone home from school, some of the teachers stayed on to mark books or prepare work for tomorrow. This is why Mrs Carpenter was still in the staff-room, in an easy chair with two piles of red exercise-books on either side of her small feet in their glossy black shoes and stockings. She was in her forties, with a grown-up son in the police. She stretched over to pick up her mug from the coffee-table. 'I keep hearing how you're going to fly off to Tahiti, Tony.'

'D'you think I could?' I stopped rewinding the flex of the Hoover and looked at her.

'Well, there's no law against it. Where do Cath and the children fit into your plans?'

'That's the problem, you see. I've been reading this book by Tom Neale ...' I told her all about Tom Neale and how he went to live on an island in the South Seas and lived on fish and coconuts.

'But he didn't have a wife and three children.'

'No, but I've discussed it with Cath, and she doesn't mind if I want to go away for a while when we get the new house, and she'll stay here.'

'Why don't you all go?'

I didn't know if she was serious or not. You could never tell with Mrs Carpenter. She seemed very sympathetic, but sometimes I thought she was sending me up.

'It's the money, you see. And Stacey, she's only five months.'

Mrs Carpenter picked up a fresh exercise-book and opened it. 'Well, you go anyway.'

'D'you think I should?'

'If you want to go and live on a desert island for a while, you go, Tony. Nobody's stopping you. It sounds like a good idea to me. And if you take some pictures, I'll help you make up an audio-visual presentation when you come back. We could tour round the schools with it. I'm sure it'd be very popular.'

I imagined working on a presentation with Mrs Carpenter, and thought I would like to do that. But we got the new council house a few days later. It was a semi-detached, two-storey house with a garden front and back, and we had a proper kitchen and bathroom at last. The house was high on a hill in West Cross, four miles from the school; and what with getting settled in and applying for other jobs, the island went out of my mind. But not for long.

There was a map of the world on the wall in Room No. 8, next to the stationery-cupboard door. It was my responsibility to lock that cupboard, and when I went in there some nights I would study the map in search of Pitcairn and the South Seas. There seemed to be a great deal of blue and I couldn't find the South Seas marked anywhere, but there were clumps of dots near New Zealand: Fiji and Tonga and Samoa. And a long string near India, the Maldives.

'Still dreaming, Tony?'

Mrs Carpenter had come in behind me. I was embarrassed. I said, 'I was just looking for an island and wondering how to get permission.'

'Permission?'

'If I'm going to live there, how do I know which ones are uninhabited? Look at the Maldives, look, all those dots. And Fiji, see? Somebody must own these places, mustn't they? They might not like it. I'd have to tell them I was coming.'

'That's true.'

'So how do I do that, then?'

'I wouldn't know, Tony.'

'D'you think I could get an address at the library?'

'I expect so,' she said absently, pinning back an eight-year-old's project that was slipping from a wall display.

'D'you think they'd have embassies in London?'

'I don't know, Tony.'

I decided to look in the London phonebooks at the library.

*

'We'll have those hula-hula girls, Tony,' said Big Malcolm. He swayed a little on his feet in the light spilling across the road from the chip shop as he buttoned his jacket over his stomach. I had missed the last bus in my efforts to drag him out of the pub, and we would both have to walk home along the sea wall. 'We'll have two each, with flowers in their hair, all right?'

'No, that's the whole point, Malcolm. I've got to find an uninhabited island.'

'That's what I said, Tony. Uninhabited except for you and me and a team of dusky maidens. Wahay!' he giggled and stepped heavily sideways. 'Shit.'

'People walk their dogs along here, look where you're going. So, you going back to Marian now, are you?' Half an hour ago Malcolm had announced that he was never going home again.

'Tony.'

He stood still. I had never spent so long getting on to Mumbles seafront in my life, it was worse than walking with a toddler. And I was perishing cold.

He put both huge hands on my shoulders and breathed a gust of lager into my face. 'Tony, Tony. You know how I've tried. The woman is a shrew. She doesn't deserve me. She's driven me to drink. I'm drinking too much. Tony, Tony. Wait. I swear to you. I'm coming with you. I'll walk right out of that flat and her bloody styling mousse all over the bathroom and she'll wake up and find me – gone.'

Cath was still awake when I came in. 'Malcolm still says he's coming with me,' I said, climbing into bed beside her.

She mumbled something.

'He says it's just what he needs, the pressure's getting to him. He's getting very big, isn't he? It's the beer. Cath.'

But Cath was asleep.

The next morning was Saturday, when we had a cooked breakfast, and I told her again.

'Oh, yes,' she said, 'and where's he going to get the money, then?'

'He says he'll get a bank loan.'

'If he can get a bank loan he wants to get one for Marian, her washer's broken down.'

'He says he's leaving Marian.'

Craig said, 'Malcolm said he was leaving Marian before.'

'Yes he did, didn't he?' grinned Cath.

'Don't encourage him, Cath.'

Craig looked mischievously at both of us, sniggered and shovelled a big spoonful of cornflakes into his mouth.

Matthew said, 'Is Dad going to a desert island with Malcolm?'

'He thinks he is,' said Cath.

Well. She would see. All the same I was glad I had somebody else to go with. That week I copied out some phone-numbers in London and started ringing up. It was funny, they all seemed a bit nonplussed if you told them you were looking for an empty island. I thought if these people had lived there, originally, they must know; but they didn't. They kept putting me through to Tourist Information or Public Affairs or the Bureau of Commerce. Once I was asked what religion I was. I spent more time hanging on than I did talking to people, and Cath said we were going to get a big bill, so I gave up in the end and started writing letters.

Late every Saturday afternoon we walked down to Cath's mam's, with Cath pushing Stacey in the pram. I didn't like it over that side. It was an estate a bit like ours, only rougher. You went past young lads sitting on the walls, drinking strong lager out of cans. If you were lucky, they went quiet as you walked by. If you weren't, they made a remark, usually when Cath was dressed up.

'Ignore them, Tony.'

I was going to anyway. I didn't fancy my chances against a dozen fifteen-year-olds out of their skulls on Tennents. Then I saw Gordon walking our way. I remembered him from Owen's school eight years ago; his mother was one of the cleaners. He was a lovely little lad, conscientious. He had got a prize for nature study, I remembered.

Now he was six foot tall with a ring through his nose and his hair in a rigid scarlet crest down the middle of his head, and he'd got black leather trousers on, with chains looped between the thighs. He strode past clanking and dragging on a cigarette.

'He never said hallo,' Cath said.

'He wouldn't have recognized us.'

She gave me a funny look but said nothing. Craig had stopped and stood on the grass verge, looking after Gordon's back view in wonderment.

'Come on, Craig,' I said.

We went down the street where Malcolm lived with Marian and her kids. It was a lot like ours, council semis, but not so much sky, down here in the valley; you'd almost think it rained more; there seemed to be less light. Their gardens were mostly weeds and some of the windows were boarded up. We passed a burnt-out car. I thought everyone down here must be on the breadline, the houses looked so neglected.

'Aren't they selling these off, then?' I asked Cath. We had decided to buy our new council house. It cost the same as renting.

'Marian says they're too expensive.'

We turned the corner into a tidy street where most of the tenants were pensioners. Cath's dad was at their gate, waiting for us as usual. He always stayed for a cup of tea with us on a Saturday, before he went off to the club.

'Walter Mitty's here,' he called indoors, and winked at Cath and picked Matthew up and carried him over the step. I wished he wouldn't call me that. I had said so to Cath, but she said there was no harm in him. And it was the only thing he ever did that needled me. When I met Cath and saw how she got on with her family it had been like a revelation, there was so much love in that household. There had been nothing like that in my childhood, nothing like all that warmth. And now, ten years on, her father might be a bit crusty at times but he still seemed like a good man, even if he did think I was a storyteller.

We sat down in the sitting-room while Cath and her mother started getting the tea ready in the kitchen. Cath's dad had had two heart attacks in three years, so he did a lot of sitting during the day. He was retired; he used to drive a fish van.

'You still writing to your islands, then, Tony?'

'I've written a lot more letters and the replies have started coming. I've had letters from Fiji and all over.'

'Have you now? And what do they have to say for themselves?'

Cath's dad sat back with his legs apart and his hands crossed on his stomach, and asked the question as if the people of Fiji owed an answer to him personally.

'I've got an address to write to over there,' I said mildly.

'You going to follow it up, are you?'

'Yes, I am. And Tonga as well.'

'Well, you've got persistence, I'll say that for you. What do they make of it, then?'

'They seem very nice. I explain it's like a survival project, to see if a modern man can survive without all this pressure and the crime. It's terrible round here. Don't you think it's frightening the way those boys hang about?'

He didn't seem interested. I don't think he understood really. Like most people he didn't see why anyone would want to get away from here. He once told me he had been very shocked when he got sent to Germany for his National Service. He just said, 'How d'you expect to pay for this little expedition, then?'

'I've got the savings, from not paying any rent all the time we were in the school house. And we've only had the one holiday in ten years.'

'Hm. What'll you do for a job when you come back?'

'I've asked the union and they say I'm entitled to six months' leave of absence because I've got ten years' service.'

He looked a bit surprised, but he was only humouring me. He never thought I'd go. Cath's mam came in with the tray just then and he turned the TV on to check the football results, so we didn't talk about it any more.

All the correspondence took time and I kept getting non-committal replies. Christmas was approaching, with the expense. There's such a lot for children nowadays, computer games and mountain bikes and skateboards, it's frightening, especially when I thought even if I could afford it I couldn't let the children out of my sight with half this stuff, in case some big teenager came along and took it off them.

I was standing amid the passing crowds in an aisle in Toys 'Я' Us, minding a trolley, while Cath went off and looked along the shelves, and I was thinking about all this, and fingering the letter in my pocket, when it hit me – I really was going.

The letter had come that morning. It was on beautiful silvery airmail paper, with a glistening green bird on the stamp. It was from a man, at least I supposed he was a man, called Kauraka Kauraka. And it said I should just come to Rarotonga, the capital of the Cook Islands, and he would arrange for me to stay on an island. But I was to bring a companion, he said, as he would not like to take the responsibility for a lone person who might fall ill and be unable to get help.

It was real. I had the invitation. The joy of it hit me

all over again. Cath came up, looking worried and carrying a shiny red cardboard box.

'D'you think Matthew'll like this?'

I grabbed her by the waist and danced her round with the parcel. Amazed bystanders scattered out of our path.

'I'm going to Rarotonga, Cath!'

'Tony, you're mad.'

Alun appeared from behind a stack of toy scooters. 'I wish I could go,' he said.

Cath and I stopped and looked at him. 'You never said before.'

'I never thought you were going before.'

'I've been telling you for months.'

'You've been talking about it for years, but you never did all this letter-writing.'

Cath went off to put the red box back. She'd seen my face when I looked at the price. A big chunk of our savings had already gone on the new house, and we were going to need to be very careful if I was to make this trip. I hadn't even found out what the air fare was yet.

'So you taking Big Malcolm with you, are you? What's Marian think about that?'

'Malcolm doesn't even know about the letter yet. It's good news, isn't it, Alun?'

'It's very good news,' Alun said, looking me right in the eye. 'But I'll believe it when I see it.'

2

'It's the fare. I haven't got £900, Tony,' said Big
Malcolm sadly. He was sober, in daylight, and wearing
a blue anorak that made him look like a big baby.

'You said you'd borrow it. Do what I'm doing, look.
I'm selling the stereo and the rest is savings. You've
got something put by, haven't you? This is a chance in
a lifetime, Malcolm.'

He wasn't going to come, I could see that, but he
wouldn't say so. Instead he stared into the window of
Boots. They had a display of cameras, shavers and foot
spas that hadn't changed since November. Imagine the
thrill of getting a battery-powered foot spa for Christmas.

'It's not that I don't want to come, Tony, but I can't.
I'm unemployed, nobody's going to lend me the money.'

I turned away. People are all the same, I thought, all
talk, and when it comes to the point they won't do it. I
intended to leave in the summer and stay on a desert
island until this time next year, and I meant it. I had
been assuming all along that Malcolm meant it too. He
seemed so desperate. He had nothing to keep him
here, no job, not even a girlfriend, since he left Marian
and went home to his mam. He would just hang
around Swansea drinking and complaining until he
was middle aged. There were lots like him.

'I tell you who I saw, Tony, who might go – Gareth
Lewis.'

'When?'

'Last night. He was asking after you. He said were you still going on about an island, and I said you'd got it all sorted, and he said he'd be interested.'

Now that was something. Gareth and I had been best friends at school; we'd gone away to London together when we were sixteen. But I hadn't seen him for a year or more.

'What's he doing now?'

'Same thing. Nothing.'

Gareth's front garden was occupied by a caravan that had not moved for as long as I could remember. He lived on an estate just outside the city centre with his wife and child. When I knocked on the door he answered it. His wife was down at the clinic with the child and he was in the kitchen with the paper. He was a scaffolder, out of work. To find work he needed to spend time in pubs getting to know people who worked on the big sites, but he was not a sociable man in that sense. He was not one for fitting in or belonging to a crowd.

The television was on in the lounge and he didn't turn it off while we talked. We sat at the kitchen-table. Gareth hadn't changed much, at least, he hadn't got a beer belly on him like Malcolm, though he had grown facial stubble and a pony-tail. He looked at me and grinned as he rolled himself a cigarette.

'So what's Cath think about all this, then?'

'She thinks it's a great idea.'

'She thinks you're going to do it, does she?'

'I'm going to do it, Gareth. All I need is somebody to go with.'

'When you going?'

'About the end of July.'

'Big Malcolm told me he was bottling out.'

'Yes. Why would he do that, Gareth?'

'I dunno. He's got nothing to keep him here. Nor've I.'

'You've got Gail and the baby.'

'They'd be all right without me for a bit. Where's this place you're going?'

I told him about the Cook Islands and the invitation from Kauraka Kauraka, and how you could survive on fish and coconuts and that I was thinking of writing a book about it.

'Think of it, Gareth. The hot sun and the blue sea. After this.'

'I am thinking about it. Where d'you sleep, under a palm tree?'

'I've got a tent already. You can get one if you hurry, Millet's sale ends at the weekend. They're £6.99 reduced from £9.99.'

'I won't need one. I'll build a hut.'

'You coming, then?'

''Course I am.'

Within a fortnight Gareth's wife announced that she was pregnant again, and the baby was due in July. So that finished that.

We were now in January, and I had transferred before Christmas to a new job. I was caretaker to two schools, with seven cleaners under me. They were Bryn Mill and Bryn y Môr, two and a half miles from our house and a hundred yards from each other. I would have to apply to the Headmasters soon for my six months' leave of absence to start in the summer.

'What am I going to do, Cath? Should I advertise for somebody to go with me? It says in the letter I shouldn't go on my own.'

She looked up from the potatoes she was peeling at the sink, slowly rinsed her hands under the cold tap and dried them on the towel behind the door. 'You're really going, aren't you?'

'Yes, 'course I am. Didn't you think I would?'

She came and sat down at the table with me. 'You've been going on about it for so long, I never thought.'

'Don't you think I should?'

'Well, you've got to get it out of your system, haven't you?'

That was one way of putting it, though not a way I liked much. It meant Cath thought the experience would be so unpleasant that I would never want to leave Swansea again.

'I don't know anybody else to go with.'

'Advertise, then.'

'Like my mam?'

''Course not. Don't put it in the lonely hearts.'

Cath looked so sweet and brave, smiling at me. I wished she could come.

'I'd be taking a big risk, advertising. It could all get taken over. There's a lot of men who'd want to go and do something like that to build up their egos, you know, to prove they could do things. Action men. It'd be all building rafts and making traps. I don't want to go with somebody who's going to order me about for six months. I want to get away from all the pressure, that's the whole point.'

'Take a girl, then.'

'Would you mind?'

''Course not.' She got up to finish the potatoes, looked at me and sat down again. She took my hand. 'Look, if you wanted to have an affair, you could have one next door, couldn't you? You don't want to have an affair, you want to go to a desert island. I know that, you've been talking about it long enough, you were talking about it the first time you took me out, I can still remember. So you put an ad in, go on, Tony. Advertise for a girl if you want to, I don't mind. Really.'

I knew I'd get a stack of replies from the paper. I remembered the postman knocking with heaps of them for our mam. When I was about seven – that was in 1968 – our mam left our father in the valleys, and took us four children to live in a caravan in Swansea. She was out a lot and it had an empty feel to it. Our older sister was thirteen and used to hang around the city centre, and the little one used to go round her friends' houses, but in that first winter in the caravan, me and Alun usually came back straight after school to try and get warm, which was difficult because the walls were made of thin stuff and the window frames were rusted and let in draughts. There was a long straight-backed seat in there, and when our mother got a batch of letters in the morning, which happened about once a fortnight, she used to open them up and then go out, leaving them all over the red plastic seat and stuck to the sink top with sticky rings from cups of tea. I read them all. Small, blue, lined pages. Men selling themselves. I am five nine and my friends say I'm good looking, exclamation mark. I drive a Cortina. You sound sexy in your ad. My ex-wife was also a petite brunette. I like country music and. My kind of woman. No strings. Phone me at work. My wife is disabled. Why don't we. See photo attached.

I was going to be fussier. However, most of the replies I got were from women selling themselves in the same way, only toned down: I am twenty-one years old, slim and have long brown hair. That sort of thing. And – because in the ad I had made it clear that this was a survival project – they often claimed to have done their Duke of Edinburgh's Award, or to have climbed in Snowdonia when they were at school. The only one who was over twenty-five was a prostitute, aged twenty-nine, who said she wanted solitude in which to write a book about her experiences over the past five years in a massage parlour in Swansea. She would be a perfect companion, she said, she had seen it all and had been earning £800 a week regular. When I didn't reply to her letter she sent another one. It had a lot of detail about family men and the services they asked for, that their wives would not provide. Quite biologically precise, it was. I showed it to Cath, who blushed.

'Are you Mr Williams?'

'Yes.'

'This is the *Evening Post* here, we noticed your ad for a companion on a survival project and we wondered if you'd give us a few more details.'

26

'Yes? What d'you want to know, then?'

'Have you had any replies yet?'

'Oh, yes, there's been quite a few.'

I didn't tell them about the prostitute, but I mentioned a six-foot blonde from Gorseinon and some of the others. The man asked me what I did for a living and where I was going. Then he wished me luck.

The next thing I knew, Cath's dad was on the doorstep, brandishing a newspaper and looking as if he was on the brink of his third heart attack.

'Let me in. I want to talk to Cath.'

He marched through the sitting-room and into the kitchen, and I followed.

'Have you seen the paper?'

'No, Tony only gets it on –'

'Well, you'd better have a look at this.' He slammed the paper on to the table, opened it up and prodded an article with his thick finger that wobbled with rage. TONY TO SPEND A YEAR IN PARADISE, it said. There was a lot about a Girl Friday who, according to the paper, was young, adventure-loving and throbbing to accompany me on the next plane to the South Seas.

'You want to get this sorted now, my girl,' said my father-in-law grimly. Turning his glare on me, he said, 'And what d'you mean, calling yourself a bachelor?'

'I didn't. I never said I was a bachelor.'

'You been advertising for some girl to go with you, have you?'

'Yes, but –'

'Did you know about this?' He turned to Cath.

'Yes, Dad –'

'You need your head examined. And you' – he was

27

talking to me again – 'what d'you mean you never said? The papers aren't going to bloody put bachelor unless you've bloody told 'em you're a bachelor, are they? What you doing, talking to this girl? You made a right balls-up here.'

He didn't mind as long as I was a Walter Mitty, but now that I'd shown him I was serious, he was really worried.

'You've got a wife and three children. What d'you think you're playing at?'

'They'll be all right. We've talked about it. It's only for a few months. I'm due a tax rebate and that'll cover the mortgage –'

'You want to pull yourself together, you do. You can't just go leaving a wife and three children.'

'We'll be all right, Dad,' said Cath.

'What d'you mean you'll be all right? Your husband's swanning off halfway round the world with a teenage nymphet, isn't he? He's supposed to provide for you, he is. He's got responsibilities same as any father. What if I'd decided to just bugger off, where would you have been? He's always been mad as a hatter. I thought you had more sense.'

He stomped out of the house soon after that, disgusted. He had never really trusted me, because I was different from him; I didn't play darts and I meditated. I had tried to explain about meditation and getting in touch with my inner self and he looked at me as though it was witchcraft. And now he thought I had used my sinister powers to make his daughter lose her reason.

As it happened, one of the replies had looked quite

promising. It didn't come across as a coy application to join some kind of harem. It was a polite and wary request for more information from a girl called Nicola in Bridgend. I rang her, and she explained that she'd done Outward Bound courses, knew how to fish, was used to living in the open air in Scotland, and was bored with her job and her life. She and her sister lived alone, and they were both keen that she should do something with her future, which seemed to be running into a rut here.

Cath and I thought she sounded fine. We went to meet her in a pub about five miles from our house that Nicola happened to know. She was a nice-looking girl of about twenty-five, quite shy, sitting in a corner drinking orange juice.

'She'll be all right,' Cath said on the way home in the bus. 'She's a listener. You need a listener, she'll be nice and quiet.' And it was true. Nicola had hung on my every word and expressed interest in all my plans for life on the island. All the same, I wished Cath could come. Seeing this other woman had set me in a turmoil. It was a kind of fear, I suppose, in case things went too far. I didn't want anything or anybody to draw me away from Cath. So far, I had shared all my dreams with her. To fly away with another woman now would be like losing a companion who had been beside me throughout a long and difficult journey.

But I couldn't express most of this, because we couldn't afford the fares for Cath and all three of the children, and since Stacey was only a baby it might be a bit risky taking her. Anyway, I could imagine Cath's father's reaction. It was bad enough me going. If he had to get his mind round the whole family setting off for a desert island, he'd probably explode in a ball of fire.

I had a companion, and an invitation, and the money to go with. I had a large collection of letters from other people who wanted to do the same thing, which I found reassuring. I had found out how to get a passport. I had even been offered money for my story, in a phone-call from a national paper that wanted me to write about the trip, but, as I told them, the whole point was to get away from pressure, so I thanked them and said no. Now all I needed was time off, and that was a question I had to confront sooner than I expected.

The Headmaster of Bryn Mill stopped me in the empty playground. He was a short fellow with a face like a knot in a hankie, who suffered from being called Mr Uren.

'What's all this I'm hearing?' he said, staring at me as if I was some kind of escaped maniac. 'I've had reporters on the phone. I've had them saying you're off to some island. It's the first I've heard of it.'

'I was going to come and see you about that,' I said. 'I want to apply for leave of absence at the end of the year.'

'You can't have leave of absence, you're caretaker to two schools.'

'I've got ten years' service, I'm entitled to it.'

'Well, I don't know about that, you'll have to ask County Hall. What's all this about a desert island?'

I explained what I intended to do.

'I never heard anything like it,' he snorted. 'See yourself as some kind of macho man swinging through the jungle, do you? You're off your head.'

I made an appointment to go to County Hall.

On Wednesday nights Cath's mam, who is an affectionate motherly person, used to take the children so that Cath and I could go out together. My father-in-law was always down the social club on Wednesdays, in fact he was there most nights because he was on the committee. We used to tell them we were going to bingo. It was easier than saying we just wanted to go for a walk on the front. They wouldn't have understood.

'D'you think I'm mad, Cath?' I said. It was dark and she had her collar up, and spray was coming over the sea wall. 'The Headmaster thinks I'm mad, your dad thinks I'm mad. But I sit in that boiler-room sometimes and I wonder, is this all there is?' I watched my feet plodding doggedly past the black gleaming puddles in the tarmac. 'I come home, we have our tea, we get the kids to bed and then I crash out in front of the television. Night after night. And then it's up again at five in the morning the next day. That seems mad to me, doesn't it to you, Cath?'

'You don't want to take any notice of them,' said Cath, her voice muffled by the wind. 'You've always wanted to go, so you go.'

'Yes, but can you see why I want to do it? It's not so crazy to want to go further than the shops, is it? You'd think it was, the way they carry on.'

'Go and ask Mr Harris what he thinks, I would,' said Cath.

One weekday afternoon I went to ask Craig's Headmaster. He seemed surprised to see me. Especially when I asked whether he thought I should go and live on a desert island.

'If you want to go, you go,' he said. Mr Harris was a nice man, Cath and me had both thought that at Craig's Sports Day, and now I knew it was right to talk to him. I told him all about the island and about my doubts. People were telling me I was off my head, I said. Cath's dad said that too much meditation had divorced me from reality.

Mr Harris didn't scoff at me, in fact he seemed to think my dream was the most normal thing in the world. And he said something that hit home. 'You don't need to ask anybody's permission, you just go. If you keep asking people, it's because you want to give yourself permission, in a way. Anyway, if you ask them they'll always look for a way to say no. Just you remember it's none of their business.'

So when I went to County Hall I felt I could assert myself. County Hall in Swansea is an arrangement of slabbed office blocks set at an angle to the main coast road. Inside, it's all long corridors and luxury lifts with carpeted walls and office ladies dressed up in jewellery. I was single-minded by now, and not to be distracted by all this grandeur, so it wasn't so much a request for leave of absence that I put in as an announcement that I was taking it; and it was granted.

I had arranged a second meeting with Nicola, to sort out the date of our flight, and was talking about it with Cath at tea-time when we went over to her parents' on the Saturday. It was still winter, around

February, and at six o'clock they had all the lights on in their kitchen and Cath's mam was cooking a rabbit. Potatoes were bouncing in a pan on the stove and steaming up the windows. The boys were upstairs, Stacey was asleep in her buggy, and me and Cath were sitting at the kitchen-table. Cath's dad had gone out early. He never stayed to have tea with us these days, he couldn't stand the sight of me.

'So who is this Nicola?' asked Cath's mam, tipping cabbage stalks into a pedal bin under the sink.

'She's a secretary,' I said. I could see that didn't go down too well. If she'd worked in a factory it would have been less of a threat somehow. Saying she was a secretary immediately put her in high heels in the mind's eye. Cath's mam looked at Cath.

'What do you think, then?'

'She seems nice enough,' said Cath. 'She lives with her sister.'

'How old is she?'

We told her. I had just launched into a comparison of the various possible routes to Rarotonga, either Gatwick to Bangkok and Auckland, then Air New Zealand to Rarotonga, or Gatwick to Los Angeles and Tahiti, then Rarotonga by an inter-island flight, when she turned round from prodding the potatoes and said to Cath, 'You'd better go with him. We'll stay over your house with the children.'

Somewhere inside me I had always known Cath would be able to come in the end. On the way home I was barely able to stop smiling.

'You look very smug. Pleased are you?' she teased me.

''Course.'

'Should think you would be,' she said. 'Saved your-self £800 a week at least.'

'She's very upset,' said the soft voice on the telephone. The woman had introduced herself as Nicola's sister. 'She feels so badly let down, you see. She's a delicate girl, you know I mean delicate mentally, she'd set a great deal of store by this trip. It was going to change her life.'

'Yes. Well, I'm sorry.'

'She's very bad now.'

'Is she?'

'Yes, she's back under the doctor, she can't keep anything down when she's like this. She gets so depressed, you see she doesn't feel her life is going anywhere. There's not much work around here.'

There is even less on a desert island, but I let it pass.

'She's not back yet and it's nearly midnight' – I didn't need telling, I had to be up at five – 'and all day Saturday she just walked around the town by herself, it's tragic. You should have taken her with you. She said you was such a nice young man.'

'I'm taking my wife.'

'Yes, she told me, but I don't think she wants to believe that, see. She feels rejected, Mr Williams.'

'I can't help the way she feels,' I said.

A reporter, a freelance he said he was, came to the door a few days later. He understood I'd made a choice of companion, he said. I wondered for a minute how he knew, but he was already asking me how he could get in touch with her.

'All I'm asking you for is a number to contact. The young lady can make her own mind up whether she wants to be interviewed.'

He was a plump fellow with spots who looked about eighteen. He had a very small tape-recorder in one hand and was already inside our hall, though he'd only knocked on the door a minute before.

'So if you'll just let me have her number, I'll leave you in peace, Mr Williams.'

'I'm not giving out any numbers.'

'I'm sorry you feel that way. You know the public has a right to know.'

'Why do they?'

'We know what our readers want, Mr Williams. All I need from you is a name and a number. If you'd like to co-operate, of course, I've got contacts on the London papers who'd be very interested in buying the full story from you, but I understand that ground's been covered already?'

I thought back to the single call from a national paper. Did the world know every detail of what I did and said, then? I was beginning to feel hunted.

'Look,' I said, 'I didn't ask you to come here.'

'Mr Williams, if you don't give us the news, you know we'll write it anyway. One of the young ladies who answered your ad is very upset that she didn't get the job, so to speak. I expect you know that.'

I decided then and there never to advertise so much as a washing-machine part in any newspaper for the rest of my life. It was like putting up a neon sign that said CRAZIES WELCOME HERE.

'I'm taking my wife,' I said.

His face lit up, he bared his teeth and shot past me into the sitting-room.

'That's fascinating, Mr Williams,' he said.

We had become news. I did not understand the significance of this at the time, but I was going to find out on the day we left.

It was an overcast morning in summer. The flight left Gatwick at two in the afternoon, so we had to get the early train from Cardiff, and Alun came at six to drive us to the station. There was a bit of a fuss out in the street, what with Craig and Matthew in the garden in their pyjamas and Cath's mam starting to cry and her dad telling Craig off for swinging on the gate and Cath's sister, in her dressing-gown with a cigarette, yawning, and me trying to heave the suitcases into the back. We had two, which we had bought for the trip to Minehead.

There were also the cameraman, the sound man, the director, a lot of cables and a light shining on my face. The articles in the papers had alerted BBC Wales and they'd rung up yesterday to find out what time we'd be leaving. I never thought a television crew would turn up. There were only three of them but you'd think they were shooting *Ben Hur*, the amount of gear they got out of one estate car.

At that time in the morning there was hardly anybody about, but then two punkish boys came round the corner. I knew both of them by sight and they knew all about me, it seemed. They caught on to what was happening straight away and started mucking about near the back of the television car. The sound man took his headphones off, walked over, slammed the car door shut and locked it. That left them nothing to do but get into the shot by our garden gate and make obscene gestures. And remarks. In general, apart from the obscenities relating to self-abuse, they were saying I was a nutter.

'Will you shut up, please?' said the tall man who had introduced himself as the director. Terse, he was. And well-spoken. It didn't get him very far. One of the lads had a nasty habit of spitting in people's faces, and I could see him thinking about it, so I bundled Cath into the car. We kissed the children while the camera was running and we were off, both of us feeling we hadn't said a proper goodbye.

It left a bad taste in my mouth. I felt confused, having suddenly realized that just by existing and being different, you can offend not only the predictable people but untold thousands of others too, people who don't even know you – people who feel that anything that is unfamiliar is a threat.

3

The sky here was a distillation of blue, the ideal of blue. There were no shades in it, no hesitations or doubts; it was endlessly, solidly blue, yet when you stared up at it you could never find the source of the blueness, the part where the world ended and heaven began. If you gazed at it for long enough your point of view changed and you were looking down from the sky on yourself, a dun-coloured dot on the sand on an islet of coconut palms in a tiny atoll in a dark ocean on a beautiful planet, slowly revolving.

On the other side of the world, in a cold, dirty, littered place, buses would be stopping, check-outs ringing, televisions talking to empty rooms. I wondered what my father would be doing, up in the dripping green valleys north of Swansea. The image of him never normally crossed my mind, but now that I was here, with warm sand beneath my back, and nothing but the sighing waves to distract me, and no menace pursuing me, I felt relaxed enough to consider him, to call up his small figure and turn it around like a doll in my mind.

He is not a big man. But he has presence, like an actor; when he comes into a room, everybody else shrinks to give him more space.

When I was small he was a miner. There were five of us children, in a semi-detached house with two bedrooms that stood with its back to the wall of our valley. In my dreams I used to pile stones up against the front of the house, to stop it falling forwards. It seemed to need to tilt back, like a person walking down a slippery slope. Everything in that house, and outside it, glowered at you. The walls seemed to be closing in and the ceiling was too low, like the sky outside. The front garden was all rocks, with scrubby grass between, and a tumble of steps down to the road. Across the gulf of the valley you could see another mountain opposite, with no houses on it, just thick green trees.

Our little brother Mark died when we lived in that house. He was a cot death. And my mother and father never spoke in the daytime, but in the night they screamed at each other. In the morning she would still be in bed when we went to school. Our big sister got me ready; she was nine, and I was four. We went out into the rain and sometimes there were fresh splits in the tarmac to jump over. No traffic up here, except the post van and the brewer's lorry for the pub. Our village was one long street incised in the mountainside, and it was bursting open, slit along its length like a wound that has been badly sewn up.

Later there were to be other funerals: the children of Aberfan, buried when their school was engulfed by a mountain of wet slag from the pits. Not far from us in any way.

When our mother was out and our father at work, Alun and I used to explore, high into the back garden. We were not allowed up there. You stood outside the kitchen door and cricked your neck looking up at the top of the hill, where the sky was white; but when you set off, you were in a kind of jungle. We never did get to the end of it. The long grass dashed drops of water on to your face, and the earth beneath your feet was soft.

My father, and the frowning mountain on which we lived, somehow identified themselves as one and the same in my mind.

We moved just before the street fell away. Not really because of the danger, but because our mother was seeing another man and our father wanted us out of there. The old village shut down around that time in any case. Warnings were given, most of the people were allocated council houses elsewhere, and one night the street six doors down from our house just gently slid into a hole. The side of the mountain, weighed down with rain and rotten inside from years of mining, opened up to the sky. The road broke like a crust and those who dared to tiptoe to the edge said you could see no end to the blackness.

We got a council house even further up the valleys, in a bleak village with no trees where my grandmother lived. A side street led to a dead-end, where a row of houses had been built across like a barrier to stop civilization from creeping any further. We lived in one of those.

'You all right, Tony?'

'Now that you're here I am.' I took Cath's hand and pulled her down beside me.

'Bloody miserable you look.'

'I was thinking about my father.'

'You don't want to come ten thousand miles to

think about that old sod,' she said briskly. 'Come and look at my shell collection.'

'Busy, busy,' I yawned, shutting my eyes again. 'You seen one trochus, you seen them all, as far as I'm concerned.'

We had been eating trochuses for weeks, since the day we got here, so long ago now that I couldn't remember when it was. Fresh fish, coconut in all its forms, and trochuses. They were beautiful, gleaming red and orange shells, and when you boiled them the creature inside trembled as the water got hotter, and shrank back inside its coil of shell. When it was dead you broke a thick caul and poked it out with a stick. They looked like giant gobbets of snot and tasted like a slice of hot-water bottle. Cath rolled away from me, sat up, hugged her knees and said, 'I'm nearly out of sun-tan oil.'

'We'll have to go back home, then. To stock up at Boots.'

'I'm serious, Tony.'

'What about?'

'Going home. I'm beginning to wonder if they'll ever come and fetch us back.'

I sat up beside her. 'I was joking.'

'I know. But when I said about the sun-tan oil, I really meant, I miss the children.'

When we first came, months ago, it had been the Cook Islands' winter, though we didn't know that, because after the weather we were used to it seemed hot. I remembered feeling physically lighter, as if the cares of home were rising from my shoulders, when we came down the steps from the plane. Rarotonga smelled of flowers.

All my life I had taken care not to offend anybody and to do what was expected of me. As a result I had experienced almost nothing outside the small part of Wales in which I grew up. But in the past few days we had crossed half the world and for me it had been a confusing experience.

Our first overnight stop in Los Angeles was frightening. The city was hot, and alive with malevolent lights winking in the darkness. We were booked into a Quality Inn, but we took a long bus ride to the one in Anaheim when we should have stayed at the one opposite the airport. Then we got a bus to the wrong airport next morning and only just caught the plane to Tahiti in time.

We had to wait for three days in Tahiti before the connection to Rarotonga. All the hotels were very expensive, but we met a man who said he would take us to a hostel; it had cockroaches. In Tahiti traffic roared past the palm trees, leaving a grey haze hanging in the air, and the policemen wore guns. We were confused and unhappy and worried about money, but when the afternoon came and we were aching all over from tiredness, Cath tried to book us in to a place called the Miramar. The woman on the desk was very rude when Cath said she wanted a room for just a few hours. We had to go back into the streets. The noise was unbearable and it was difficult to cross the road, so we kept returning to the airport. I thought they had a nerve selling this place as a tropical island, it was misleading.

But Rarotonga was different. The passengers on the plane fell silent as we flew over the deep blue Pacific and saw it far below us, like a green emerald ringed with white. Imagine sweating in a dark noisy room, and opening a door on to blue skies and the gentle splash of water beneath green plants. That's what Rarotonga is like. The little aeroplane settled and cut its engines, and there was very little noise outside the airport. Waiting for us, when we left the customs desk with our suitcases, was a huge beaming brown man in a smart suit, shirt and tie, with no shoes and socks on. He knew us right away. We were the palest people in the airport. I had never been conscious of my whiteness before, and here it was unusual. And we were both thinner than we had been when we left Wales, after five days of airline food and snacks. As we stood with him, I felt the two of us would have fitted snugly into his jacket.

Behind Kauraka Kauraka trailed a smiling plump lady in a neat blouse and floral skirt, who spoke no English. 'This is my aunt,' he explained. We all shook hands awkwardly. His English was perfect but his aunty spoke only Maori. He talked the whole time, but all I could think about was the smell of fruit and flowers and the warmth of the air, so sensuous on the skin. We got into a taxi and were driven past endless ocean on one side and low houses in luxuriant gardens on the other. There were no high buildings, just soft protective greenery clothing the high mountains inland, and the perfect emptiness of that blue sky over the Pacific.

Our big smiling guide took us to a motel. He had paid for a room for us, for our first night on the island.

43

His kindness was unforgettable. I don't know what I had expected, when I saw the name Kauraka Kauraka on the neatly typed letter that arrived in Swansea in the rain last winter. He had been a civil servant then. In the months that followed there had been a change of government, he told us, and, as he was identified with the party that had previously held power, he had been edged out. Now he was suffering from stress, and an in-patient at the hospital on top of the mountain. His aunty was quietly caring for him when he came to meet us. None the less he was able to get away on his scooter, find a friend who would lend us a scooter too, and conduct us on a tour of Rarotonga.

Imagine a scattering of islands. Two scatterings in fact, one to the north and one to the south, spread over six hundred miles of ocean where the sun always shines. Of the southern group, Rarotonga is the biggest, the most populous and lively, and is mountainous and volcanic and fertile. It consists of steep forested mountains, rock formations and waterfalls in the middle, with a ring of plantations and villages and beaches round the edge. There are two main roads: the new one, closer to the beach, which goes right round the island, and an inner circle which is a very old road called the Ara Metua, which was originally made of coral.

We followed Kauraka bouncing along on his scooter, with his red and yellow shirt billowing. We bowled along in the warm salt air beside the beach and climbed high into the jungly interior, where fresh water tumbled from high peaks into vegetation as thick as fur.

With such variety Rarotonga seemed like a miniature world, isolated in contentment and untouched by history. Here it is possible for the islanders to live without working. As Kauraka pointed out, the houses we passed, little fibreboard and tin bungalows gaily decorated with scarlet and orange flowers, had gardens and plots of land adjoining that made them self-sufficient. You spat a pip, and a tree grew. People had bananas and papayas and coconuts and pineapples flourishing in their backyards.

'It's the same on all the islands,' he told us. We had stopped on a beach, at a place called Black Rock, and he pulled out a cellophane bag of caramels and offered them to us. Chewing on a toffee, he told us how the spirits of the dead set off from here to return to Havaiiki, which is their Paradise. 'You can live easily here. There is none of the western world's pressure to change and improve. Existence is perfect already.'

Kauraka was a clever man, who loved his island. He had written a book of poetry, he told us, in Maori with an English translation.

'Many of my poems are about the difficulties of being an islander nowadays.'

'It doesn't sound as if there are any difficulties.'

'Wait until you know the islands better. Notice the bars and the video stores – and now we even have computers in the offices,' he said sadly, unwrapping another toffee. 'We are torn two ways. I wrote a poem to my father – one day I shall read it to you. It is about my guilt. When I learned the new skills, I forsook the old.'

We sat on the sand and gazed out to sea, where the

sky was turning the colour of apricots. Two slender girls in long wrap-around skirts, with flowers in their hair, strolled along the shoreline, deep in conversation. Why, I wondered, had I spent so much of my short life in Swansea?

The streets of Avarua, the port on the north side of the island, were full of people. Kauraka told us it was the week of the Constitution Celebration, and islanders from all around had come, many of them by the big government boat which made a stately round-trip of the islands (a distance of some thousands of miles) to pick people up and bring them to Rarotonga to join in the dances and cultural displays. I slipped cautiously along the street between laughing brown people who talked to one another in Maori. Passing scooters honked and young men stopped, shouted greetings, leapt off and clasped long-absent relations in bearhugs. The tourist shops were full of little wooden figures of a man with a head as big as his body, a penis as long as his legs, and his hands clasped over his stomach.

'Why's that little man everywhere? I saw one of those figures at the airport.'

'That's Tangaroa,' said Kauraka. 'He is the symbol of the islands. Most of the early statues of him were taken away by missionaries. You must go and see the island girls dance,' he added mysteriously, in a way that didn't seem to follow. However, when we saw the dancing later, I understood what he had meant. Kauraka's aunty let him take us to an Island Night, where girls from the island of Pukapuka gyrated suggestively

46

on stage to a soft and rhythmic drum beat. One of them, her hips swaying, stepped slowly down into the audience and came towards me. I could feel my face on fire as the brown tummy-button wiggled closer, and the audience clapped and shouted Maori words that I thought were probably indecent. I was trans-fixed. Kauraka nudged me and lazily lowered his eye-lids in a slow blink.

'She's thinking of Tangaroa,' he whispered. 'Pu-kapuka girls – whew. Do they have a *reputation*, those Pukapuka girls.'

Kauraka knew a great deal of island history. He col-lected stories of the islands before the white man came. 'We put them in the pot at first,' he said, straight-faced. 'Very good they were too. We called them *Papa-a*, the white men. *Papa-a*, mm,' he said, and rubbed his tummy and rolled his eyes before he dug his big brown fingers into a fresh bag of toffees. Cath giggled. I felt uncomfortably as though I ought to change the subject.

'So which island d'you think they'll let us stay on?' I asked.

'Give me a couple of days,' he said. 'Manuae would be fine, but it is a little remote, and you would have to go to Aitutaki and wait for a boat. Takutea would be all right. And you can go to Suwarrow whenever a boat goes there but –' He shrugged his big shoulders. The island men have a boldness and liveliness about their faces; everything about Kauraka seemed larger than life at that moment, as his skin glowed chestnut colour in the setting sun. 'If you go to Suwarrow, you may not come back for a long time.'

47

'Why not?' asked Cath.

'There is no reason to go there. Boats drop in sometimes, but you never know when the next one is coming. If you went to a nearer island, somewhere within a few hundred miles, we could arrange for a boat from Rarotonga. But the only boats that go anywhere near to Suwarrow are on their way to the pearl farms at Manihiki. It's a hundred miles off course, so they only call in if they have a very good reason.'

'So how long . . .' I wanted to go to Suwarrow because of Tom Neale. That was where he had spent six years as a hermit. I was beginning to see how he had managed to stay away from people for so long.

'A year maybe. Nine months.'

'No, we can't go to Suwarrow, Tony,' said Cath firmly.

'I'll sort something out tomorrow. I'll talk to people in the morning while you go to see William Richard.'

That night we strolled through Avarua after dark. On one side of us was the harbour, with a collection of yachts, cargo boats, and little fishing vessels in port for the Constitution Celebrations. On the other, banana palms and shops, small houses and lanes and the backdrop of mountains against the sky. Hanging signs advertised bicycle hire, the Snowbird Laundromat and diving schools. A notice told us that Tuesdays and Wednesdays were Island Nights at the Rarotongan Hotel. A burger van stood on the waterfront. A jeep drove cautiously along the street. A few Australians were heading for the Empire Cinema, which was showing *Rambo*, while some local youths laughed uproariously as they ran over the road towards TJ's Night-club. It could have been Saturday night in a coastal resort in Wales, except for the warmth and the high violet sky – and the way people carelessly left their scooters at the roadside and ambled off, without locking them up or eyeing the neighbourhood suspiciously as they took off crash helmets.

The Banana Court Bar was easy to find. We had been aware of it all day, because so many of the young male islanders that we passed, riding scooters or strolling amiably from point to point, wore T-shirts with BANANA COURT written on them. We turned off the street under a palm tree and paid our admission fee to a fat lady sitting at a card-table. Inside it was a great barn of a place, full of enormous islanders in colourful shirts and shorts, their faces knobbly as walnuts. The ones who weren't shouting at each other in Maori and waving their glasses to illustrate a point were roaring with laughter. It seemed rather a rowdy place to me. I ordered a couple of bottles of Cook Islands Lager at the bar and felt conscious of my pale skin and general lack of beefiness. If this had been the dockyard in Swansea, I'd have feared for my life.

'You a Limey?' shouted an American voice near my shoulder. I looked around and saw the top of a bald head and a thin hairy arm, reaching under mine to place a glass on the counter. A bespectacled white face of about fifty looked up into mine.

'You what?'

'You bin here long, you know your way around?' He was peering up at me and I caught a gust of unpleasant breath.

'We've only just come,' I said.

'Shame, I coulda done with some information. Can't get a fuck in this place.'

'Pardon?'

'No offence, but you come to these places you know what to expect, right?'

I was silent.

'My wife died four months ago,' he shouted.

'Oh. Sorry to hear it.'

'Buncha crap after the Philippines. The women are all over you there.'

He must have realized he was getting no sympathy from me, because he vanished into the crowd. I took the drinks and wove my way back to Cath. Big fellows edged politely out of my path. Cath was sitting bolt upright. She had been joined by an elderly islander who was drinking beer with whisky chasers and looked much the worse for it.

'This gentleman here,' said Cath as I sat down, 'he says he'd like to meet you to discuss the War.'

I sighed, and nodded and smiled at our new friend. I always get them.

William Richard was the great-grandson of a nineteenth-century British castaway, Kauraka had told us. I said I'd like to meet him, and Kauraka rang up and told him to expect us. The next day we explored the south of the island on foot, looking for his house.

A young woman waved absently as she chugged by on her scooter with two big rings of doughnuts strung on a palm leaf over the handlebars. No cars passed us. We saw very few cars on Rarotonga generally, and when we did, their suspension often looked as if it had given up the battle with the islanders' tendency to put on weight. We strolled under tall palms, smelling the scent of hibiscus and feeling warm sun on our backs. Chickens pecked lazily in front gardens and occasionally an old brown lady in a floral dress would smile and wave as we passed the path to her house.

Finally we found the place we were looking for, a big bungalow set well back in a garden. The front door was open.

'*Kia Orana*,' said the bouncy sweet-faced girl who answered our knock. 'Hallo?' William Richard appeared from the room behind her, beaming and grasping our hands. The girl was introduced as Mary, his daughter. She had a very pretty face and a roly-poly figure. As we followed her voluptuous haunches into the kitchen, I remembered Kauraka telling me how the young girls were traditionally fattened up to show off their curves in the erotic dance that would attract a husband.

William Richard was a school inspector in his fifties who wore the usual T-shirt and long shorts. He greeted us with dignity and kindness. His wife spoke very little English, but she smiled a lot and sat us down at the table and plied us with chocolate cake. The garden glowed outside in yellow sunlight. Later we discovered that it was like a kind of tropical park, with bananas, and meandering dusty paths, and an outhouse with a boat in it and some chickens and large carefree black pigs.

The household consisted of William, his wife Tepu, their daughters, and a baby granddaughter called Mary

Ann, who was about Stacey's age and made us feel a bit misty-eyed. Once or twice while we talked a smiling young person would wander in, be introduced as the son or daughter of a friend who was working abroad, and would drift off again; they all seemed to live here, it was open house.

William Richard's name had been William Marsters until he changed it because of confusion at the Post Office between him and all the other Marsters on the islands; there were about three thousand people of that name altogether. I knew part of the Marsters story from Kauraka, and I wanted to know more, because the first Cook Islander of that name had been an Englishman, and already I identified with him as I did with Tom Neale.

William Marsters the First came from Gloucestershire, and was a ploughboy who ran away to sea in 1858. He set forth, from Bristol maybe, on a barquentine, a three-masted sailing ship, bound for Australia, and he can't have been happy because he jumped ship at Penrhyn, which is one of the northern group of islands. I wondered at the homesickness of the sailor who had named Penrhyn.

It seems that the islanders of Penrhyn were not at all happy to have this newcomer in their midst. However, one young warrior helped him to build a canoe, and waved him away as he paddled out to sea. Marsters must have been given good directions, because he fetched up on Palmerston, another Cook Island about eight hundred miles south-west. By the early 1860s he was settled there with a wife who was a local girl. He later took two more wives, and by the time he died, at the end of the nineteenth century, his three wives had borne him scores of children and there were hundreds of grandchildren, all of them bearing his name. The William who sat opposite me now, brushing a crumb of cake from his T-shirt, was a great-grandson. His grandfather had been one of the last children born before William Marsters the First died in 1899.

'How did they travel between the islands?' I asked William. Mary and her mother were sitting at the table with us, chopping pineapples and tipping them into a bowl.

'Come and see.' He rose slowly to his feet and said something in Maori to his wife, who made a quick reply. William grinned, and led Cath and me down the garden. His legs shone like old leather and he walked barefoot on the stony yellow path. Alongside it the grass was cropped short, perhaps by the pigs. I saw a rangy black one snuffling under a coconut palm.

In a three-sided shed roofed with long pandanus leaves we found a boat, up-ended above the floor on blocks. It was a canoe about twelve feet long, with three or four thin frets of timber that projected from one side. These supported a fish-shaped wooden pole running parallel with the boat's side. 'That's the float,' William explained. 'Or the balance, or whatever you call it. We always use this kind of boat to fish from. At least we used to, when everyone had a boat.'

'Doesn't everyone have one now, then?'

'No need,' he said crisply. 'Tinned tuna.'

I looked at the boat. Its timbers had worn to a bluish-green dryness like weathered copper. Paddling from Penrhyn to Palmerston in that, you'd be like an ant crawling the length of a school hall.

'So William Marsters got to Palmerston . . .'

William sat down with us on an old iron garden seat. 'I'll tell you the family story,' he said.

According to William, when Marsters first arrived on Palmerston from Penrhyn, he found a European called Jeffrey living there. 'Jeffrey already had a home on Aitutaki,' William explained in his deep, confident voice. Kauraka had told me that all the Marsters rolled their *r*'s still, as their Gloucestershire great-grandfather must have done. 'But he was having trouble with his wife. You know – they get fidgety. A woman doesn't like to leave her mother's family and go to such a remote place. Palmerston is one of our southern islands on the map, but even now it feels like Suwarrow or one of the northern ones. It's only two kilometres square, there's nothing much there, and it's not on any of the trading routes, you see. It's too far out, it's two hundred and seventy miles from here – people don't want to live there.'

'Who lives there now?'

'Palmerston? Everyone is a Marsters. It's a family island still, a small place. Anyway, to go back to the 1860s, when William Marsters came, Jeffrey gave in to his wife and said he would take her home to Aitutaki. He didn't want to leave, because he had undertaken to look after Palmerston for the owner, but he thought William Marsters could take his place.'

'Who was the owner?'

'An Englishman who lived in Tahiti. What made him the owner is not clear to me, but he had assumed rights. Anyway, no sooner was Jeffrey out of sight over the horizon than William stocked up his canoe

54

with mangoes and coconuts and set off to return to Penrhyn.' I thought of William, so recently a plough-boy, and marvelled at his navigational skill. 'When he got back to Penrhyn he asked a local girl called Matavia to marry him and come and live on Palmerston. She said yes, and they were married, and when they got into the canoe they took her younger sister with them. She was seventeen. Matavia took the name of Esther, and I don't know what the sister was called originally but in the family we know her as Adeline.'

'How did they think he was going to get them back over all those miles of ocean?'

'They had faith in the Lord,' said William firmly. Cath smiled at me. I thought of all the people who had said I'd never make it to the South Pacific and smiled back.

'William had children by Esther, and then married Adeline as well –'

'D'you mean – I mean how –'

'He conducted his own ceremony. He had to. And soon Adeline was pregnant. And as soon as her first baby was born he set off for Rarotonga in the canoe, and bought chickens and a sow in farrow and a cow and some tools and seeds –'

'What did he do for money?'

William grinned. 'There are a lot of family stories about that. I'm sure you'll hear them one day. First he brought all these things home, and with them a new wife, called Naomi.'

'Did she have babies too?'

'Certainly she did. Now, with so many children it seemed to William that he should make his future secure. Back he went towards the northern islands, to collect a team of men and all the growing coconuts they could carry. This was a clever move, as you will see. The men planted the coconut palms on Palmerston, and on the little *motus* around it.'

'*Motus*?'

'A little island is a *motu*. Nobody lives on the ones around Palmerston. You see an atoll like Palmerston, it is really the top of a volcano with bits of the edges showing around the crater in the middle, which is the lagoon. And in Palmerston, when the tide goes out, the edges of the volcano are so high under the water that ships can't get over. It's like a wall that shelters the lagoon from the open sea. The bits that project above the surface, where sand and vegetation occur, those are the *motus*. William Marsters's men planted coconuts on them too. Five hundred trees altogether.'

'And the men, did they stay on Palmerston?'

'No. William made sure they all went home. He didn't want any competition.'

'So did they have any other visitors?'

'Yes, they had trading ships call in a couple of times a year. And as the years passed, and the children grew into good swimmers and the trees produced coconuts, William Marsters the First began to trade in copra and pearls.'

'It sounds idyllic.'

'Of course. But there was one problem. After ten or twenty years William had a big tribe of wives and children and no security in the land, you see. Now, news came to Aitutaki that the owner of Palmerston had died far away in Tahiti. The man Jeffrey inherited Palmerston, so he set off, as soon as he got news of the death, to claim it. William received him in one of the houses – each of the wives had her own house built of driftwood; Naomi's, my great-grandmother's, is still there. But to go on with the story. The two men had a fairly friendly meeting. Jeffrey explained why he had come and William was courteous. Jeffrey could have the land, he said, but the trees belonged to him. The coconuts and the copra from them had been his livelihood for the past five years. So many people depended on them for sustenance that, if Jeffrey wished to persuade them all to leave, he must pay proper recompense for the trees. Jeffrey asked the price. "One guinea a tree," said William. He was a cool customer. He knew Jeffrey couldn't pay.

'Jeffrey went home to Aitutaki, feeling gloomy, and decided to take William to court. Now, this was just after the British had claimed the Cook Islands but before they had put a resident on Rarotonga. I suppose letters went back and forth to London – it must have taken a long time. This was the 1880s remember, and there was certainly no regular mail service to Europe. In the end somebody in London decreed that the court case should be heard in Fiji. So off went my great-grandfather and pleaded his case.'

'And he got the island.'

'It was a little more complicated than that. Jeffrey got the right to buy the coconut trees at William's asking price within three years. But if he couldn't pay, the trees and the land on which they stood would revert to William. Three years passed, no money arrived, and William became ruler of Palmerston.'

*

Master of all I surveyed. The phrase came from some-where.

I sat up carefully, so as not to disturb Cath asleep beside me. She had cried a little, thinking of the children. I gently stroked a curl of hair from her forehead and wondered again about Tom Neale. I had been enchanted by his book, and by how self-sufficient he was; but then when I got to Rarotonga I had had a shock. We found that he hadn't been a bachelor at all but a man with a wife and three children. We even met a schoolgirl who was a granddaughter of his. It had been quite upsetting for his wife, I heard, to be left out of the story as if she never existed. He simply left her behind. All the time he was building and fishing and growing things on Suwarrow, and apparently facing up to the ultimate challenge, she was struggling to bring up their family on her own.

My dreams were the same as his, but I wasn't going to realize them in the same way. I couldn't just leave Cath and the children and live on a desert island and claim to be independent. It was harder than that. Real independence for me had to include my family.

I wondered when Tutai would arrive. He and his crew had brought us here to Takutea, on their way to Manihiki to do some pearl-diving, and had promised that they would pick us up on their way back. They had been described to me by Kauraka and I had found their little green and white boat and approached them in the port at Avarua.

'Excuse me.' I felt awkward, calling out to these sailors. They seemed to be possessed of arcane know-ledge. There were two of them sitting cross-legged on the planking of the boat, and they were engrossed in what looked like an engine, or engine parts, disassembled and spread on a square of tarpaulin on the deck. The older one looked up and stared at me. It was that golden time again, the ten minutes when the light caught all the coppery tones of skin and hair and shone it back at you.

'Are you Tutai? Kauraka Kauraka told me you might be able to help us.'

I explained that I wanted to go to Takutea. The big man seemed genial. Of course, he agreed, as soon as his boat was seaworthy he would take us. It would cost $700 for the round-trip, he told me, his white teeth flashing, his eyes shaded by an arm shining with engine oil.

I told him I'd think about it.

'We can't afford that much,' I told Kauraka the following morning. Cath and I were visiting him in the hospital on the mountaintop. His aunty said he had had a relapse, though he seemed just the same to us. He sat in a straining cane chair, heavy-lidded eyes watchful, as nurses passed along the corridor beside us.

'Offer him $300,' he said. 'He'll say yes.'

Tutai accepted $300 at once. The following morning he and his two friends set off with us across a hundred and twenty miles of ocean to Takutea. He turned out to be an interesting man who read a lot, and said he liked to listen to my Welsh accent. He made me say a few things in Welsh.

When at last we saw the low island on the horizon I was speechless; I couldn't believe we were really here.

It was a small place, covered in low shrubs and coconut palms.

Little fishes scattered in the clear water beneath the prow of the boat. The engines stopped and the boat came to rest some way out from the beach. There was silence except for the sound of sea birds crying. I climbed into the water gingerly; it was tepid and came up to my chest. Cath fell from the side into my arms and I nearly toppled over with her weight. One of the crew said something in Maori to the other and they both laughed. I had only just told them I couldn't swim.

Cath swam a few yards and was first on to the beach. She shrieked; the sand was boiling, and mixed with thin sharp broken shells.

Tutai waded ashore to show us where to find trochuses and how to spot the shadow in the lagoon that was a shoal of fish. He told us that the big island we would see from the other side of Takutea was Atiu, but that it was not reachable from here, as the currents were too dangerous for a small boat to cross.

'I have to hurry on,' he explained. 'We've got to get back on course before dark. But first I'll show you the fresh water place.' We followed him as he ducked and dived through the gaps between low bushes for a few hundred yards and approached the middle of the island.

'This is it,' he said and pointed downwards. There was a sort of puddle about a yard across amid the grass. 'But of course there is coconut water.'

We thanked him, and he grinned and walked with us back to the shore. When he had clambered aboard again he handed down the fishing net William had lent us and our two suitcases. The other men watched as we struggled ashore with the cases. They shook their heads and grinned. They would have found it even funnier had they seen us after they had chugged away and were just a dot on the horizon.

We began by putting up the tent in the middle of the island, where we were about fifteen feet above sea-level, and Cath said we would be safer from a freak wave. We had only experimented with the tent once before, in the garden at home. We now discovered that the moist dark earth of Swansea was a lot easier to tread a peg into than the dry tussocky sand here. Besides we had nothing like a hammer, which would have been useful. In the end we made shift as best we could by pinning the ropes down with stones. That was when we discovered that the grey things that looked like small boulders were big crabs. There were crabs everywhere in the sand, babies that scuttled along the shore and bigger varieties like these; it was their island.

We looked up and saw coconuts above us like bunches of golden grapes. They are not like the fair-ground coconuts, when they are on the tree; they are more like big footballs, and have soft white flesh inside and a couple of pints of sweet clear water. I had seen boys climbing for them on Rarotonga; I had even seen William, a man in his late fifties, swarming quickly up a coconut palm. So I grasped the tree-trunk right round and got a foothold, then another one. I had seen how it was done and I wriggled my arms up a bit, which scraped the soft insides and hurt. Then with an almighty effort I got myself a few inches higher. And higher. And again. My chest was squashed against the palm-trunk and I looked up barely able to breathe. I saw graceful fronds of palm dancing against the reddish sky of evening, coyly sheltering their tempting harvest from the sun. Another heave. I was having to hold very tight and I began to wonder how I would get the coconuts down when I got up there. I couldn't let go to pick one, I would fall off. I looked down, saw the top of Cath's head just below my foot, and began to swoon.

'I hate heights,' I gasped, landing heavily on the ground behind her. 'I can't do it, Cath.'

'You can't swim, you can't stand heights, what can you do?' she said scornfully. 'Look here, give me a bunk up and I'll get them down.'

I got her on to my shoulders and we wobbled about a bit until she got a good grasp of the tree. Then she got a foot on to the trunk, and her other foot on my shoulder, then on to the trunk, and I ducked slowly out of the way, and there she was, clinging to it, one leg higher than the other. She moved one leg. She seemed to stay there for several seconds before she slid down the trunk as firemen slide down a pole. When she got to the bottom with the insides of her legs scarlet there were tears in her eyes and she swore violently. All redheads have a bit of a temper, so I ignored her.

After that we found a stick and knocked down some coconuts that were on a very low tree, and had supper.

It was nearly dark, so we got into the tent; but not before Cath had made me bring both the suitcases inside. You never knew, she said.

*

Tutai had said that he and his crew would return in 'a couple of months'. I had deliberately not kept any record of the passing days. The wisdom of this seemed obvious. I had been clock-watching all my working life; I had been expected to turn up on time for at least two, sometimes three shifts a day. My life had been governed by the clock for far too long. Yet almost against my will I retained a vague idea of the number of nights we had passed in our tent.

Cath was awake. 'I think they're late back,' she said softly, sitting up beside me. The thought that we might really be castaways occurred to both of us; but we did not voice it.

If you ask a person to draw a desert island they put a curved line, and a single palm tree on it. Takutea was not quite like that. But it was almost as low in the water as the imaginary version. A big wave would swamp the beach, and from one end to the other is only about half a mile. We had camped out on it for weeks now, not really becoming part of it, but camping as we would have done in the Brecon Beacons, in our £6.99 tent from Millet's.

It was very exposed; the sun seemed to reach us wherever we went. We moved the tent down to a shady spot on the sands once, but the birds attacked us. These were big frigate birds, white with scarlet tail feathers and beaks. They swooped at us with their menacing red mouths agape, making angry cawing noises.

'We're in their space,' Cath said. She was right. We had parked in the middle of the runway they used for taking off and landing. We moved the tent back to the middle of the island, and the birds left us alone.

We hadn't brought any books. I had seen Cath looking longingly at a display of paperbacks at Tahiti Airport. 'We're supposed to be leaving the twentieth century behind,' I said. Besides, by that time I had realized how expensive everything was.

'If you say so,' she said doubtfully. 'What about my medicine, then?' She has to take two tablets a day for epilepsy.

'That's different. You need those.'

'I might like something to read as well.'

'Yes, but you won't *need* it. That's the difference.'

A long time had passed since then. Without books, or television or radio or even eight favourite records, we had nevertheless fallen into a routine. In the morning I knocked down a few coconuts with a stick. Cath looked for trochuses or crayfish. After breakfast Cath arranged her shells while I strolled off to the other side of the island. There I knelt on the beach in the *seiza* position, which I learned when I was twelve at an aikido class in Llanelli, and meditated.

We picked some drinking coconuts and then fell asleep for the hottest part of the day. I meditated again later in the afternoon, practising standing on my head in the sand. In the evenings we walked into the shallowest part of the lagoon with a net, and pulled out some fish. Cath boiled these in coconut water over a Primus stove. Having eaten, we talked.

You can live with somebody for years in Swansea and never talk the way you did before the children were born. Because of the hours I worked and the free time I had during the day, we had spent more time together than most couples. Yet after ten years the things we talked about were shopping, my work, and our family and friends. We never discussed what we really felt or wanted. Before we got married we had sat on the seafront with a bag of chips and talked about our dreams. Cath wanted to be a nurse, and I wanted to live on a desert island. Those conversations had been the most intimate ones of our marriage – until now. On the desert island all our little pretensions and artifices were left behind. If Cath wanted to leave the tent to go to the toilet in the middle of the night, I went with her, because she was afraid of the dark. When she went into the lagoon, she didn't expect me to swim with her, because she knew I was frightened of the water.

Modestly, we both wore shorts, though after the first few days Cath left her top off. I expected to feel rampant lust, but most of the time I was too hot.

We were honest with each other about our fears and failings, and what we wanted. And now that we knew each other, and felt we had found a calm centre to our relationship, Cath reminded me that I missed the children as much as she did.

But Tutai didn't come.

Cath was rearranging her shells and I was lying on my back with an arm over my face against the sun. My skin smelled like the salt sea.

'When Tutai comes,' I said, 'and we go back home, d'you think the children will want to come out here with us?'

'Stacey's a bit young to decide.'

'No, not Stacey. You know. Will Craig and Matthew want to come, d'you think, Cath?'

'Craig wanted to come this time.'

'When they've seen the photographs d'you think?'

''Course they'll want to come.' She stroked my neck tenderly. Cath is affectionate in a natural way. Her whole family is. They're not like my mother and father, who never touched any of us. I remember being quite shocked when I first saw how Cath's parents cuddled her when she was miserable. In my family there were whole sequences of human interaction missing. You couldn't be miserable, or angry, or express dissatisfaction in any way. Us children learned very early to get by without expressing feelings. The four of us were as taciturn and impassive as lamp standards or taps.

Cath kissed me. After a while she said, 'We'll have to find a way to get the children out here next year. No, not next year. When we can afford it.'

'They don't charge for children under four on the plane.'

'I know, but it's still a lot of money.'

'Three years, d'you think we could save it in three years?'

'We've got the loan to pay back, remember.'

I had taken out a loan for a car, to pay for Cath's fare as well as my own. It was easy. You filled in a form at the bank and were interviewed on a Saturday morning in the banking hall, right beside a queue of shoppers, by a youth who looked like a school-leaver. He kept telling me I'd get a better deal on a car with the cash from this loan but I ought to take out insurance on it, which was an extra £3.89 a month. It was like listening to a robot. Anyway they put the money in my account and off we went. When we got back I would have enough money left to buy a car anyway, but I would also have to deduct a chunk of my salary for several years to pay the loan back. I felt as if the sun had gone in.

'I wish you hadn't said that, Cath,' I said. 'It's like being back home. Stress and loans and bloody money, if the children were out here now I'd never go back.'

I heard Cath exclaim and sat up. 'What is it?'

Cath was standing up already, waving madly. 'It's Tutai. Look! Their boat's out there.'

I took her firmly by the shoulder. 'Well, go and put a top on, Cath,' I said.

4

I woke to a knock on the door downstairs. I could hear Cath talking to the postman and I turned over under the bedclothes and opened my eyes. Rain was crawling down the outside of the window panes and hissing sadly in the gutters. Nothing had changed here. The dressing-table was in the same place, and Cath's jar of face cream on it, and my digital alarm on the floor by the bed. We had been back only a few weeks and it was as if we had never been away.

Cath shut the front door and came upstairs. I could hear the children talking and a blare of synthetic cheerfulness from the radio in the kitchen.

'Recorded delivery,' she said. 'It's for you.'

I got up, scratching my head.

'Don't scratch. You know what the doctor said.'

'What's he know about tropical diseases?'

'That's not a tropical disease, you heard him, it's a fungal infection. Come downstairs, I'm making a cup of tea.'

It felt like a tropical disease; hot and itchy. And it looked horrible. Scaly. Our first weekend back we had gone into Malone's Wine Bar in Swansea and I overheard something about dandruff from hell. Since then I had been avoiding public places.

When Cath had gone I opened the letter. It was from Mr N. Whitlock, who had 'Chairman of Governing Bodies' under his name. He and the Headmasters of the two schools thought that the 'current situation was unsatisfactory'. They wanted details of the itinerary we had followed and my 'intentions for the immediate future, in terms of you returning to work'.

I knew Whitlock. He was a big bearded man with half-moon glasses who had a shop in the market.

'Cath!'

West Cross is a small place. If you didn't know it you'd think it was just another part of Swansea. It doesn't look like a village, and nobody goes in and out of each other's houses, but in our estate everyone knows everyone else's business all the same. Young men marry into families they know, having been to school with cousins or brothers of the girls they meet. They don't leave the district. They have children young, and fall out of work easily. They have no idea that they might do better somewhere else, because they don't know anybody who's gone away. The outside world exists on the box in the corner.

There are very few people who come in from outside Swansea either. My mother's father was a Londoner, and Cath's brother-in-law too, but apart from that everyone in our families is local. When we came down here from the valleys when I was eight, speaking only Welsh, you'd have thought we were aliens at school instead of coming from less than fifteen miles away. You are expected to work in Swansea and send your children to the school you went to yourself. There are some strangers round here of course. The University has a lot of foreign students, some of them with families. But they don't mix with people like us.

So when we came back before Christmas, there was talk. After all we were famous; we had been on TV. I felt that there was a lot of resentment, but the only people in authority who voiced any doubts were Mr Whitlock and Mr Uren.

Maybe I was mad to expect any different. Somebody told my father-in-law that at the governors' meeting it had been said we'd never left the British Isles but had been hiding out in Scotland all the time. If that was true, it was no wonder these governors wanted to see my itinerary. All the same I couldn't see what right they had to demand my return to work, because I could prove I'd been given unpaid leave of absence, in writing, until the 8th of January next year.

I said all this several times on the morning I got the letter.

'You want to ring the union,' Cath said. We had walked the children to school and were on our way down to the shops, squinting into the rain and wind.

The union said I could ignore the letter if I wanted to. 'They've got no right to demand an itinerary from you,' said the man on the phone. 'In my view it's none of their business if you've been to the moon and back.'

I decided to go and see Mr Uren anyway. I rang up and made an appointment with his secretary.

On Saturday I bumped into Mrs Carpenter, the teacher from Plasmarl, in the street.

'I heard you were home,' she said. She had just come out of the newsagent's with the *Guardian*, and looked tired. It was the weekend, so she hadn't got her make-up on. 'Was it what you expected?'

'It was better,' I told her. By now I was dying for

somebody to talk to. I had found that after the first day or two, Cath's parents didn't want to know about the islands. Even my brother changed the subject. Mrs Carpenter had been interested from the start, so I knew she'd want to hear about it now. I expanded on my description for about ten minutes. She fidgeted a bit as people edged past us on the pavement, and we seemed to be doing a circular dance, with me chasing her round so that her back was to the shops. I finished up, 'We was going to work on a talk to take round the schools, wasn't we?'

'Well, if there's material there,' she said. She was a lot less forthcoming than she had been a year before.

'What sort of material?'

'Oh – slides, local flora and fauna, you know.'

'Local – yes, we've got slides. Yes, I know about the birds and the trees, but it's the people, you see, the Marsters family that I found interesting.' It was frustrating. I kept shuffling round as her eyes wandered, but I didn't seem to be communicating the way I felt, my amazement at finding a real desert island and a real family descended from a castaway from over a hundred years ago. Mrs Carpenter folded her newspaper into quarters and pushed it into her shoulder-bag.

'Well, we'll see. I must get along now, Tony.'

'I heard Miss Roberts did a talk.'

'Yes, very successfully.'

Miss Roberts was a teacher who had taken six months off to go to Australia with her boyfriend.

'She only went to Australia. You'd think people would be interested in a completely different style of life, wouldn't you?'

'Yes, of course. If you want to do a talk, it's a question of asking County Hall.' I noticed that it was a question of me asking County Hall, not the two of us together. I wondered what I had done to offend her.

Cath and I went off to my appointment with Mr Uren at Bryn Mill. I wore my suit and Cath looked very nice in a new jacket. She waited with me outside his office for fifteen minutes, on hard chairs in the corridor with small children coming past, staring, knocking on the Headmaster's door and gaining admittance before going away again. There was already somebody in with Mr Uren; it was a man, and we could hear a burst of laughter now and again.

When the secretary showed me in, Mr Whitlock was sitting in a corner behind Mr Uren. Mr Uren was at his desk. Neither of them got up.

'Good afternoon, Mr Williams,' said Mr Uren. 'You know Mr Whitlock, don't you.' It wasn't a question. Whitlock had been a Conservative councillor until recently, which made him well known; but in any case, as chairman of governors, he was supposed to be important enough for me to recognize him on sight, and indeed I had often nodded to him as he left the school after meetings, in the bitter dark nights of a winter term.

'Yes.'

'Now we have to clear up this matter.'

I didn't say anything. I could feel my face smiling, but I was angry. I sat down on the hard chair in front of the Headmaster's desk.

'Well, Mr Williams? What's your explanation for all this?'

'All what?'

'Now, don't come the innocent here. You can't pretend you don't know what's going on. You're caretaker for these two schools, in case you've forgotten.'

'I've got leave of absence.'

'To go away, yes. But you're back now. You should be at work.'

'Yes, I'm getting medical attention. I've got a scalp condition. It's a fungus I got in the Cook Islands. I'm having blood tests.'

'I suppose you know some doubts have been voiced about whether you've been to the Cook Islands at all.'

'Well, I have. I took my wife.'

'Oh, indeed. I don't know how much we're paying you, but I want to know how a school caretaker can afford to take his wife to the South Pacific.'

'We had savings. And in the first place it was going to be just me –'

'And that's another thing. All this publicity. We don't want this sort of thing at the school. Getting yourself in all the papers, everybody knew you worked here. I was getting calls from God knows where. Sunday papers in London – all this talk about some woman, and you married. And to cap it all now I sit down for my tea one night and what pops up on the TV screen but your face.'

'I didn't go seeking publicity, I –'

'How do we know you've been to some island?'

'I've written about it. I've told everybody. It's called Takutea, we lived on fish and coconuts. It was a survival project.'

I was feeling really paranoid; I thought I heard him say something about a helicopter dropping us off.

'How d'you get there, then?'

'It takes ten hours to get there from Rarotonga. We got a boat that some men were taking to Manihiki, where the pearl farms are.'

'Pearl farms.'

'Yes, they farm pearls on Manihiki, that's a lot further on.'

They stared at me. Mr Uren said, 'Now look. Enough is enough, Mr Williams. I want you back at work at once.'

When I got back into the corridor, Cath said, 'Well? What did you tell him?'

'He says I've got to go back to work Monday.'

'You should have told him where to stick his job.'

I didn't go back to work, and waited to see what would happen.

On Takutea I had filled six exercise-books with writing. I described the island and what I had thought about when we were there. A lot of it concerned my childhood. I got it typed by a girl who advertised in the *Evening Post*. And on a Saturday morning I took the manuscript into the city centre to get it photocopied.

Me and Cath were coming out of the print shop when I ran into my father. 'What you been doing in the print shop, then? What's that you got there? Written a book about your world travels, have you?'

'Yes, I have.'

'Oh, really. That'll sell well, I don't think. You're a big bag of wind, you are. You only been gone half a year. Less. What you going to fill it up with? Your childhood?'

'Yes. There's a lot about you in it.'

'You know bugger all about me. Your mother marched you off as soon as you could walk. You're a liar, you always were. Look at you, you shifty little devil.'

Cath grabbed my arm and dragged me down the hill.

'I don't know why you even bother to talk to him,' she said angrily. I wondered myself. But somehow when he was there, in front of me, I was transfixed, like a rabbit by a ferret. I wanted to keep him there because in the back of my mind, I always thought I could make him see how he had treated me and be sorry. Instead he attacked me, every time, and I couldn't bite back.

Both the schools seemed to be getting on fine without me. Christmas was approaching, and one night when I went past Bryn y Môr I saw the decorations up, cotton-wool snow neatly curved against the bottom right-hand corners of all the windows, and red and green paper lanterns that were kept the rest of the year high up in the stationery cupboard. I would be scouring the parquet for dropped drawing-pins when I went back in January.

I had to go to County Hall to explain why I hadn't gone back to my job the minute the plane landed. The Assistant Director of Education wrote me a nice letter and said it would help if I could take airline tickets or other evidence of where I'd been. When I got there, and went into the room and showed him my souvenirs, he laughed and shook his head. He said he didn't know why I'd wanted to go to a desert island and it would have saved trouble all round if I'd taken a fortnight at Tenby. It was good enough for him, he said, he'd never been out of Britain in his life. But somehow, in the days that followed, he soothed the troubled waters at Bryn Mill and Bryn y Môr.

I liked my job. I was entitled to take some time off from it, and happy not to have to go to work for a few months, but I liked it all the same: the feeling of achievement when you locked up at night, knowing everything was tidy and clean and polished; the smell of traffic wax; feeling that the children had been kept warm and safe for another day. It was a good job.

I kept coming across another kind of resentment, not so much outrage that somebody like me could travel, but jealousy that I had attracted attention because of it. There was a barmaid at Malone's Wine Bar who expressed it exactly. She was French, and had travelled all over before she fetched up in Swansea. She told me she had come overland from the Far East. She said to my face what the others only implied, or whispered behind my back.

'People go away a lot, all the time. Why is there all the fuss? I have lived on an island in Malaysia. I saw nobody there for many days. Why is it that you are on television?'

After the first time she never spoke to us, and I overheard her telling somebody in the bar that we gave her a pain, me and Cath.

She didn't understand about West Cross. For her, travelling was normal: you asked your father for a cheque. It isn't like that for people like us, and I wanted to explain, but when I heard her saying how we gave her a pain, I decided not to bother. I talked to the barman instead. He was a nice young Irishman called John and he said we were an inspiration to him. This was his second Christmas in the bar and he told me it would be his last. He said he'd always wanted to travel.

People round us on the estate were not jealous but they seemed suspicious. They didn't know anybody else who had been on television. And if you were in the papers because you were in your firm's football team that had won, they cut it out. It was a big thing. So stories about me made people shy. They thought I was different from the person they had known, now that I had been abroad. Being different is bad; it's a disability. People are nice to you to your face, but behind your back they talk.

Christmas was a bit lean, with three children to buy presents for and no money coming in, so I was looking forward to starting work again at the end of the first week in January. I had big plans for saving all my overtime to go away again.

On New Year's Day we walked along the front from West Cross to Mumbles. I could do that walk in my sleep. Craig and Matthew were running along the beach below us, sometimes stopping to try and throw pebbles as far as the water's edge. The sea was dark grey, and miles out. The beach was brown and wormy with miles of silver sky above. In the distance the pretty little town of Mumbles clung to the shelter of the headland, the chip shop and the newsagent's and the bus stop, and a few boats in a chilly huddle under the hillside. The view held no surprises. I wanted Craig and Matthew to know what I did about white sand and warm sun and coconut palms. They shouldn't grow up with their minds stunted like the people round here, thinking this was all there was.

I didn't need to tell Cath what was on my mind; she knew I had been reading about Captain Bligh all morning.

'How long will it take us to save up to take the children, Cath?'

'Years, at this rate,' she said. Stacey was asleep in her pushchair as we trundled along the front. 'She'll be needing shoes soon.'

'Don't you miss it, Cath?'

''Course I do. I'd rather be there than here. But they've got to go to school, Tony.'

'We could take them for the summer holidays, just for six weeks.'

'We'd still have three fares to pay, even if Stacey goes for nothing.'

It would be well over £3,000, even without spending money or funds for emergencies or insurance. And I was still paying off the loan for last year's trip.

'We'll do it in the end,' I said. 'Maybe the price of cigarettes will go up.'

We called our savings the cigarette money because that was how we had got the money for my fare in the first place. One day a couple of years back I had been talking to a woman I knew – she worked in a fruit shop and had a terrible life with two delinquent sons –

78

about travelling. She was puffing on a cigarette as she totted up the day's takings, and she said she wanted to go to New Zealand. She had always wanted to, but how would she ever get the money? I said I'd tell her how: all she had to do was give up smoking. I took a piece of paper and borrowed a pen from her and worked it out. She spent about £16 a week, even then. I multiplied it up to see how she could save the money for New Zealand in less than a year.

'She can't do that. No more than I can,' said the man who owned the greengrocer's. He was sweeping out at the time.

She gave him a filthy look. 'It's an addiction,' she said to me.

'I know, but if you really wanted to go to New Zealand, you'd give it up and put the money away,' I persisted.

She seemed quite offended. 'It's my only pleasure,' she said, and ground out the one she was smoking on the lino tiles as his broom approached.

When I told Cath about this we began the cigarette savings. We pretended we smoked twenty a day and put the money in the Christmas biscuit tin. We were addicted, we told each other; we could not do without cigarettes. Not a day would pass without spending that money. Every Saturday morning I took the tin up a ladder into the loft, where I tipped the coins into an old cash-box with compartments.

We enjoyed switching brands occasionally. Cath usually pretended she smoked Dunhill and I was an Embassy Regal man. On Budget Day, when they announced ten pee on the price of a packet of cigarettes, we knew we had to save more, or look around for a menthol-tipped brand that would be cheaper.

The union had told me I'd have to watch out for myself when I went back to work.

'What, you mean I might still be in trouble because I took leave of absence?' I asked the voice on the phone.

'No, of course not. But I suggest you keep a low profile.'

On my first day back I found things had changed in my absence. Each of the two schools had acquired an industrial-size floor buffer. The cleaners took turns in using these machines, which didn't just polish, but also held water and scrubbed tiled floors. They were a marvel and when I got back, never having seen anything like them, the cleaners had a bit of an edge over me. They acted superior about the machines; in fact you'd think they'd invented the things. But when it came to shifting the beasts from floor to floor, it was my turn.

Porterage was one of my duties, so I got on with it, but the job hadn't seemed so hard since they did away with coal. I would be heaving the machine upstairs at Bryn Mill at six in the morning and then dashing down the road to lift the Bryn y Môr machine on to another floor. And then back up, and then down, and at each school the cleaners would want the buffing machines moved.

So the cleaners were glad to see me back in my job, even if only because I was like a human lift. But some of the teachers were different. They had been friendly towards me when I was planning my trip, because they thought I was a dreamer. They had encouraged me, like Mrs Carpenter at Plasmarl, and had said they would like to do the same thing. Now that I had done it, while they were still stuck in the same place, with the same problems, I was an achiever, and a threat. I made them confront something about themselves. They were wary of me and, like Mrs Carpenter, seemed to have cooled off.

But there was something else that I could not yet define: a kind of impatience with me, a dismissal of me, a jealousy. Where some people seemed to think that I was lying, that I just talked about desert islands and hadn't really been to one, one or two school-teachers seemed jealous, like the French barmaid at Malone's. I suppose they thought because they were more literate than me and had degrees that they had a right to an audience and I didn't. That was why Mrs Carpenter was cool towards me now and why the teachers didn't want to know. I had been in the papers and they didn't think I deserved to be.

I was back in the routine: work from five thirty till nine thirty, home until three, and then work till six or, if there was overtime, until ten at night. There were Lettings in the evenings, and I had to be on call while they were there to make sure everything was secure.

At the old school in Plasmarl I had occupied these evening hours in the Headmaster's study, looking through school registers from the last century: big maroon leather volumes with marbled edges to the pages and columns of sepia copperplate handwriting inside. You'd haul the book down and read *Form Two*, and the old names: *Ethel*, *Myfanwy*, *Blodwyn*, most of them Joneses and Powells and Thomases like today, but the sicknesses different: *diphtheria*, *scarlet fever*, *bilious attack*. And long absences sometimes ending in *dec'd*.

Now, at schools where there were no old volumes to read, I usually walked down to the shop once the classes were settled in. I would buy a snack for my tea and hurry back with my collar up against the cold, thinking about money. I was always working out how much overtime I'd done and adding it up and mentally checking it against plane fares.

I worked all the evenings I could, and began again early; in a hard week it felt as if I was at school all my waking hours. And then one morning at seven o'clock I was hauling a buffing machine up the steps at Bryn y Môr when my back locked.

Maybe it was stress, or maybe the thing was too heavy for me. Whatever the matter was, I was rigid with pain, as if I had a boulder on my back, and I could feel the hefty machine pulling me forward, down steep steps on to a hard floor. It slipped from my fingers, turning slowly as it careered to the bottom with a crash. I must have cried out because in no time I was surrounded by people, an ambulance had been called, and I was in hospital. As they lifted me on to a stretcher, I kept thinking about the overtime I would miss if I was off sick, and I could have cried with frustration.

It would be longer still before we had enough money to go away. How was I going to earn the cigarette money now?

5

I was on pain-killers so as Cath left the ward she looked a bit out of focus, but I heard what she said. 'Don't worry, I won't be telling your mother this time.' I managed a grin and a wave as she went away.

It was the second time in my life I had been in hospital. The first time I was seventeen. I hadn't been going out with Cath long and I got appendicitis, with some complications. I was too far gone to know what was wrong with me, but Cath had been told, and she went up the estate in a taxi to fetch my mother. I don't think my mother would have cared, since she had barely seen me since I left home two years before, but Cath came from a different sort of family and didn't know this.

She had to throw a stone up at the window because there wasn't an answer. The haunted face came to the window, with the hand at the mouth dragging on a cigarette as usual, and looked down and disappeared. Cath waited. The front door opened. 'What you doing up here?'

'It's Tony,' Cath said. 'He's been taken ill, he's in the hospital, they're operating.'

'Oh, yes, how's that, then? You couldn't lend me a couple of quid for cigs, could you? I can pay you back tomorrow.' She threw her dog-end into the garden.

Cath just stared at my mother in disbelief, turned round and left.

I couldn't understand what my mother's feelings

were. She never laid a finger on us when we were children, she always looked after us herself, and yet, because she never showed us any affection, it was hard to know what she thought she was gaining by keeping the four of us.

She kept advertising for a man. I suppose she thought she would find one who would rescue us from being poor. A farmer wrote her from Yorkshire once, and sent her fare. My eldest sister, who had just married at seventeen, stayed home with her new husband and our mother took the rest of us there by coach and bus. It was a low old house, miles out on a moor, not a bit like the valleys but windswept, and there was a big dog. I saw the fellow's face when he opened the yard door and the dog snarled and she stood there. Us three were loitering in the background with hold-alls. I don't think he'd expected children. He made us go to bed at seven and after about three weeks he threw her out. We set off up the farm track with our luggage, with our mother and the man still having a row because she didn't have the fare home. The door slammed on them. Then she came on after us, and got us back with her on a coach to Swansea; it must have been expensive, all the tickets.

Not that we cost a lot, day to day. She was often not there at tea-time so we all learned to get money for food, except for our little sister, who was usually sick. After about three years in the caravan the doctor had visited so often for my sister's bronchitis that he kicked up a fuss with the Guildhall, as County Hall was then, and got us a council house.

★

I went home to West Cross. I was supposed to be convalescing. There were medicals, organized by the West Glamorgan Education Authority, which I thought I must have passed. I wasn't in great pain so I waited to be told I could go back to work.

The spring term was almost over when I got a letter telling me that I had been permanently incapacitated by my injury and in view of that, my employment would be terminated and an index-linked pension granted. I had to read it over and over, and discuss 'permanently incapacitated' with Cath and her family and my brother, before I believed it.

The union told me I must sue for compensation and I was only too willing. I thought I should never have had to haul industrial buffers up flights of stairs, and I said so to the solicitor they found for me. She was a nice woman, with an office in Cardiff city centre, who explained to me and Cath that I was certainly entitled to some money, but it would take years before the case came to court.

'Years? How many years?'

She shrugged. 'I couldn't say. Two. Five. It's the system, I'm afraid.'

We found ourselves out in the street, in weakly commiserating sunshine, walking to get the train home. I thought about how I had been able to tell people I was a caretaker, and now I wasn't one any more. It had meant a lot to me, having a good job; more than just the money. I took pride in it.

People with shopping-bags passed us, going about their business; people with jobs. They bustled into Our Price and Boots and Next, knowing that they could spend money. I was going to have to bring up the children on a pension equivalent to income support. Cath got some money too, as an epileptic.

The island seemed almost out of reach now. I could take the whole family out there when the compensation came through, but that might be years. I would be half buried in this place year after year with no end in sight; I couldn't stand it.

I could, of course.

I managed the same way everybody else does. Days began, pottered by and ended with relief that they had passed. Summer came, then winter, then another summer. Rituals made the time pass, like telegraph poles along a road: rabbit stew and the late feature on TV at Cath's mam's on Saturdays, a walk along the front with the children on Sunday afternoon, library on Mondays, a drink at Malone's with Cath on Wednesday nights. John, the Irish barman at Malone's, was still saying he'd be off travelling after next Christmas, and three years had passed since he started saying it.

My brother talked about coming with us when we went back to the Cook Islands. I told him about William and his family and how they took stray teenagers into the household in their laid-back, friendly way; we should have met them when we were at school, I said. I could see it sounded inviting to him. But he had wriggled into a comfy place in his rut. I knew he wouldn't leave Swansea.

It was about six o'clock on a winter's evening. All had

been quiet in Craig's and Matthew's room for a while, when I put my head round the door and found that they had put out the light. This was very unusual because Craig had just started at senior school and he generally had a lot of homework to do after tea.

'What you two doing?'

'Watching.'

As my eyes got used to the black, I could see that they were kneeling on chairs, with their heads between the net curtains and the windows, avidly watching the street.

'What are you watching?'

'There's gonna be a race,' said Craig.

'What race?'

'Last night when I said I saw two cars going fast, well, it was a boy at school's brother and they're going to do it again tonight.'

This was too much. 'They're not allowed to have races in the street.'

'They keep having them, though,' said Matthew, aged seven. 'Look.'

I could hear engines roaring up the road. I strode to the window in time to see one blare of headlamps and then another, that had to swerve to avoid Mr Thomas's car parked on the opposite kerb; they must have been doing seventy.

'How old's that boy? The brother?'

'Sixteen.'

So now it was our estate. It had been happening in the city centre all summer. On Friday and Saturday nights, child drivers in baseball caps gathered at the top of Kingsway outside a multi-storey car park, and one after another shot down the road and did hand-brake turns at a mini-roundabout. And that was the 'city centre'; a place empty enough in the evenings for stunt racing to go on without the police being called.

The next time Craig complained of being bored, Cath and I took him along to enrol in the Swansea Grand Youth Theatre. It ate into our cigarette money, but I didn't care.

'He's always bloody moaning, your Walter Mitty,' Cath's dad said to her. It was Saturday night and he had stayed in for once, to eat the rabbit. He reached across me to grab the salt cellar. 'You go on about crime you do, Tony, but I don't see you joining the constabulary if you feel so strongly about it.'

'It's more than just crime, it's the way people are round here.'

'What would you know, you've lived here all your life, what makes you think people are so much better anywhere else? And don't start about Rarowhatjama-callit,' he warned. 'I've had it up to here with you and your travels. You're a married man with three children, it's time you settled down.'

So I watched television.

I watched television, and Cath cooked the meal and washed up, and Craig played with his computer or did his homework; I thought he got too much of it, for a child of eleven. He had grown quieter and seemed under stress since he started at the senior school. He was up till ten o'clock at night sometimes. But he blossomed at rehearsals for the Youth Theatre at week-ends. He was going to be Baby Face in *Bugsy Malone* after Christmas. The younger ones played with their toys. You couldn't expect them to play out when the weather was cold and wet, and in any case with the crime in Swansea now there was no question of letting them out after dark; and it was dark by four. We didn't have a big house but it seemed to have a different room for everybody.

Cath and I were together most of the time, but we didn't have much to talk about except the price of things. We couldn't go out more than once a week because we were saving so hard, and the longer we saved, the dearer the fares became: Stacey's fourth birthday had passed, so we would have to pay half fare for her now. I envisaged the prospect of another winter like the last one, and decided to do something drastic.

He was a little fellow, a bus driver, he said. When he unfolded the crisp new notes from his wallet, I wondered if he'd been to the bank for a loan, same as I had three years ago. The car sat outside our house, looking better than it had done for months. I had done a nice job on the scraped paintwork and waxed it ready for sale and I'd only had the ad in one night, when this bus driver turned up. He said the car was for his wife, but she didn't come round.

I watched him drive off in it and went indoors.

'That's it,' I said, coming up behind Cath at the sink and putting my arms round her. '£2,100. Plus the cigarette money and I'll ask £300 for Craig's computer and the music centre. We're on our way, Cath.'

William Richard had made me promise to let him know as soon as we were on our way back. I rang him at half past ten that night and told him we would be over with the children some time next year. He sounded very pleased.

'But you won't be able to stay on Takutea again,' he said. His voice was deep and rolling, and I saw him in my mind's eye like Neptune crossing the waves. 'They've made it into a bird sanctuary now.'

'Where will we go, then?'

'I think you should stay on one of the Palmerston islands, since you're interested in my great-grandfather. I'll see what I can organize. There is one called Primrose.'

'Is it a nice island?'

'It's a beautiful island. Not as remote as Suwarrow but very far from anywhere. Leave it with me.'

I thanked him and rang off, but not before I could ask about the weather. He laughed. This puzzled me until I remembered that our winter is their summer. Mary had just picked some bananas from the garden, he said.

It was lucky that the journalist rang when she did.

'I thought I'd chase you up,' said an enthusiastic girl's voice on the telephone. 'About your being a castaway. I've got a note here from, erm, 1989, that you were planning to take the children when they were a little older, and I wondered whether you're still going.'

'Oh, yes,' I said, confident now that the car was sold and things seemed to be moving. 'We're going in the New Year.'

She said she wrote for various magazines. She came

down to see us a few days later, with a photographer. He had a shaven head covered in a small black hat and wore a long overcoat; the journalist wore a leather jacket and a micro-skirt. Cath said the neighbours would think we were letting rooms to students. But the girl was very friendly, drank tea without milk and took notes on everything. I gave her an old aerial photograph of Rarotonga and told her how I wanted to see William Richard again and how I had spoken to him on the phone, which was true; I told her all about how fish and coconuts were an adequate diet. The photographer waited for Craig and Matthew to come back from school and took their picture in the front garden with Stacey. The article didn't appear for weeks, and when it did, there was nothing about William Richard in it.

But somebody must have seen it, because we got a telephone call from the *Daily Mirror*.

The *Mirror* sent Harry Arnold. I had seen his picture in the paper sometimes, a very small picture the size of a postage stamp that they printed in the middle of the page when he did a report. He had a square face and glasses. However, when he stepped out of the station taxi I was not prepared for anyone so opulent. He had a mobile phone, a leather briefcase and a wallet that he flourished at the taxi driver like somebody in an advertisement. Very dapper he was, and I could see curtains twitching over the way as he came up the path.

He was not nearly so intimidating once he got indoors. He was very friendly, and put his phone and his briefcase on the floor and sat down with me at our low table while Cath made a cup of tea. He asked a lot of general questions before he got round to the island. I told him what I had told the girl journalist about William Richard, and how we hoped to go in the New Year. I was getting tired of saying it by now, I just wanted it to happen. He asked me the children's ages and what we would live on and whether we would have a boat. He wanted to know what had happened to the photographs from our last trip and was very interested in our cuttings from the *Post*.

'So exactly when're you going, Tony?'

'After Christmas I hope,' I said. 'It's the money, see. We've sold everything so we've nearly got enough, but there's still a bit of saving to do.'

That was an understatement. In my more pessimistic moments I confronted the fact that we needed another £1,000 at the very least. But there was no point in dwelling on negative aspects; we'd never go if I did that.

'Difficult, is it, financially?'

Cath was coming in with the tray and I caught her eye. I knew what she was thinking: oh goodness me no, not at all, anyone on a works pension can go to the South Seas, no problem. Care for a little more caviare, Mr Arnold? I told him it was difficult, financially. He asked me how long we were thinking of staying. Whether we'd be taking photographs. There were a lot of questions like that, but whenever I mentioned the people of the Cook Islands and how relaxed and friendly they all were, he seemed to steer me off the subject and back to what he saw as the hardships of life on a desert island with three children.

'There won't be any hardships,' I said. 'Not compared with here, and the crime. You don't know how we live here. We're afraid to let the children out of the house after four o'clock in the winter time, there's bullying. Out there they can run free and climb the coconut trees. There's none of these thugs on the islands. It's very healthy for them. It's a natural life.'

He looked dubious and went back to London.

A day later he was on the phone. 'I think I may have got a deal for you,' he said confidentially. I was amazed. I had asked him about sponsorship before he left, but, as I said to him then, I didn't suppose anyone would be interested in sponsoring people nobody was going to see. It wasn't as if we could flaunt *Daily Mirror* T-shirts to impress the hermit crabs and the frigate birds, was it? He must have thought about this because now he said, 'I think we may be able to get your flights paid for.'

'What?' My voice rose to a squeak. 'Do you know how much it is?'

'I shouldn't worry about that.'

'It's thousands.'

'It's worth it to the *Mirror* if we can tell your family's story, Tony. We'd want exclusive rights to coverage of the trip, and in return we'd finance your flights and the first few nights' stay on Rarotonga when you get there. Would you be happy with that?'

I caught Cath's eye. She looked mystified, presumably by the expression on my face.

'I'll think about it,' I said.

January is not the warmest month to be on the beach at Mumbles.

'Smile. Big smile, everybody. That's it!'

The photographer – a tall man called Harry Page from the *Mirror* – had us running along the sand in order of height: me, then Cath, then the children strung out behind like ducklings. All the kids were wearing the rucksacks we had bought for them, in brutal emerald and magenta and crimson nylon that looked out of place in this light. An icy wind cut into our faces. The sands were brown and ridged and damp underfoot. People in anoraks leaned over the sea wall to see what was going on.

'I'm bloody freezing,' I said through gritted teeth.

'All together now! Say "cheese"!'

I said it. Several times, I said it. We posed while the photographer ran around us, framing our pinched faces in his viewfinder, and getting us all to smile. The children were a lot less distressed by this than I was.

'I think I've got enough,' he said at last, panting slightly. I felt sorry for him. I imagined having to spend a winter's day working on a freezing beach in Swansea.

The photographs, when they appeared in the *Mirror*, told the story of how we were leaving Wales for a desert island. But again I got that odd feeling of disassociation. I couldn't relate the grinning family in the picture to us, the children bounding up and down stairs and me and Cath going to the greengrocer's or waiting for the tickets to come through the post.

'It'll all seem real when we get there, Tony,' said Cath. I would have thought the same, but the *Mirror* was talking about sending Harry Arnold to join us for a few days.

'How we going to manage with a journalist on the island?'

'What d'you mean, how we going to manage? Think I should pack a few extra guest towels, do you? Stop worrying, Tony.'

We went to the doctor's so that the children could get vaccinations against tropical diseases. There was a sort of catching of breath when we trooped into the waiting-room. Conversation stopped. We occupied most of one wall, and I was aware that people were staring at us. I knew most of them by sight, and they certainly knew us, from the papers.

Cath took the children in one after another. When Matthew came out and Stacey went in, I caught a glimpse inside the surgery, where a nurse in a white overall stood preparing a syringe. The door closed behind Stacey and almost immediately a great yell went up.

'I dowanna go to the island! I dowanna go to the island!'

This was followed by howls of unhappiness, and everybody in the room avoided looking at me. Craig and Matthew nudged each other and grinned. The yelling persisted. People crossed their legs and got up and put their magazines back on the table and blew their noses. I could see they were all formulating a thought about cruelty to children.

At last the door burst open and Stacey shot out, her little wet face like a beetroot, pulling Cath by the hand. Cath was pink too, with embarrassment, and looking back as she was tugged along and apologizing to the doctor. We left the waiting-room in silence, and, as I turned to shut the door, I saw faces of various ages turned towards me accusingly.

When we told Cath's mother we had the flight booked and paid for, I half expected to see my father-in-law stay home from the club the next Saturday so that he could spend some extra time with us. We might not be back till next Christmas or later, and I thought that a man who had had two heart attacks would care to see his grandchildren while they were here. He loved them a lot. But I got on his nerves these days, so he never stayed home, although the next week Cath's mam said, 'He wants to know what you're doing about insurance.'

'What insurance?'

'Health insurance, Tony. He says you want to buy some. One of the children might get an appendix.'

'It would cost hundreds of pounds, Mam,' said Cath. 'We can't afford it.'

'I thought you'd got your flights paid for?'

'We have, but we still need our savings. Just getting the phone cut off you get the bill in, then there's the mortgage when we're away, then we've had to buy a new tent, and we've got to get ourselves to Gatwick and back, and we might need to stop on Rarotonga for a bit before we go on to the island. Then we'll have to pay somebody to take us there, and that's five more fares.'

'Well, I don't know. I don't know what he'll say but you can thank your stars you won't be here to hear it.'

Cath's dad kept out of the way until one Saturday, he was just on his way out when we all arrived outside in my brother's car that I'd borrowed for the evening.

'Come on, I'll take you up the club.'

It was raining and he couldn't resist. It isn't a long way but it's awkward, lots of parked cars and turns through the estate and then out on to the main road in the dark, so it takes a while. So he was able to sit in silence beside me for quite a few minutes before he said, 'How is it on this island, then? How you going to live?'

'Same way me and Cath did. On fish and coconuts.'

I thought he probably didn't even know how we had lived the first time. I had certainly never been able to talk to him about it so unless his wife had said something he was suffering in ignorance.

'You can't bloody do it!' he shouted suddenly. I looked across and saw that he was sort of bouncing in agitation strapped in behind his seat-belt. 'Are you bloody mad or what? You'll have three children with you! What happens when they want something? Supermarket on this island, is there? Bloody supermarket?'

We were outside the club now and I braked. I turned to him with the intention of explaining calmly and coherently what we intended to do and what we would get out of the trip, psychologically and physically, but he had unstrapped the belt and it shot back with a snap and he was already struggling out, a heavy man, in the light from the club doorway.

He slammed the door and after a minute I drove off. As I drove back to his house, I had what Alun calls a flash of insight. My father-in-law knew perfectly well we would be all right, it wasn't our health that was bothering him, it was the shame of it. The shame of having a son-in-law like me. I had only been up the club a few times and I didn't drink much and I couldn't get interested in darts or snooker, so I was a bit of a social embarrassment as far as he was concerned. I couldn't even talk about football or rugby. At the club there were the men, who did the activities, and there were the wives, who came in one night a week and drank shorts and shandies, and as far as I was concerned, the wives (they were mostly women of about fifty, but kindly) were better company.

The weekend before we went, Cath's dad relented and came with all of us to see Craig in *Bugsy* at the Grand Theatre. Craig was brilliant; we were really proud of him, and at the party after, he was in there talking to all the adults, not a sign of shyness. I hung back, but he was born to be sociable. Out of three hundred kids in the Youth Theatre he had got the name part in *Oliver*, he was so good; but because of our trip he wouldn't be able to do it. I felt guilty about that after seeing him on stage, and I told him so as he sat in the back of Alun's car on the way home, but he said it was all right. I was in the passenger seat and I twisted round to see if he meant it, and I saw him sitting cramped between the others with a big smile on his face. He said a boy at school had asked him if his dad was Indiana Jones.

Gareth came over on the last day before our flight, to board the house up for us and take us over to his house, where we would spend the night on the floor in their back room. I had borrowed an extra suitcase and, as I put all three cases into the car, I wondered what made them so heavy. I had bought a very expensive life of William Bligh specially, but Cath had said she'd get something at the airport, so it wasn't books. Gareth had given me a plastic box of fishing hooks and a rod and line. There were saucepans – a nesting set of three for camping that we had got from Millet's, though I couldn't see what we'd want three for, we'd only have the one fire – and the tent of course, a four-man tent it was called. And some plastic plates and cutlery and clothes and soap. We couldn't think of anything else we might need. Cath had all the important things like passports and her epilepsy tablets in her black quilted shoulder-bag with a gold chain. It was hard to know what to wear to the airport, February being so cold here, but we wouldn't need our winter jackets again until we came back, at least six months from now.

Craig and Matthew and Stacey had backpacks full of schoolwork and books and toys. Mr Harris was Headmaster to Matthew and Stacey now and he had been very encouraging about them going. 'It's not schooling they'll get when you take them,' he explained. 'But it is education. They'll learn new skills. Different skills. It will all feed into the work they'll be doing when they come back here.' He had said he thought six months away would be a broadening experience, and I found this very encouraging.

Gareth spent most evenings at home drinking beer he made himself, but he gave it a miss the night before we left because he had to get up at five to see us off. The alarm went in pitch-darkness and I got up and peered out between the curtains. Gareth's house is on high ground, and beyond his back garden Swansea was spread out in a twinkle of street lights, glimmering through teeming rain. A draught knifed through a gap between the window and the wall. I dressed quickly against the cold.

While Cath got the children ready I sat with Gareth at his kitchen-table. In the evenings when I came round, he would be sitting in his kitchen drinking a glass of home brew by the light of a candle stuck in a bottle. You don't have breakfast by candlelight, and the kitchen looked a lot worse under a fluorescent strip. So did he; the light did funny things to his skin. He gave me a cup of instant coffee and sat down, turning his chair away from the wall. He sat back with his head against a pinned-up drawing his little girl had done at playschool, and shut his eyes.

'I remember you coming round our Mam's and talking about Canada,' he said. 'We was going to go away and find gold, do you remember?'

''Course I do.'

I had read about gold-diggers in the library. I thought I would grow up and get out to the goldfields and be rich. As it happened, when we were sixteen me and Gareth did go away. But we only got as far as Paddington. I hadn't known London was so big. Gareth used the return half of his train ticket the same night and went home, leaving me in London on my own.

It was strange, starting a journey across the world from this kitchen, with the kettle on and Gareth sitting there unshaven like it was a normal day. It would be for him; when we'd gone he'd probably catch up on a bit of sleep, watch telly at lunch-time. It'd be raining here; it'd started already, I could hear it outside. We'd be miles up in the sky this afternoon. And by tonight, hurtling over another continent thousands of miles away. It was nearly four years since me and Cath had made that journey for the first time.

At last we crammed into a taxi that took us to Cardiff for the 7.05 InterCity to Paddington. We got a trolley and trooped on to the platform. There was no train yet, but a lot of people were waiting in the cold. The children had never been to London, or even on a train, never mind an aeroplane, and they were excited.

We waited with all the early-morning businessmen. There was a loud clearing of the throat on the tannoy. No London trains would be running, boomed a voice, because of water on the line. Taxis would be provided for passengers who could pick up the eight fifteen connection at Bristol Temple Meads. British Rail apologized.

We struggled into another taxi. It was an ordinary saloon and everybody was squashed, except me in the front passenger seat. We rumbled along the inside lane of a dual carriageway never exceeding forty and got to Bristol in the rush hour, fifteen minutes late.

The train had gone, said a guard. We could catch the nine fifteen, take a taxi across London and get the Gatwick shuttle from Victoria.

We sped on our way at last, and five minutes out of Paddington the train slowed down and stopped. We stared out of the window for a bit, at the backs of big white houses and other, empty railway tracks.

'We're going to miss the plane.'

Cath had a watch on; I had sold mine. As I saw it, time had no meaning on a desert island. It wasn't as if you needed to get up to go to work, so what was the point? The children had packed their games away, ready to get off the train, other people were already standing near the doors, and here we were, stuck. A voice over the intercom system announced that there was a security alert at Paddington. British Rail apologized.

Everybody seemed to be listening for something. Another train passing, or a distant explosion. Forty minutes elapsed before the train crawled into the station.

London was crowded with high buildings everywhere and roaring with traffic and I hated it. I felt frightened by all the people hurrying about looking confident. How could they be? How had they learned to live here? We got to Gatwick on a packed train with fifty minutes to spare before take-off and dozens of people on the walkways and in the airport. There was too much to take in at once. The Air New Zealand desk was the only one with nobody queueing at it. Against it leaned a tall man with a camera: it was Harry Page. As I panted up with our trolley he said, 'Let me help you.' He started hauling cases on to the weighing machine, looked round and spoke to me like a conspirator. 'We've got to get through here fast, there's a bloke from the *Sun* looking for you.'

Cath took our boarding cards from the desk clerk. Harry Page whisked us outside the airport building on to a windswept balcony and took our picture. Then he saw us to the departure lounge and said goodbye.

'See you in a few weeks.'

'What?'

'Didn't you know? I'm coming out with Harry Arnold.'

'To our island?'

'Yes.'

'We'll have no privacy,' I said weakly.

'Get away,' he said, hitching his camera bag higher on his shoulder. 'Think of the public interest.' Whatever that meant.

6

I breathed in a draught of scented air, sat up and squinted into the sunshine. Most of the people here were from Australia or Germany. They were either honeymoon couples who looked on us in a way I found condescending, or elderly people who ate a lot and lay by the pool like sausages grilling. The Cook Islands are a long way to come for a holiday with children and we seemed to be the only young family here.

Craig and Matthew had their T-shirts off and their thin bodies were white as paper. They sat on the lawn, talking to a couple of islanders their own age. Cath was in a bikini with her eyes shut, on a sun-lounger beside me. Stacey squatted beside the sparkling paddling pool, solemnly trawling the water with a bucket. Behind her, framed by palm trees trembling in the heat, lay the blue Pacific.

I felt like a cheat.

I had phoned William Richard from Swansea to tell him our time of arrival. He expected us to stay with him as we had promised, and he had cleared a space in the garden for our tent, he said. I did not have the courage to tell him that the *Daily Mirror* had arranged for us to spend our first two nights at the Edgewater Resort Hotel, with fresh white sheets, private showers and a full English breakfast. As a result I felt churlish.

I had rung him at breakfast-time this morning when the courtesy bus dropped us at the Edgewater, and when he told me he had come to meet us at the airport in the middle of the night, I felt worse than ever. I explained that the flight had been delayed, which was true, but it was a lot harder to tell him that our tickets had been bought for us by a newspaper.

Stacey was sitting on the edge of the pool with her feet stuck out, pouring water over them from the bucket.

'I wish we'd never taken those tickets,' I said suddenly.

Cath opened her eyes. 'They offered,' she said.

'I know, but now look what it's leading to.'

She propped herself up on her elbows and looked at the palm trees, the blue pool, and the tourists ambling contentedly across to the bar. One of the island boys was showing Matthew how to climb a coconut palm.

'Yes? What's wrong now?'

'I feel like a publicity stunt.'

'You don't look like one. You want to put some Factor 15 on those shoulders, Tony.'

'Yes, but don't you see, if I have to tell William the *Daily Mirror* paid for us, he'll think we're here to make up a story for the papers. And I've been interested in the Cook Islands for a long time, we nearly had the money to come here anyway, so it's nothing to do with the *Daily Mirror* –'

'So what's the problem?'

'Oh, I don't know.'

'Then maybe there isn't one.'

I don't know if William Richard felt, as I did, that I had somehow turned my dream into a commercial enterprise. If he did, he never let it show. He was as hospitable as ever. The next morning after breakfast he arrived on foot to collect us. There were tears in my eyes as I met him. He looked just the same: hefty, brown, his teeth like piano keys flashing a giant smile of welcome. I felt I had been close to him for years, yet I was still afraid my motives might be misunderstood, now that I had to explain about the *Daily Mirror*.

He listened as we walked past the golf course on our way to his house. Cath trailed behind us with the children. I had been talking quickly for about five minutes when he said, puzzled, 'What is the *Daily Mirror*?'

When I told him it was a national paper in Britain he just shrugged. I couldn't believe he had never heard of it.

'I expect you know what you're doing, Tony.'

I wished that was true. Then I thought perhaps it wasn't my own predicament that was making me uneasy, but something to do with Rarotonga. Staying at a hotel had made me see it from the tourist's point of view, and it didn't seem so sleepy as it had four years ago. New hotels and guest houses had sprung up, and more diving schools and walking tours and signposts directing visitors to the studios of local artists. Because we had led the children to expect so much, I looked at everything as though I had a personal responsibility for it, and these changes disappointed me. I had expected Rarotonga to be suspended in time like Sleeping Beauty in the fairy story. But I had noticed a sign when we left the airport yesterday morning: KEEP THE COOK ISLANDS AIDS-FREE, it had said. It reminded me that the world I wanted to leave behind was creeping up insidiously like the tide.

As we turned away from the coast to go to William Richard's house, there was fencing across the road ahead, and a thump and roar of machinery. I looked through the bushes behind the fencing and could scarcely believe my eyes. Earth-movers were crawling over a vast gouged-out hollow of red soil, biting great mouthfuls out of the fertile island, tossing banana plants and young palms into small hillocks of unwanted greenery.

'It's the Sheraton they're building,' William explained sadly. 'They're digging out new lagoons and importing sand. They're even importing fish. All the earth they've dug out is silting up the lagoon that was there in the first place. And we can't get to the sea – the people who live over at Titikaveke have to cycle round the back of this site instead of going by the coast road.'

At the house Mary beamed at the children and took them into the garden, while we followed William into the kitchen and hugged Tepu. There seemed to be a lot more people here than last time. We were introduced to two young men who were Tepu's nephews, whose parents had gone to New Zealand, and a girl called Pepe and another girl of about eleven who shyly smiled at us and then skipped out to continue sweeping up the garden. Mary Ann, who had been a baby Stacey's age, was now a little girl just like her, but taller. There was a new baby called Memory in a bassinet in the kitchen.

The island children drifted out to the garden as we talked.

'The person you must meet,' said William, with his mouth full, 'is John James Marsters. I'll take you down to Parliament House to meet him. If he supports your application you'll get permission from parliament to go to Primrose. If he doesn't, life could be quite awkward for you.'

Tepu said something to him in Maori and he grinned. 'John James is very religious,' he told us. 'No swimming on a Sunday while you are on Primrose.'

'Will he be able to see us from Palmerston, then?'

'Well, no, but I wouldn't put it past him to check up!'

William told us John James was the eldest male descendant of William Marsters and Esther, the first wife, which made him important on Palmerston. He was a chief there. He was on Rarotonga now because he needed medical treatment, but he would soon be going back to Palmerston.

Across the grass, under a coconut palm, Craig and Matthew and Stacey and Mary Ann and a large black pig were standing in a row watching as Mary prepared to do something. She slowly kicked off her thonged sandals, hoicked up her skirt over her massive legs, grasped the trunk of the tree and set off steadily upwards like a giant turtle. I could hardly believe my eyes. Mary must have weighed at least twice what I do, yet she climbed with grace and without hesitation for thirty feet. Four years ago I had spent several months relying on coconuts to live on, but still I would not be able to get above my own height off the ground without feeling giddy and getting sore feet.

Everyone else in the kitchen was oblivious to what was going on outside. William was talking about his cousin Tom, who was in the Cook Islands parliament. The whole set-up in the Cook Islands seemed to be a manageable size. I wished I was part of it. It wasn't like coming from West Cross, where your access to somebody in Parliament was about a million times removed. I tried to say this to William but he was sceptical. He implied that things were more complicated than I thought.

'Oh, goodness,' said Cath suddenly, staring over my shoulder.

I looked round. Craig had got a coconut stuck on a pole ready to husk it the way the islanders did, and, as Mary looked on fondly, he hacked at it with a machete big enough to slice a tree in two.

'Don't worry about him,' said William. 'He's got to learn.'

Craig looked up and saw us, and grinned triumphantly, heaving the coconut off the pole and holding it out to us so that we could take a long sweet drink.

I don't know what I expected the Cook Islands parliament to look like. Perhaps I half thought that somewhere in the forests of the Rarotongan interior there might be a version of County Hall in Swansea, six storeys of concrete and glass with thousands of bureaucrats and water-coolers and computers. After all, the Cook Islands cover thousands of square miles, and Swansea doesn't. So I was surprised to find that Parliament House was a low white building rather like a smartly painted Nissen hut with a corrugated roof and a veranda. The tropical plants outside were tamed, clipped and arranged in beds beside a lawn.

William and me and Cath and the children met John James Marsters, who was tall, elderly and dignified. With him was a younger man who wore a suit and was a member of the government. I understood that he would have the final say about whether or not to let us stay on Palmerston.

Everybody smiled warily and shook hands. We entered a cool room, which was bare like a spare classroom but had a long table in the middle. We stood around it awkwardly as John James bowed his head and led a short prayer for guidance. Then we sat down and began.

'Mr Williams, I believe you would like to stay on Primrose for some months and write a book about it.'

I launched into my description of how we wanted to make the island our home, following in the footsteps of Tom Neale and William Marsters and all the other Europeans who had found happiness through escape to a desert island. The young man looked puzzled and said something in Maori to William. John James said to me in English, 'People come here all the time, and go away and write books about themselves and how adventurous they have been, and they never come again. They give nothing to the islands. We make them welcome, but all they want to do is sell their fantasies. They don't really want to become part of our community. They don't want to know about our history or culture. They are conscious only of themselves and the importance they imagine they can gain at home in Europe or America.'

I shrank. I felt as if I was wearing a badge saying SPONSORED BY THE DAILY MIRROR. The airline tickets might as well have been converted into thirty pieces of silver. John James had white hair and piercing eyes and as I turned to plead my case with the younger man I felt I had probably lost already.

'I won't exploit anybody because it's the Cook Islands that I'm interested in. I'm not coming here for publicity, I'm coming because my own country is more than I can stand.' I told him about the long winter nights and how the children couldn't go out after dark because of the danger of crime. Miserably I thought of having to return to Swansea, to the joy-riders and the boy down the road who had threatened to punch Matthew. I told all of them that crime was the scourge of my country and I had to take my children away from it to survive.

John James looked doubtful and the younger man turned to William. William spoke to him in Maori and then turned to me. 'He can't understand a word of what you're saying,' he said apologetically. 'You speak very quietly and it's your Welsh accent.'

'A lot of people say I speak quietly,' I agreed. 'It's because of the abdominal breathing, see – the aikido that I do, and the meditation.' I could see that this was beyond even William so I hurried on. 'You see, the purpose of taking my children to the island is to teach them a better way of life, to show them that we don't need all this so-called civilization with the pollution and crime –'

The young man looked as though he'd got the

general idea and began a rapid exchange in Maori with William and John James. Towards the end of it William said something that made him throw his hands in the air and laugh. William turned to me and smiled. 'This gentleman cannot understand so we have told him that we understand you, because we are from Palmerston and have a British ancestor.'

John James added, 'I take you at your word that you are sincere and want to spend some months on Primrose. I've said that you can come with me when I go home to Palmerston.'

Everybody was smiling encouragingly so I tried not to let my dismay show. John James had told us that he was waiting for some friends with a yacht to take him to Palmerston, and they were not expected on Rarotonga for 'several weeks'.

'We haven't got several weeks to spare, Cath,' I said. After the interview me and Cath walked in the midday sun down to the harbour with the children. I was too hot. I had never been in heat like this in my life before. William had said it was about ninety degrees and I wasn't used to it.

'What do you think, Cath? Several weeks is too long, isn't it?'

'We can afford to wait here this time. We've got enough money if we stay in William's garden. He'd like us to.'

'I know, but I didn't come here for a holiday on Rarotonga.'

Craig and Matthew had stopped to look at the boats in the harbour. We crossed the dry dust road in front of a single motor-scooter and looked into the window of a general store. This was the hottest part of the day, and business was sluggish for a few hours. Most of the tourists were on a shady beach somewhere, or tramping after guides into the interior. Stacey drew circles with her finger in the dust of the glass as we peered through it.

'Look, mosquito netting, see? Remember last time?' Cath had been covered in bites on Takutea.

'It's very expensive.'

'They've got knives, look, for hacking down coconuts.'

'We should get mosquito coils, shouldn't we?'

'We ought to ask William what we should take.'

We called Matthew and Craig and set off to walk past the airport to the pearl shop to see the owner, who was a woman we'd met four years ago. Outside Avarua the road was empty, its edges merging into gravel before falling away to the beach on our side, and dense jungly plots of pineapple and banana on the other. Stacey was whining that she was too hot and thirsty, and wanted to be carried. I picked her up.

'Now we've got here it seems a bit of an anticlimax if we have to wait for weeks on end.'

'There's no point in going on about it, Tony. We can't change it –' Cath turned away and looked behind us at a vehicle that was approaching – 'You will keep on worrying at things. You're never happy. You're a bundle of nerves, you are. Just enjoy the day, can't you?'

A small truck bowled noisily past us and stopped. It was open, like a jeep, with two middle-aged European men in it. One of them leaned out. 'Want a lift?'

We all piled in and they introduced themselves as Jeremy and Alastair.

'On holiday here, are you?' I asked, squashing Matthew on to the back seat beside me as we set off.

'Oh, far from it. We've lived here for twenty-eight years.' Jeremy wore a floppy linen hat and a cravat and was very English. Alastair, who had very short red hair and a wizened gritty face, was driving, steering very slowly and carefully along the empty coast road. He said, 'You're the couple who lived on Takutea, aren't you?'

'Yes. Now we've come back to stay with the children, you see –'

'You must be sorely disappointed.'

There was something rather uppish in the voice. 'How's that, then?'

'Well, Takutea's a bird sanctuary, as you must know. They won't let you go there a second time.'

'Yes, but we've been told we can stay on Primrose instead. It's off Palmerston.'

'Who told you that?'

'John James Marsters from Palmerston, and I went to see the man in parliament.'

'What man?'

I was confused by this aggressive questioning. 'What was his name, Cath?'

Cath didn't know. Jeremy took a small brown tightly rolled cigarette from a soft packet, tapped it on the back of his hand and lit it. He puffed out some reeking smoke before he said, 'I think you'll find that John James Marsters is in no position to give you permission. There are very strict rules about camping on the islands. It's not allowed.'

'Palmerston's not like the other islands, though, is it? They raise the British flag, don't they?'

Jeremy sniggered and Alastair growled something about Palmerston being independent like the rest of the Cook Islands. I was so used to people here being friendly that I didn't know what to say.

William laughed when I told him.

'Take no notice of them, Tony. All the foreigners who live here are the same.'

'How d'you mean?'

'They don't want other Europeans to come. They want to be unusual. And also, they believe that because they're white they have the right to decide what happens here. That is not the case.'

'They made me feel the way people in Swansea do. They were so nasty, I'm not used to it here, you sort of expect it in Swansea, but I didn't know what to say.'

He looked at me curiously and changed the subject.

'So. I don't suppose you want to wait for John James Marsters to go to Primrose.'

He was right, but I would have been too polite to say so if he hadn't brought the subject up. As it turned out, while Cath and I were window-shopping William had solved our problem. He had spoken on the telephone to his brother and sister, who lived on Aitutaki, about a hundred and forty miles away. His sister Teré would take us to Maina, he said.

'Where's Maina?'

'It's just a small island in the Aitutaki atoll. She

spent a holiday on one of those islands herself a few years ago,' he said.

It seemed strange that if you lived on a tropical island you could get away from it all by sailing across the lagoon to somewhere even more remote.

'A boat is leaving for Aitutaki tomorrow night.'

'But what about permission?'

'Nobody's going to come looking for you, Tony. And when John James sails, the yacht can come and pick you up and take you the rest of the way to Palmerston.'

Now that we had an island to go to, I was suddenly cast into a panic, and began looking for excuses to put off leaving.

'We'd better get some things in the shops, hadn't we, Cath?'

'You've got your tent, and your saucepans,' William Richard said reasonably.

'Yes, but we were looking in the shops and we saw a machete. And I'll need a fishing net.'

'Palmer will give you those things. Get some citronella oil against the mosquitoes, but don't spend your money on nets.'

'Who's Palmer?'

'He's my younger brother. And our father Richard Marsters is there. You'll be able to ask him about his own father, who was the youngest son of William Marsters the First.'

We spent our last night on Rarotonga in the big open-sided shelter in William's garden. He still kept the long canoe in there. I was sad when I saw it; it represented a whole way of life, yet it wasn't used any more. I could see that it was just the sort of thing that a hotel proprietor would use as a feature suspended above a theme bar, with cocktail waitresses in grass skirts and tourists drinking out of coconuts with a straw.

The next morning we went to see Kauraka in his airy new office in the National Cultural Centre. He was slimmer and had stopped eating toffees. He confided that his private life had been a mess when he saw us before, because his marriage had broken up and his only child was in New Zealand. But now he had work he enjoyed and a new young girlfriend from Samoa. I thought he could not have looked more smug if she had come from Pukapuka.

For the afternoon of our departure Tepu and William had prepared a feast in the traditional island oven, underground in the garden. Early in the morning William burned some wood to a fierce heat at the bottom of a hole, and lowered a couple of wide flat stones on top of it, so that they heated through. Then Tepu wrapped a big fish in banana leaves and placed it on top of the stones, where it cooked to a smoky deliciousness, covered by an oblong iron plate it took two of us to lift. In the last half hour of cooking time I helped William move it so that Mary could add vegetables in foil.

I had been sitting with Mary for a while, asking her about her life. I wondered why she had not married. She was very beautiful, as round and golden as a nectarine or a plum. Her movements were dainty and precise as she stripped and peeled and chopped the vegetables on a board in the garden.

Smoky, spicy smells drifted across the grass from the oven. Somewhere among the banana palms Craig and Matthew were playing a rowdy chasing game. Cath was on the veranda at Tepu's feet, watching her weave a crownless hat from flowers and pandanus leaves.

'My brother should have come,' I said suddenly. 'You should have married my brother. Alun is his name.'

She wriggled and squirmed like a little girl.

'Oh, Tony, *Tony*,' she said, and batted her eyelashes and giggled and rocked back and forth. I wished the feast were a marriage feast; I wished that William and Tepu and Mary were really my family. With their hospitality and kindness they seemed to have adopted our family, the way they had adopted all the children whose parents had gone away to find money, and mortgages, and traffic jams.

Our overnight trip to Aitutaki was spent under canvas on the deck of a small rusting ferry. I was awake at dawn, kneeling to meditate on a folded towel I had laid on the planks of the deck. We chugged past several long islands on our left which were covered in foliage.

One of the crew came up from below decks. He was a good-looking boy from Manihiki with an engaging smile who had spent most of the last evening practising his English on us. He asked us to call him Joey.

'You see the island behind the others?'

I could see a long, deep green shape like a crocodile.

West Cross, Swansea: our house is second from the right
(*Daily Mirror*)

(*left to right*) Craig, Cath, Stacey, Matthew and Tony
in Mumbles Bay (*Daily Mirror*)

Inter-island transport in Rarotonga harbour (*Daily Mirror*)

(*clockwise from left*) Tony, William Richard, Mary, Craig, Matthew, Mary Ann, Stacey

(*from left*) Stacey, Tony, Matthew, William Richard

Maina (*Daily Mirror*)

(*above*) Stacey after the storm
(*right*) Matthew fetches breakfast (*Daily Mirror*)

Gathering materials for the hut (*Daily Mirror*)

Making a shady roof (*Daily Mirror*)

Stacey, the champion fish-picker (*Daily Mirror*)

(above and below)
Cath constructs a domestic routine (*Daily Mirror*)

Planning the kitchen extension (*Daily Mirror*)

The canoe we used for our flight from Primrose

'It's Aitutaki. We go around Aitutaki past the air-strip at the far end, then in through the gap in the reef on the other side.'

Cath and the children woke up. We rounded the tip of Aitutaki and Joey pointed out the airstrip which had been built during the war, where little planes landed from Rarotonga. It was almost hidden from us by coconut palms and dense plantations of banana which grew right down to within a few feet of the sea.

I didn't know what time it was or how long the trip had taken; I knew only that the sun had been up for several hours. Although Cath's watch was working, I had urged her not to bother changing it to Pacific time. In the same way I was not interested in exactly where we were. Maps showing which direction we were facing in were irrelevant, I thought. I hadn't looked at any maps since the one on the wall at Plasmarl, and, as I knelt in my meditation position with the deck rocking gently beneath me, I decided that it was impor-tant to leave that kind of analysis behind and concen-trate on immediate sensation. It was all part of getting in touch with the present moment. I had tried to explain this to Cath last night, but she only giggled and said it was a good thing the Captain knew what he was doing.

Joey had two close friends among the crew of six. Once during the night I saw the one who was not on duty arm in arm with him on the steps from the bridge. Unfortunately Joey's two friends did not get on well with each other, and were constantly squabbling over who should do what, until Joey had to shriek at both of them, which brought tears to his eyes while each of the boys turned on his heel, snarling. This pattern repeated itself several times before we got off the ship, and the ferry was still only half a day out of Rarotonga. Cath said it would be a miracle if they got to Manihiki without murdering each other.

The little boat nosed into the lagoon through a narrow passage between the underwater walls of coral. I could see the town of Arutanga, bright against the deep green interior: a string of low shops and houses, a little wooden church, and near the wharf crates of bananas piled as high as a house. We leaned on the deck rail. A small group of people was watching the boat's approach expectantly. They were a large lady in a white hat, a girl, a tall young man and a man in his thirties who was almost spherical, wearing shorts and a vast shirt.

'The lady will be Teré,' said Cath. 'The big man will be Palmer, and I don't know who the others are.'

'The girl's probably got a mam and dad in New Zealand, like Pepe,' said Craig.

'What makes you say that?'

'Mary told me. She says nearly all the islanders have got spare children that they bring up while the parents work in New Zealand. That girl's probably spare.'

'I know what you mean, but don't say she's spare when you meet her, she'll think you're being rude.'

'It's not rude,' said Matthew. 'We could be spare. We could live here while you go back home.'

'Oh, yes? Mind yourself on that rail, Matthew.'

'Mary would look after us, she said.'

'They've got it all planned out, Cath.'

'So I see. You do your best for them and they can't wait to get rid of you.'

Teré, William's sister, was a widow, and Palmer, their brother, had a family in New Zealand. Here on Aitutaki, Palmer lived in Teré's house, as did Richard Marsters.

Teré said she would take us to Maina the same afternoon. We straggled on foot along the gravelly coast road to her house. Palm trees waved above us, and on one side, framed between their trunks, a strip of silver sand sloped into blue water. I remembered our daily walk along Mumbles seafront to the shops, and suddenly I felt so happy to be here that I'd have paid for Cath's mam and dad to come out, if I'd had the money; I felt sorry for anybody who had never seen this.

All this time Cath had been telling Teré about our journey.

'William said you're all ready to go,' Teré said.

'Yes, but we haven't got fishing nets.'

'Palmer will give you those. Junior!'

Junior was the tall youth from the quay. He came running from the back of the group where he had been walking with Stacey and Matthew.

'Yes, Teré.'

'Make sure Palmer finds them some fishing nets.'

'Yes, Teré.'

'And get them some limes and some cabin bread.'

'Yes, Teré.'

He loped on ahead to talk to Palmer, whose round

figure was rapidly covering the ground ahead of us. Palmer was talking to Craig and the young girl, and waving his arms, which looked like Indian clubs. His hair was very black, while Teré's was snow-white, and I remembered William telling me that there was a big gap in their ages.

Teré's house, in a garden overhung by trees, had grown organically like coral. It was ramshackle and surrounded by an assortment of ancient discarded rowing boats, old oildrums and gardening implements abandoned to the jungle. The first few rooms had been erected for Teré as a bride by Richard Marsters, her father, who was a clever carpenter, besides being a missionary. This house of Teré's must have started out as a modest dwelling, and as Teré's family had become more numerous, first a veranda had been added, then walls were added to the veranda, so that it became a room; and the new room had to have a veranda of its own, which was gradually furnished with table and chairs and hooks on the back wall until sides were added, and it too was on its way to being a room. The house now occupied most of what had once been the garden, and the inside rooms all had windows giving on to each other. You knew which way the inner core of the house lay by the curtains, which hung on the insides of the windows in the walls of the innermost rooms. Also, by the cries and banging noises that came from deep in the house. Teré had a beautiful daughter who had been accidentally brain-damaged during a routine medical check, and lived like a wild creature in a room somewhere near the middle.

Teré hung pictures high up near the ceiling, the way

we did at home, and for some reason this made me feel comfortable in the house straight away, in spite of the sounds of suffering. I was tired. Everything had happened so quickly: two nights at the resort hotel, the feast at William's, last night spent sleeplessly on board ship. I asked if we might stay overnight in one of the outer rooms, but Teré said it would be better if we didn't. We would have dinner and she would take us to Maina this afternoon. She would not like to leave her daughter alone near the children, she explained. The girl meant no harm but she might frighten them in the night.

We were eating delicious fried chicken when the girl, her eyes blank as marbles, emerged from behind the curtain. She crouched near the wall and then raced forward, howling, and leaped on to the table to seize a biscuit.

'Get down! Sit!' commanded Teré. The poor creature dashed into a corner, licking the biscuit and gibbering and smearing it over her lips like lipstick. It was the unpredictability of her that was so frightening.

'She was an ordinary schoolgirl, my youngest daughter,' Teré said, answering questions we had not dared to ask. 'And one day she went away to the hospital for a lumbar puncture and came back like this.'

I thought if she had lived in Swansea, the social services might have helped care for her; it must be hard for her family to cope on their own.

We could see part of Maina from the beach near Teré's house; it was a tiny blur further along the coast, about four miles beyond the wharf at Arutanga.

A rowing boat lay up-ended in the sand. Palmer and Junior and some local boys hauled it on to logs and rolled it down to the water, while Cath and me and the children stood nervously with our luggage beside Teré. Teré insisted that we must take a bag of limes, to use as an antiseptic, and some cabin bread, the kind that sailors kept in barrels aboard the old sailing ships. Palmer lent us two fishing nets, a machete and a metal container full of water. There was no fresh water on Maina and Stacey had announced that she thought coconut water had a nasty taste and she would not drink it. We were also taking a spear-fishing gun of Junior's, in case he saw dinner on the way. Teré was carrying a vast, brightly coloured umbrella to protect herself from the sun, but I saw her looking at Craig.

'The boy looks a little burned,' she said to Cath.

'I made him put some sunscreen on this morning, so he should be all right.'

Palmer and Junior heaved an outboard motor on to the boat, and Junior climbed in and shoved it into place as the boys stood in the shallow water, holding the boat steady. When it was still, Teré waded out and climbed aboard, which made it cringe into the water as if a giant forefinger had pushed it down. Palmer helped all of us to scramble in with our possessions, waved cheerfully, and the boys gave us a push out into the lagoon. Junior spun the engine and we roared away from the shore and away, it seemed, from Maina.

'We have to zigzag,' explained Teré, seeing my puzzlement and making herself heard over the noise. 'The reefs are very dangerous.'

The water we were crossing was a clear turquoise,

paler and greener than the surrounding ocean. Maina is harder to get to than the other islets in the Aitutaki atoll because there are treacherous coral reefs close to the surface along the route. Sometimes we sped along quickly, Junior staring intently at the water all the time and not seeming to look where he was going. Then he would suddenly cut the engine and allow us to bob about while he manoeuvred us with an oar over a coral outcrop underwater. Once or twice he had to pivot the engine right out of the water so that the rudder could clear an obstacle near the surface.

Craig and Matthew were trailing their arms in the glistening lagoon and Stacey snoozed happily on Cath's lap.

'You must cover the children,' chided Teré. She had a way of raising her voice without shouting, so that I could understand her above the roar. 'They will be burned by the sun.'

She fussed around trying to cast a shadow over Stacey with her umbrella. I had my shirt off and the hot sun felt good, although my skin had peeled a bit since we arrived.

'You'll have blisters, Tony,' she told me.

'I always go a bit red at first,' I explained, 'then I go brown. When were you here for a holiday, Teré?'

'It wasn't Maina,' she explained. 'It was Akaiami, over there on the other side of the lagoon. There are a couple of huts there left over from when it was a seaplane harbour. We came for a week when the children were small, all of us with my husband – one of the neighbour's boys brought us. It was lovely, we took the oil from the coconuts and fried the fish in it.

And we cooked a big fish on the hot stones in an oven in the ground, the way you've seen William do it – oh, it was melting on the tongue. And I must tell you that when you have finished with the coconut oil for frying, if you have some oil left over, keep it until it cools and then salt it, and put it in a dark place and you can use it again. Maybe you can have fried chicken. There are wild chickens on some of the islands. If you're lucky there'll be some on Maina.'

'Are you listening to this, Cath?'

Cath was near the front of the boat watching Matthew, and she turned and smiled and waved vaguely at her ears to show that the noise of the motor was too loud.

'Well,' Teré went on, 'we had a lovely holiday and the end of the week came and we could see that the weather was getting bad. There were waves in the lagoon and the sky on the horizon was dark. My husband said there might have been a hurricane warning on the radio, and as it turned out he was right, because there had been, and the boy's mother had told him not to come. But just as the wind was coming up we saw him, that crazy boy, and could he sail! – because he tacked right round to where the seaplanes used to land, and we were so glad to see him. He came up the beach and told us about the hurricane warning and when I said we mustn't risk our lives to return to Aitutaki, he was so worried! He said, "Oh, Mam!" Because his mother would think that he had capsized. And the weather was so bad that we had to stay an extra week and he had to stay with us. Junior!'

Junior had just cut the engine again and he turned round, squinting in the sun.

'Big one! You'll need the spear.'

Junior grabbed the spear-fishing gun from its hooks along the side and peered into the water. We all saw a long dark shadow in the depths, but it seemed to see us at the same time, and vanished. Junior pulled a face, put the spear back, and ripped the cord of his engine again. Teré sighed and to divert her I shouted over the noise, 'Your father told me the weather was bad yesterday.'

'It was! There were big waves only twenty metres out. I thought a storm was coming. But this morning, it was all sunshine again.'

Maina was close now: smaller than Takutea had looked, and slightly greener and higher out of the water. I could see a dusty bank four or five feet high, like a miniature cliff, running along the back of the beach and dividing it from the interior. It was as though the land of the island had been abruptly scraped away by a spade. Behind the beach I saw dense undergrowth out of which thirty or forty tall palm trunks rose at intervals, softly brushing the blue sky. A colony of blackish birds swooped and cried beneath the crowns of the trees. They did not know that they would soon be sharing their home with strangers.

7

It wasn't much easier to erect the tent this time than it had been on Takutea, because once again I had not thought to bring a hammer. We had found a good spot, though, in a grassy clearing on top of the bank near the beach, near to where a fallen palm tree grew diagonally from the side of the ridge. It was shaded by a tree with long leaves that stood up from the ground on high, dainty roots like walking fingers.

Cath stood back and surveyed our new home. She smiled at me and glanced out to sea.

'Look, Matthew, you can just see them still, look.'

Far away in the blue Teré and Junior, her striped umbrella a little blodge of synthetic colour, zigzagged home. We were going to be properly alone with the children for weeks on end now.

We got the tent anchored at last. Its orange nylon looked as bright as a traffic cone in the shade under the tree.

'Zip it up, Tony, or we'll get sandflies inside.'

My legs were itching already. Everywhere you walked these things rose up in clouds.

'I could murder a cup of tea,' Cath said. 'Keep your shoes on in the water, Stacey! Matthew, run and tell her.'

'Now you're the one who's jumpy,' I said.

'You've got to watch out for them, haven't you? Where's Craig gone?'

'He said he was going to look for coconut husks.'

'Did he have his top on?'

'No.'

'You're a fine example, you are.'

'I'm not burning.'

'You are, your shoulders are all red.'

'They'll be brown tomorrow. Relax, Cath.'

She shook her head hopelessly at me and went to talk to Stacey and Matthew.

We had picked a good place. Outside the tent a couple of graceful palms framed a sunlit vista of sand and water and sky as far as the eye could see. There was silence, except for the rustle of the hot wind and the susurration of the waves against crushed shells. And behind the tent, undergrowth too dense to penetrate.

I propped the empty suitcase, which had had the tent in it, against a coconut palm and opened the other one. There was a cassette-recorder with batteries in here, and I was determined to commit our first impressions of the desert island to tape. It was warm when I took it from among the jumble of T-shirts and plastic plates. The sun had penetrated deep inside the case.

Already I was so much at one with my surroundings that the cassette-recorder seemed the strangest artefact, a hard little black box with efficient-looking buttons, so freakish and unworldly that I wouldn't have been surprised if it could have beamed me up into space. And ripping the cellophane wrapper from a cassette was an unnatural act. I had nowhere to put it. Should I bury it?

'You're sitting right in the fireplace,' said Cath,

dumping a few coconut husks alongside me. 'We need some twigs, Tony, come on, I'm starving.'

Wherever you go there is pressure.

'It's no good building a fire till we've got some fish to cook,' I said reasonably, and put the recorder back in the suitcase. I left Cath to find the twigs, while I scrambled down the bank to the lagoon to show Craig how to fish. I crossed a few feet of chalky rubble and twisted driftwood with small lizards and crabs slipping out of my path. The sand near the waterline was crunchy with broken shells and little dry twigs. And then I was on the beach, where the sand was hot, white and silky against the ankles. Stacey came running towards me, holding a small crab by one claw.

'Look, Dad!'

'You can get lots of those, Stacey, and we'll use them for fishing with.'

Craig appeared beside me, looking excited.

'I've just been down the shore, Dad, there are some really big crabs along there.'

'We only need little ones for bait.'

'I thought we had to walk out with the nets.'

'Last time,' I said, revealing a plan I had thought up while I was meditating, 'me and your mam used the nets. But we can get bigger fish if we do it another way. We get two big sticks and put one in the water and one on the sand and run a line between them, with crabs hanging off just under the surface. Then when the fish bite, we've got them.'

We wandered about near the edge of the beach, looking for sticks that would be long enough. There was quite a lot of dry grey driftwood, and Craig and I soon found one straightish branch each, smooth, silvery, a couple of inches in diameter and taller than a man. I plunged mine into the soft sand at the water's edge and wiggled and tugged it down as deep as I could, which was not very deep. Craig said it was a pity we had not brought a spade, but I said the first islanders hadn't had spades, and they had managed all right. When the piece of driftwood was steady and vertical in the sand I walked out into the lagoon with the other one, and Craig followed. When I got to waist-height in the water he started to swim out, and I passed the branch to him. He had to dive down into the water, which was about six feet deep at that point, and plant the stick as I had planted the one on shore. He did this, after a few tries, and we strung a bit of spare nylon cord that had come with the tent slackly between the two poles so that it hung just above the water. At intervals along the cord I tied strings, and at the end of each one, hanging into the glassy sea, I put a hook with a bit of dismembered crab on it.

'The sun's still hot, isn't it, Cath?'

She had come down to the water's edge and was holding Stacey's hand and paddling.

'There's a lot of sea cucumbers here,' she called. 'We'll have them for supper, will we? I'm tired of waiting for the fish.'

I stayed silent rather than reply to this kind of sarcasm, but Craig let go of his pole once he had tied the line on and swam a few strokes inshore. Matthew said eagerly, 'Let's see, Mam.'

Because I was curious I waded over to look at the sea cucumbers too. In the very shallow water there were dozens of them, dotted about singly and clinging to the sand underwater, like slugs after a rainy night. It was their slug-like appearance, black and slimy, that put us off eating them, though William had said they were a great delicacy. I remembered him telling me that a Japanese company had wanted to farm them here and airfreight them from the Cook Islands. 'But we would not let them,' he had said, self-righteously. The Cook Islanders, or the Japanese, were welcome to the world's entire supply of sea cucumbers as far as I was concerned. I had trodden on one on Takutea once, and the insides rolled out red and beige like bloody worms.

'It's what you're used to, I suppose.'

I waded back to the line between the poles. Unfortunately once the first strings were tied on and my back was turned, the two poles had lurched gently sideways in opposite directions, pulling the line out of the water. It stretched taut between them, the strings with their tempting bait dangling several feet above the surface. Craig and I tried again, but whatever we did with those poles, they rocked from side to side and fell over.

'Keep the bait up in the air like that, you might catch a flying fish.'

She can be so cutting, my wife. Before I had thought of a reply, she said, 'Let's just walk out with the net, Tony, the way we used to.'

'This is a much better way of doing it, if I could get the sticks to stay up, Cath.'

'You can't.'

'Mam, I'm hungry,' said Stacey.

'Look, I can't keep the fire going unless I can stay beside it,' said Cath impatiently, 'and I can't stay beside it unless you help me do the fishing now. Come on, do it with me. Craig's never done it before, you can teach him tomorrow.'

Reluctantly I let go of my pole and took an end of fishing net from Cath. Palmer had lent us two nets: one with big holes for catching snapper and other fish out in the lagoon, which I needed to be able to swim to use, and since I could not, it stayed in its gauze bag; and this one, with fine holes. It was a big white lacy rectangle. One long side had floats on, and we knew from Takutea that we could weight it down by tying lumps of coral into the other side.

'Tell us where the shadow is, in the water,' I called to Matthew. From his vantage point on the beach he studied the area near us and pointed to a small shoal of fish. All Cath and I had to do was approach it carefully, spread the net between us, slap the surface of the water to drive the fish in and walk around in a circle to meet each other. When we pulled the net up from the sand it was full of little darting silver forms, the size of sprats.

The sun had just dropped over the horizon, the light was dim and the sky had all the violent colours of a bruise. We had eaten our fish, boiled in coconut water over a fire made of twigs and coconut husks, and we were tucking into some papaws Craig had found on a tree further inland, when we heard a baby crying.

Fear rolled over us like a wave. If I hadn't been so hot I would have shuddered. As it was, we all stopped chewing and sat motionless. Stacey whimpered.

'Ssssh, Stacey.'

None of us dared move.

After long seconds of staring at each other we heard it again. A hungry, discontented baby.

There was nobody else here. How could we be hearing this? My eyes flicked towards the machete. William Bligh's stories about cannibal tribes flashed through my mind. Joey had made a joke about the first Mr Williams on the islands, the missionary reverend who came in 1821. All the islanders knew of him, and they all, it seemed, knew that he had finished up as a roast dinner, somewhere in Vanuatu. I was sure Joey had been teasing me, but I wished he hadn't bothered. The cry came again, *just behind the tent*, followed by a crashing and fluttering – and then the baby wailed far above my head. I jumped to my feet.

'It's a bird. It's all right, it's a bird.'

'Oh, thank God for that, my heart was pounding,' said Cath, her hand on her heart and her face white in the gloom.

'Mam, why does that bird sound like a baby?'

'I don't know, Stacey.'

'What sort of bird is it?'

'I don't know. Eat up your papaw.'

By morning we were still ignorant, but now we knew that there was not just one bird crying like a baby, but hundreds. We had passed a terrible night. Being zipped into a tent with four other people was like being buried alive, but if you slept out in the dark, clouds of hungry mosquitoes descended on you. Cath and me lay lengthways and the children slept across the width of the tent and we all smelt strongly of the citronella oil we had smeared on when the sun went down.

I lay on my front because the slightest touch on the toasted flesh of my back felt like a whiplash. Outside, a whole nursery full of babies cried, and heavy forms rustled and clicked and ground across the crushed shells and remains of the fire. My feet were against the zipped-up part of the tent, and outside the zipper was a storage area with no groundsheet. I felt something hard pressing and moving against the canvas and realized that the big coconut crabs were foraging in there. I heard metal grinding against metal as they shoved the nesting pans about, and hoped Stacey would not waken and want to go outside to the toilet because I would have to clear the crabs out before she went through.

I was dozing after hours of discomfort when a rooster cock-a-doodle-doo'd loudly outside.

'Listen to that, Tony.'

'Aagh!' Cath touched my shoulder and in agony I lurched on to my knees, which was as far as I could go without hitting the roof.

'You hit my sunburn.'

'I only touched you. I'm sorry, love.'

'Mam, my back hurts.'

'Go on out of the tent, Craig, and I'll have a look.'

I shuffled round, bent double in the orange glow of morning, and unzipped the tent. In the storage area our pans and Primus stove were all tipped over, but I hardly noticed this, because I was so glad to get out into the air.

A large cockerel which had been prodding at our pile of coconuts took one look at me and bounded into the undergrowth. Before me I saw the sand, the lagoon and the blue sky. All to ourselves.

For a moment I felt the exhilaration that had been missing since we arrived on Rarotonga: the sense of freedom that had been my goal; the sense of power over my own destiny and delight in a world that seemed made specially for me and my family. Then reality intruded.

'Tony.'

Cath and Craig had crawled out of the tent behind me.

'Look at Craig's back.'

Craig was crimson all over and big blisters had puffed up on his face and shoulders.

'You're in the same state he is, Tony. I don't think much of that sunscreen.'

'It got washed off, didn't it?'

'They should tell you to keep putting it on. I never knew.'

'I never been in heat like this before.'

One by one the family disappeared into the bushes. I had told them yesterday to cover what they had done by scraping at the earth with a stick, so I hoped they were doing as I had said. On Takutea we had not done this properly and there had been a lot of flies.

We split up and went looking for papaw for breakfast. The fruit swelled in golden bunches from the trunks of low, pretty trees with a few shady leaves. As the morning went on, the sun grew hotter, and one by one we dozed off in the shade. I had an uneasy feeling; I couldn't have said why.

★

I woke up because there was a chicken pecking at the ground near me. She was a dirty white colour and when I leaned on an elbow and stared at her she stared right back out of two red eyes. We were both too hot to do much else. The whole island seemed unusually quiet. The water of the lagoon was even flatter than usual, and slid on to the sand like oil.

Something moved near my head. I looked hard at the thin erect roots of the strange tree near the tent and saw nothing at first, and then made out the shape of a lizard, the size of my hand, mottled and wrinkly like an old man's skin. In the ground near me were dimples that I knew concealed hermit crabs. Some would come out at night as they had done on Takutea; some were slowly moving near the tent even now.

The chicken stabbed the ground with her beak and picked up a small black beetle.

'Tony!'

Cath's voice made the chicken trot away squawking. My whole family appeared below me on the beach, framed by the coconut palm growing out of the ridge. They were all scarlet. Craig and Cath were squinting against the sunlight reflected off the beach, trying to see me among the leaves. Matthew and Stacey splashed each other in the water behind them.

I skidded down the embankment.

'We been looking for eggs.'

'I could do with a nice boiled egg and soldiers.'

'Fat chance, we couldn't find any. You coming to fish for supper?'

'Let's have some *pod* with it.'

I set off along the strand with Cath to look for a

sprouting coconut. When coconuts fall from the tree and are undisturbed, they slowly settle low into the sand and sprout palm leaves from one end. If you pull them up and open the coconut, you find a substance that looks like white candy floss inside, which you can eat like any other kind of starch. Tom Neale in his book calls this *uto*, but we had learned to call it *pod*, because that is how William referred to it. When you've scooped it all out of the shell, you find coconut oil for putting on your sunburn.

Cath and I tugged up a couple of coconuts by their leaves and carried them back towards the camp.

'What did you do when I was asleep?'

'Craig kept nodding off. His face is in an awful mess, Tony, I do feel bad about it but I never knew it would be so hot.'

'He should have worn that hat Teré gave him.'

'Yes, well, it's too late now.'

Matthew came running up with a couple of crabs. 'Can we eat these?'

'There's nothing much on them, Matthew,' said Cath. She put her *pod* on the ground and I did the same.

Matthew looked disappointed. I said, 'If you boil them in the water with the fish it'll make the fish taste better, won't it, Cath?'

I was willing her to say it would, but when she replied doubtfully, Matthew pulled a face and put the crabs on the sand. They creaked stiffly towards the sea.

'You can help me with the cassette-recorder later,' I said to him.

'What you want to use the cassette-recorder for?' Cath asked me. She was leading me down to the water to where I had left the nets on the sand this morning. I had noticed before how she edged me towards acting in the way she wanted. She started asking questions and walking away so that I had to follow her with my answer, and while I was giving it something was put into my hand, something to do, like now, when before I had even got my thoughts together I found myself walking round in a circle in the water again, getting fish.

We had our set of three pans for camping, with one detachable handle. Cath made the fire with twigs in the middle and coconut husks round the outside because the fibres of the husks burn slowly. She rested the pan of coconut water on the twigs but when they burned low, she had to hold the handle with both hands to keep the pan just above the fire, so that the water kept boiling without the whole fire collapsing. The burning twigs made a lot of smoke and Cath's eyes watered a lot. It was at about this time, with a saucepan full of boiling fish in her hands and smoke in her eyes, that Cath heard me asking what her impressions of the island were, and asking her to speak up. She was quite rude about the cassette-recorder.

She has got a temper sometimes. She was feeling guilty about the children getting sunburned and I thought she was taking it out on me. So I made no reply. We did not sit round the camp-fire for long that night, because the atmosphere seemed to be in all senses oppressive. Instead, we retired to the tent when the sun went down. It was much hotter than last night.

8

I took a deep breath, but no air seemed to go into me. The roof of the tent hung three feet above my face and, although my eyes were open, I could see nothing.

When we were at the dead-end house high up in the valleys, my brother and I used to stay over at our grandmother's, my father's mother's house down near the crossroads. Alun would never let me sleep on the wall side, and I dreaded getting squashed into the bed between him and my gran.

I waited for her to creak heavily on to the mattress. A great hard arm like a bolster would be shoved around my neck and my face pressed into her bosom as she rocked me to sleep against her peach nylon nightie. It was suffocating, it was stifling.

It was like this.

I opened my mouth and heaved some air in. This was smellier than Gran because we all stank of burned flesh and citronella oil. One gulp and the air supply seemed to be exhausted. I opened my eyes into the blackness and raised a hand to my face, barely believing that there could be no obstruction.

The others were asleep. The children were exhausted from heat, exercise and the pain of sunburn. Cath and I rolled away from each other sulkily when we settled down, and we both fell asleep at once. The birds and crabs which had kept us awake last night seemed to have gone away. I wanted to sit up or even turn over, but I didn't want to wake the others. I lay with my eyes open, wondering why it was so quiet outside.

As soon as daylight came, I would be in control. I pictured myself striding about, taking whatever we wanted, hacking and stripping and building and fishing and digging, converting the island to suit ourselves. But at night the original inhabitants took over; it had been like that on Takutea. Now, in the silence, I could almost fancy that some great meeting of the animals was taking place on the other side of the island, some big discussion about our arrival and the formulation of a plan of campaign.

Yet I knew from Takutea exactly what was outside the walls of the tent. If I sat up, bent forward and opened the flap of the entrance, if I crawled past the water-container and the ashes of the fire and stood upright, the heat of my skin would attract a dense cloud of mosquitoes dancing in the torchlight. And if I beamed the torch down the slope to the beach, I would see crowds waving, crowds of hermit crabs packed as close as ruddy-faced trippers on a hot Bank Holiday at Rhyl, nudging and bumping and waving their claws helplessly in the light.

Tonight was quiet. Tonight was different: there was a stillness about it. It wasn't just the choking heat. Not so much as a rustle came from outside.

One of the children turned over with a sigh. I dozed.

It was too hot to sleep. This tent would not do. We couldn't sleep like this for months on end. There was a spot where I thought we could build a sleeping hut. I had seen it today, though at a time when Craig was running on ahead and I wanted to warn him about something, so I hadn't mentioned it. It overlooked the ocean, where there was more of a breeze and fewer mosquitoes. We could weave a roof out of palm fronds. Cath had done something like that on Takutea – she made a mat. That's what we would do. We would build a shelter against the sun, with a woven roof, and use it as a school hut in the day. We could make walls. They didn't need much support; with nothing more than a constant breeze, occasional rain and hot sunlight to contend with, the flimsiest house would last for months. Teré had said there'd been no storms for a long time now.

I thought about cutting branches for a shelter with the machete, and felt that I had made a decision. I would start tomorrow.

The machete was outside, stuck into the side of a palm tree.

Nobody else around.

Nobody who could use the machete.

At this moment I was the single conscious human being on this vast blue curve on the surface of the globe.

'Tony.'

It was so dark that I didn't know whether my eyes were open or not, but the roar was loud enough to be right inside my head.

'What is it?'

Cath's face was close to mine, but it was hard to hear each other over the noise. She groped about near my head.

'Aagh! Mind my sunburn.'

She found the torch and switched it on, shielding it with her hand so as not to waken the children.

Black shadows danced over the roof, which bellied down in places, like the underneath of a deck-chair with a fat lady sitting in it. There was a groaning and shuddering above the roar of the surf, and the guy ropes were creaking and rain was beating a tattoo above us and we could hear the trees wailing and screaming as they bent before the wind.

'Dad.'

'Don't sit up, Craig, you'll hit the tent.'

Matthew woke up and didn't say anything. He lay there rubbing his eyes while his brother looked blearily at me.

'Is it a storm, Dad?'

'Yes, Craig, don't worry about it. Go back to sleep.'

I don't suppose he was the least bit worried about it. He had me looking after him, after all. This brilliant father who had successfully brought him ten thousand miles from home. A father who could catch fish from the sea and get us and our suitcases through Los Angeles International Airport. Craig tried to pillow his ears against his arms to keep out the roar which was now rising to a howl as the sides of the tent strained upwards from the ground.

He wasn't thinking that his brilliant father had managed to get them all to Maina just in time for what sounded like a hurricane.

Matthew whimpered a little. 'Mammy, I don't like it.'

'It's only a storm,' said Cath quietly. 'Nothing to

143

worry about. Now don't talk any more or you'll wake Stacey.'

Cath switched off the torch and we lay on our fronts beneath the low-slung canvas, not speaking above the tumult. You'd have had more space at the coal-face. I pressed my chest against the groundsheet, trying to extend as much of myself as I could along the ground to keep the tent from lifting up. The gale was trying to dislodge it, to prise it from its moorings as carelessly as my fingernail had flicked a thorn from my leg this afternoon. I had heard of islands disappearing in hurricanes. Everything above the waterline, trees, living things, just torn away and flung into oblivion by the cruel wind. Tom Neale had written about it.

Under the groundsheet I could feel movement. Rainwater was filling up the sand . . . In the village with our house on the mountainside the stony unmade road used to crack in wet weather, as oak struts settled in the mines hundreds of feet below. With horror I imagined the island simply collapsing inwards, subsiding into the sea.

I struggled to turn over, supporting myself on my elbows.

'Watch out, you'll get water in.'

'Sorry. How long's it been like this?'

'I been awake hours. I heard the suitcases go.'

I could hear them myself. It sounded as if somebody was banging doors. There was a mad poltergeist out there, flinging suitcases, pots and pans, the water-container, the T-shirts which had hung motionless in the sunset from the bark of a coconut palm – tossing all this across the beach, battering the hermit crabs, pushing at the trees, trying to uproot us. I thought of the machete. Then I pretended I hadn't thought of it. I preferred not to. I had never wanted to be the target in a knife-throwing act.

I had heard stories. There was no reason to think that this violence was being suffered anywhere else. It was like a judgement: we had only just arrived, and the elements were directing their power at us in a way I could never have foreseen. A bolt from the blue: I had heard the phrase. A thunderbolt, what was that? Perhaps the spirit of the place had risen up and was out to get us. Tangaroa ... Kauraka had told me how the Reverend Williams had destroyed images of the island's god. Maybe this was Tangaroa's revenge. Perhaps the god had been mortally offended by having a Williams on Maina. And the other living creatures had deserted us and left us to weather the storm alone.

I felt a pang of guilt. Thanks to me, Cath and the children were in danger. A suspicion that I had never admitted to before wormed its way to the surface. What if they had come not because they wanted to, but because they didn't want to disappoint me – what if this was all just a charade, to humour me in my stupid over-confidence?

'It'll pass,' whispered Cath. 'We're fine here.'

I dragged my mind back to reality. 'Is that the lagoon?'

'That's the roaring, isn't it?'

'Yes. D'you think it sounds too close?'

I could hear layers of sound, pick them out, interpret the thundering sound-track that was running outside. I had never seen waves in the lagoon, yet there was a rumble, a crash, high on the beach. Too close. But what bothered me more was the constant thudding and banging.

'There's coconuts falling all over.'

'It's a bit late to worry about that. There isn't anywhere else to shelter.'

Her fingers linked mine and we lay still amid the uproar. Craig and Matthew were awake. When your sons think you're invincible, you're better off keeping your mouth shut.

I kept thinking it would go away but it didn't. The storm seemed to rage for hours. At last the rain slackened, and I saw a twinkle of grey light where the zipper of the tent ended.

'I'm going out.'

I crawled through the opening and was still on all fours when I saw why we should move. The scene before me bore hardly any resemblance to the paradise of yesterday. The fine white sand was beige and wet, the sky yawned grey as a Swansea sky, the arching, straining palms were a dismal monochrome; coconuts bounced furiously across what was left of the beach, and, most terrifying of all, the sea was black and vicious and hurtling forward in waves as high as a man. It rolled up and spent itself against a coconut palm only six feet away. I turned, still on my knees, to go back into the tent, and the gale seemed to take me by the shoulders. Somehow I scrambled back inside in an eddy of leaves and dust.

'We must move.'

Cath must have seen the alarm in my face, but she

knew better than to frighten the children. Craig and Matthew were sitting up, hugging their knees like little elves and shivering now under the sides of the tent.

'All right, you boys, now pack up everything you can into your rucksacks.'

We hunched in the gloom with our legs stretched out in front and scrabbled around Stacey, who was dozing floppily with her thumb in her mouth. I shoved things into bags. Bright little messages flashed by: DURACELL: FOR LONGER LONGER LIFE. RAROTONGA: THE LAST PARADISE. Cath seized the brown paper-bag of cabin bread which Teré had given us.

'We'll have to go into the interior.'

It had been a joke before, this: 'the interior'. It sounded like an expedition to the source of the Amazon. But I had to get them away from that wall of black water.

'Is the sea coming up?'

'It's very close.'

It was too close. I thought of Stacey, and the wind out there.

'She won't be able to stand up in it, Cath.'

'I can hold her.'

Stacey was waking up now. Her mother pushed her hair out of her eyes.

'Come on, sweetheart, we've got to go now.'

She was half asleep. I could see she would have to be dragged from the tent or she would lapse back into a doze. She was so small, lighter probably than the suitcase with the cassette-recorder and batteries in it that had been lifted and hurled against a tree. I thought how difficult it had been for me to move into the wind.

'I think we have to stop the children getting blown away. We have to tie them to something.'

The others were following me as I hauled myself out into the storm. There was water in the wind, whether rain or sea-spray I couldn't tell, and as I stood up I could see the deep pools of water that swung across hollows in the tent canvas. Cath staggered and grabbed my arm as she stood upright.

'Can you hold Stacey?' I shouted. Then I didn't wait for an answer. 'She might get swept away.' I needed rope to lash Stacey down with, and there was rope within sight, but it needed cutting. As I turned towards the place where the machete had been, the wind took me and I hurtled towards it as if frog-marched at great speed. The machete was still wedged in the tree. I jerked it out and strained double on my way back to the tent. The others were on their way now, all holding hands, bending into the wind, plodding bravely along the top of the beach. Cath was struggling to carry a suitcase and keep tight hold of Stacey's hand as she led the children a little way along the edge of the undergrowth. At that point there was a gap between two bushes where you could pass through to the interior.

They left me ten yards behind them. I was hacking at the guy ropes with my machete. Rain lashed into my eyes and the salt-spray smacked the trunks of the coconut palms. I tugged pegs out of the ground. Once it was released from the ropes' tension, the tent collapsed under the weight of water. It was so heavy and sodden that it did not immediately fly away. I could not lift it. Instead I battled to roll it up, dragged it behind me, clutched the long ropes that I had cut from it and staggered after the others.

I caught up with them in a stony clearing between trees. We were all gasping from the struggle against the wind. I dropped the end of the tent that I had been hauling.

'Come over here, Stacey,' I shouted. She let go of Cath's hand and took mine.

'Hug the tree for a minute,' I yelled. I got down on my hunkers as she obeyed, stretching her little arms around the hairy trunk of the coconut palm. It was when I passed the tent-rope under her armpits that she turned around and I saw a stricken look in her eyes before the wind blew her hair over her face. She let out a great yell. 'Mammy!' It was the yell you hear right across the playground when somebody else's four-year-old is being bullied at going-home time. 'Mammy, I dowanna be tied, I dowanna, he's tying me – '

She wriggled furiously. She wouldn't keep still. I was struggling to hold the machete with my foot to stop it from skittering away in the wind, and the tree was groaning back and forth like a drunken old sailor while I tried to tie a proper knot in the rope. I was no match for Stacey. She got away and clambered into her mother's arms with a tear-stained face.

'It seemed like the best idea,' I muttered.

For the rest of the morning we huddled in the clearing. There was whitish rubble underfoot and above us sixty-foot coconut palms swayed so forcefully that the ground beneath us seemed to heave and roll with them. I had no sense that we were on dry land. I felt as if we were on board a flimsy ship amid a raging ocean.

Heavy rain began again and we fought to put up the tent. I tied some of the ropes around trees and kept the rest anchored with big stones. We crawled inside with all we had managed to save from the beach, and sat, breathing the foul scorched scent of each other's skin.

Breakfast was flying about in the sea and wind outside, and I wasn't eager to risk hunting it. The cabin bread didn't look like breakfast. It was like thick dry slabs of cardboard. After a few hours of '*I Spy*' and answering questions like 'Why is the wind so loud, Dad?', we fished it out of Cath's bag and ate it. It tasted like a sample left behind by Captain Cook. But it staved off hunger, and we sucked limes that Matthew had stuffed into his rucksack in the flight from the tent.

As the day wore on the sun emerged, the sea grew calmer, and the wind died down. We went out. The island looked littered and wrecked, like a dustbin over-turned by stray dogs.

Tomorrow we would build a shelter. Tonight would be our last in the tent. I would rather lose all the blood in my body to mosquitoes than spend another night in that inferno.

Nothing happens quickly on the island. The next day, a calm and sunny one, was well advanced, and we had barely made a start on the shelter, when I saw a speck bobbing across the lagoon from the direction of Aitutaki. I was fishing at the time, with the small net. Cath was up to her waist in the lagoon, washing clothes, which the children had picked up from all over the beach after the storm. The children were near the camp, playing. The sun was past its height and had the beach not been littered with debris, smashed shells, driftwood and broken branches, this would have been an idyllic scene.

I hauled the net on to the sand. Then I turned to stare at whatever it was that I had seen. A boat, certainly. The men from the *Mirror* might turn up at any time, but we were unlikely to see them so soon; I was dreading their arrival; they would want something from me, and I was not quite sure what it was.

I comforted myself that it was most likely just Teré and Junior in the boat. Well, they would see that we had been through it and survived. I looked proudly at my catch: fresh silvery little fishes gleaming in the evening sun. They would be delicious cooked in coconut water over the fire and served on an empty coconut shell with a squeeze of lime. There would be plenty for everybody.

I made a space clear of fallen branches and sodden driftwood, sat on the beach in the sunset and began to clean the fish. I grew engrossed in what I was doing. Practical tasks like this are therapeutic. You learn to do them efficiently and it frees your mind for other things. I was thinking about *Bligh and the Bounty*, my thick book with a stiff grey cover which had blown into the lagoon and had been hurled back to shore on a wave. It was the only book I had and I dearly hoped it would dry out all right. Some of the children's schoolbooks had been ruined by the water. *Blue Book One* and *Blue Book Two* had gone the way of William Bligh, but we still had Roald Dahl's *Charlie and the Chocolate Factory* and *The Story of Henry Sugar* and some pens and paper.

I looked out to sea. The boat wasn't coming in a straight line, because of the reefs, but I thought I could see three or four figures in it. I would look again when they got closer.

Above the soft slapping of the waves, I could just about hear the children and an occasional interjected word from Cath. Sitting here, gutting fish with my fingers, I was attracting thousands of sandflies. I could feel sharp shells pressing painfully into the skin on the backs of my legs, and I shifted, sending the cloud of tiny flies high into the air for a moment. I stood up, scraping sand from my legs, and looked out to sea again. Two white blobs and two dark ones sat in the boat.

The storm had been very stressful and we had had little sleep since we came to the island. The sun was now warm, pleasantly warm on my face. I lay down for a moment, shielding my eyes with my arm.

Cath woke me up. 'Look!'

Teré and Junior had stopped the boat's engine and the craft sat calm on the lagoon. A pink figure in tight denim shorts, with his back to me, was struggling over the side, gingerly holding a pair of sandals high above the water. Another man, much taller, was standing up and wobbling against the horizon.

'It's Harry and the other Harry.'

The two figures, the tall and the short, both wearing large-brimmed sun-hats with fringed straw edges, waded towards us. Cath and I waved to Teré. We stood at the edge of the lagoon like a welcoming committee, the Mayor and Lady Mayoress of Swansea on their best behaviour for the arrival of royalty. Under their hats Harry Arnold and Harry Page looked earnest. Their skin was burned scarlet by the sun but you could see white flesh where their shirt-sleeves began. They were both sweating. They stumbled through the last few feet of clear water.

'Ow,' muttered Harry Arnold. Harry Page made a hissing noise behind his teeth. The shells are quite sharp underfoot if you're not used to them. I said, 'You found us all right, then.'

Harry Page looked at me as if I was mad. As for Harry Arnold, the Savile Row look that had seemed so out of place on our front step had been left far behind. I wished the neighbours could have seen him this time. He had a sort of cutlass stuck into his belt. He said, ''Scuse the shorts.' He mumbled something about his honeymoon and the shorts having spent twenty years in a cupboard.

The children lined up behind us.

'He's got hairy legs, Mammy.'

'Ssh, Stacey.'

Cath and Teré began a shouted conversation across the water. Harry Arnold, wincing a bit on the sharp shells, trod cautiously up the beach with me and the children. His sandals were made of very thin plastic. I guessed he had bought them in Tahiti. Glancing behind me, I could see Cath looking mortified, like when somebody comes round and she's sorting washing all over the kitchen floor. Harry Arnold stopped, shifting his cutlass slightly, and stared in dismay at the torn foliage and broken wood. He must have thought it always looked like that.

'Were you aware of the cyclone at all?' he inquired.

9

The island seemed crowded. Just four more people, and it was uproar. The beach felt like Minehead. Everywhere you looked there was somebody.

Harry Arnold followed me towards the shady patch by the tent, warily clutching the knife on his belt. Harry Page unslung a camera and a pair of sandals from his neck, left them in a heap on the beach and walked away from all of us. He looked a bit greenish, under his hat, I thought, not at all the cheery character we had met at Gatwick.

'The sea doesn't agree with him,' said Harry Arnold, who had a hunted look and kept sneaking glances over his shoulder. He was conscious of Teré behind him. She had stepped majestically on to the shore, holding her umbrella aloft, surrounded by Cath and our children, and was scrutinizing the two Harries from a distance. Harry Page marched alongside the lagoon.

'Big Harry! Don't go into the water without your sandals!'

The tall fellow hesitated and stopped. Teré scanned the beach for Junior, who had jumped out of the boat and was pulling it ashore.

'Junior! Give me my bag from under the seat there.'

Junior heaved a huge laundry-bag across the water to her. She subsided on to the sand with it and began rummaging. Cath sat down to talk with her.

At the clearing outside the tent I sat on the ground.

Harry Arnold did the same. Then he noticed a crab shooting into its hole and got up.

'I never thought you'd come this quick,' I said, as he selected a new position and hesitantly sat down again. I was at a bit of a loss. Now that he was here, there seemed to be no social emollient to smooth the path, somehow. No coffee or tea to offer and not a lot of point in asking how they had got here. He explained that anyway.

'We got the inter-island flight to Aitutaki yesterday afternoon. This is just a recce, just a brief visit to find how the land lies. We'll do the pictures and the interview tomorrow and the next day . . .' Harry was peering at me with a horrified look. 'You seem a bit rough, if you don't mind my saying so. What's happened to your back? And your face?'

'Sunburn.'

'The children are burned as well. Didn't you bring any sunscreen?'

When I explained that we had not expected such intense sunshine, he looked unimpressed.

'Well, maybe you'd better wear a T-shirt for the photographs.'

The children came running up from the beach with Cath walking behind them, smiling.

'Teré's gone to sleep on a coconut,' Craig said. I could see Teré's form, prone on her side near the waterline. Her head was indeed resting on a coconut. The devoted Junior was sitting beside her, gently waving a palm-frond fan.

'She's asleep, is she?' asked Harry hopefully. 'Does she go to sleep often?'

'She goes to sleep when she's eaten her spaghetti,' Matthew explained, as though he was giving guidance to the habits of some rare wild creature. 'She's got cans of spaghetti and corned beef in her bag.'

'Reminds me of Queen Salote,' murmured Harry. 'Dynamic woman, isn't she?'

'She's very good-hearted and kind. It's her brother who's William Richard in Rarotonga, that I told you about, you know, they are the third generation since William Marsters, who came from Gloucestershire in the last –'

'Yes, I believe you did tell me. Is this where you sleep? Where do the children sleep?'

He struggled to his feet as I showed him the tent. He didn't say much. In fact he had an air of disbelief.

'Just the one tent?'

I explained that we had wanted to burden ourselves with as little luggage as possible. I told him how we had made a start on a hut. Harry Page emerged from the bushes and muttered something about failing light. They prepared to leave.

'We'll be back tomorrow,' they promised. Harry Arnold said Teré had told them it was important to return to Aitutaki in daylight so that the reefs were visible underwater. They set off, looking grave, I thought.

'I told him I wished they'd waited a bit before they came,' I said to Cath, as we strolled down to the waterside to collect the fish I had caught before the boat landed. 'The place does look in a terrible state, doesn't it?'

'I hope they don't think it's always like this,' Cath

said. 'By the way I told Harry Page he could take pictures of us putting the hut up tomorrow.'

But I was not to be distracted. The visit had made me uneasy.

'Suppose your dad sees Craig's blisters in the newspaper,' I said. 'He'll be on the next flight, Cath.'

My father-in-law had once threatened to come out and fetch us if he thought anything was wrong. The idea that he might have meant it made me dread the day the *Mirror* printed our pictures. I could see the headline now: MAN RISKS FAMILY'S LIVES ON DESERT ISLAND. And Cath's dad in his committee suit with his face puce, marching across the hot tarmac at Rarotonga Airport for a confrontation. I hate confrontation.

Cath took my hand. She kissed it; it was the only bit of me that she could kiss, the rest was too sunburned.

'I wouldn't worry. If Dad ever did come it'd probably mellow him out a bit. He could play darts with Kauraka.'

We had not long finished our breakfast next morning when Teré's boat again appeared on the horizon.

Cath swore under her breath. 'Help us get the washing-up done, Stacey. Matthew, go and tidy up the tent. Craig, shift some of those coconuts, will you, they're all over the place.'

Cath and Stacey were just finishing washing up in the lagoon when the boat came within shouting distance. I walked across the sand to meet it. I strode into the water, smiling. Everyone on board was yelling at me. After a while I understood that Teré and Harry Arnold were asking me to grab the front of the boat and pull it into shore. Cath had followed. She turned away in embarrassment when she saw that Harry Arnold had got a video-camera on his shoulder, and he was taking our picture as we tugged the boat in.

Harry Page took no notice of what the other Harry was doing. He swung out of the boat with a lot of camera equipment, muttered a greeting and tramped past me up the beach. His face was shaded by the fringed edges of his hat brim.

'The other Harry's taking video pictures, is he?' I inquired as he sloshed by. 'What's that for, then?'

'Plans for you,' he grinned. 'Big plans for you. Career in television.' He unslung his gear on to the sand, squatted beside it and started fiddling with lenses and light meters. A crab waddled away at the sound of velcro ripping.

This time Cath helped Junior to heave Teré's bag off the boat.

'I shall wait for them again,' Teré announced, up to her ankles in the water of the lagoon. 'The Harrys are going to work for several hours, they tell me. Junior! Fetch me two coconuts.'

Teré created a little force field of energy wherever she walked. As soon as she looked at you, you felt you should be doing something. She strode up the beach to the place where our low coconut palm grew diagonally from the ridge, and sat in its shade. She settled herself into the sand with grace, straight-backed and cross-legged, closed her eyes and waited for Junior to bring her the biggest green coconuts he could find. I could see him in the background, shinning up a tree. She opened her eyes.

'Little Harry!'

Harry Arnold was gingerly exploring the spot where I had been fishing yesterday and he pretended not to hear her. The sand was hot and damp and he was paddling, carrying his sandals.

'Don't go into the water without your shoes!'

Approaching him, I saw that he had got that hunted look again.

'What's all this palaver about shoes?' he asked in a quiet voice as if Teré, who was fifty yards away, might hear.

'There're stone-fish,' I explained. 'They're very rare, but they lie in shallow water and have spikes. If you trod on one accidentally it'd be fatal.'

He quickly shoved his feet into the plastic sandals and tried to look composed. It was a very warm day already, though the sun hadn't been up more than three or four hours, and I could see that perspiration stood in beads on his forehead.

'Interview first,' he said. We strolled back to the tent where Cath and me and the children, knowing that visitors were expected, had tried to collect those of our possessions that had been damaged by the storm, and pile them neatly alongside our suitcases. The heat of the sun beat through my T-shirt to my back, making the blisters ache. There was quite a strong breeze, but it felt about the same temperature as a car exhaust.

Harry Arnold sat down with all of us. Harry Page prowled around the edges of the group, taking pictures.

'Don't mind me. Just ignore me.'

Craig, Matthew and Stacey found this easy to do. It was as if the most natural thing in the world was to be drinking from a coconut in the mid-Pacific, with some fellow from Surrey in a floppy hat crawling out of the undergrowth with a camera to take your likeness every second gulp.

'The children are very adaptable,' I said to Harry Arnold.

'They need to be. Oh, by the way, I told you I'd bring a surprise.'

He jumped up and ran down to the boat. Harry Page took more pictures; I felt a complete fool. I wanted Teré to be in the picture but apparently her being present would ruin the story.

The other Harry returned carrying a large plastic bucket that looked heavy. It turned out to be full of crushed ice. Nestling in the middle were tubs of ice-cream, one for each of us, and milkshakes for the children, whose eyes shone.

There were cans of lager for the grown-ups. I pulled the ring-pull and thanked him, though I never drank lager normally. I got that sense once again that I was touching an artefact from an alien planet. I would have liked to explain this: that cassettes and cameras and cans of lager belonged to another world, that they were invaders, and that on this island I could drop out of the century and the culture into which I had been born. This was the point: here, on the island, there was no sense of the twentieth century.

But somehow when I said all this it didn't seem to impress him with the same force that it had me. He was concerned about our distance from medical assistance, he said. With Cath being an epileptic. Did we have the flares the *Mirror* had provided? I had brought them in one of our suitcases, though it seemed highly unlikely to me that of the thousand people who live on Aitutaki, one of them would happen to be awake at night at exactly the minute when one of our flares shot across the sky, if it ever did. I had no idea how to use them, and in any case those flares repelled me. I didn't want to have them with me. They signified mistrust of the island. I felt no mistrust – especially now, since the storm was over and I thought that we had survived the worst that could happen.

So I would have liked to throw the flares into the sea and not to drink the lager, but I was too polite.

I told him about the Marsters family and how they own land in Palmerston and how it was thanks to John James that their parliament had given us permission to stay on Primrose for a while. I urged him to interview Teré and Junior, but he said the story was about us, not them. He seemed more interested in the risks he thought we were taking. I said, 'When I was small my parents had us up in the valleys, there was no telephone and it was a long way for an ambulance, so how can you think this is any worse?' But I don't think Harry Arnold had ever been up the valleys.

Remoteness is more than just distance. I would have liked to explain this. You can be isolated anywhere. In the council house in the dead-end that we moved to after our first village crumbled into the mountainside, we were isolated with our mother and father, although there were houses on both sides. It was a house faced in grey concrete, streaked with rain. We were at the end of a spur that led to nowhere, half a mile away from the crossroads where the village was; and you could feel the emptiness.

'So what did you do first?' Harry Arnold was asking. He had got his notebook out and was taking down what we said in shorthand. He had to keep stopping to wipe his sweaty hand on his shorts. 'Did you, ah, dig a latrine?'

'A what?' I said, suddenly distracted. I had been thinking in Welsh. We only spoke Welsh, up there in the valleys.

'When you got here first. I suppose the first thing was to make sanitary arrangements. What they call a latrine, in the army.'

'No, you just scrape a hole in the ground and cover it up afterwards.'

'I see. Erm – oh, by the way, are you doing any gardening? Teré's got a watermelon for you in her bag, I thought that would be a good idea because of the pips, maybe they'll grow. Have you got plans to grow anything?'

'There's no need, is there, Cath? We've got our fish and coconuts, haven't we? Anyway, we're going to be on Primrose, you see.'

'Did you bring a spade?'

'No.'

'Have you got – erm – tools, other implements, a saw and so on for building the hut?'

Cath looked at me and I looked at her.

'We've got a machete,' I explained. 'You've seen it, it's the one Craig was using for husking the coconuts.'

'Bit rusty, isn't it?'

'Yes. It's borrowed from Teré's brother Palmer.'

'What else have you got?'

'Well –' Cath and I exchanged desperate looks. We wanted to help. We could see that he had an idea of what he wanted to discover, and it was a Swiss Family Robinson idyll of homespun industry and resourcefulness; but unfortunately I hadn't come to the island to practise DIY and survival skills, so he was trotting up a blind alley. His questioning was relentless.

'If Palmer hadn't lent you that machete, would you have brought something of your own?'

'Oh, yes. We was looking in the shops, wasn't we, Cath? But William's family wanted to lend us things, and it would have been rude to say no.'

Harry Arnold looked nonplussed.

'We did have a spade,' Cath contributed. 'You got a collapsible one at Millet's, you remember that, Tony?'

'Oh, yes, that's right.'

'So you have got a spade.'

'No, I left it behind.'

Harry Arnold scribbled busily in his notebook.

'There's a good lad,' Harry Page told Craig from behind his lens, the motor drive whirring obediently.

Harry Arnold had stretched his hand up the trunk of a coconut palm to provide support for one of Craig's feet. He had shoved my son as high up a coconut palm as he could reach, and Craig was clinging on desperately while at the same time turning and grinning down at the camera.

'He hasn't learned to climb them yet,' I muttered, for about the fifth time.

Harry Page trod on my foot and swore under his breath, and I dodged sideways. 'Harry,' he said to his friend, 'give the boy the coconut.'

'Got it?' said Harry Arnold through his teeth, holding the coconut above his head. Craig let go of the trunk with one hand and wobbled down and grasped the coconut to his chest. He never stopped smiling.

'Stay right there. That's great. Smile. That's excellent. Keep smiling. Get your hand out, Harry.'

I stood at his shoulder and said, 'If his sunburn shows I don't want that in the paper, it'll upset the relatives.'

'Yup, yup,' he muttered, stooping to get an angle on Craig, who was stoically grinning as he clung to the tree with his feet and clasped the coconut in his arm.

When Harry Page had got enough shots of Craig up the tree, he beckoned Cath over.

'Washing shots, dear,' he said, like a conspirator. 'If you could get a few clothes together and wash them in the lagoon for me, there's a good girl.'

He wandered about snapping the vegetation while Cath hurried to collect some T-shirts from where they had been drying on a branch. Harry Arnold was making some adjustment to the video-camera and he said, 'You could show me where this hut is that you're building, Tony, if you would. Then maybe when Harry's finished with Cath, you could both do a bit more building for the video.'

'It's over there.' I had taken a couple of steps when I heard a choking cry from above. The green coconut banged heavily to the ground and Craig shot down the trunk after it with a suppressed squeal. His face was red and so were the insides of his legs.

'God, sorry, Craig,' said Harry Page, evidently concerned. 'Completely forgot you were up there.'

Craig hobbled after us to the hut. Stacey took his hand and Matthew followed, carrying half a dozen of his figure-men. These were models about four inches high which represented various soldiers, terminators, Viking raiders and fierce creatures from space. Since we had rescued the figures after the storm he took them with him everywhere, and was quite likely to slope off at any moment and enact a short drama with them, murmuring to himself in the voices he had given to their different characters.

The storm had made a clearing a few hundred yards from our tent, overhung by a couple of low palm trees. We had begun to stake out a four-sided hut in this space, using the palm trees as one gable end and two tall sticks in the ground as the other. The walls would be made by sticking palm fronds into the ground.

Harry Arnold saw what we had done. 'Oh, it's quite straightforward, isn't it? You don't need to weave them together or anything.'

'That's right, and you make the roof the same way.'

I went off with Craig and Matthew to find some more palm fronds and saw Cath up to her waist in the lagoon with a bar of soap and some brightly coloured washing under the noonday sun. Harry Page stole along the shore in his hat, snapping shot after shot.

'We usually sleep at this time,' I said, approaching him across the sand. He said something about having a day's work to do and asked me to walk towards him with the children and some palm fronds. The white sand reflected blistering heat on to our faces as we dragged the fronds towards him and Harry Arnold, who had now got his video-camera on his shoulder and was busy directing us from the bushes.

'Right, if you could all do that again, that's right, smile – now take the fronds off and do it again from the top, come in from right of frame, that's it, SMILE please, Tony.'

Obediently we trailed our fronds towards the hut again. I thought it was stupid to keep smiling, it's not what you do on a desert island. Cath came to join us. I wished I was lying down in the shade. Harry Arnold stole forward in his little shorts with the purposeful knife in his belt and the video-camera on his shoulder.

'Get your arse out of my picture, Harry,' growled Harry Page.

'Whose story is this anyway?'

'Christ knows, but you're not supposed to be in the shot, mate.'

We stood around while they argued and then Harry Arnold said, 'What I want you to do, Tony, if you wouldn't mind, is say a few words to camera.'

'There you are, Tony, you're going to be a film star,' said Cath cosily.

'What words? What's this for?'

'Promotion. Sunday night in the middle of *Poirot*. All we need is something like – "I've come ten thousand miles with my family to live on this deserted island and you can read why I did it in tomorrow's *Daily Mirror*."'

I positioned myself where he said and when he said 'Action', I began.

'I've come ten thousand miles to live on this deserted

island and you can read all about it in the *Daily Mirror*. That wasn't right, was it?'

'I'll write it down for you.'

He tore off some pages from his shorthand pad, wrote the sentence in big letters and got Harry Page to stand beside him, holding them up.

'All right, action.'

'There's something moving beside your foot, Harry.'

Harry Page spoke and Harry Arnold jumped in the air with his video-camera.

'It's only a crab.'

Stacey solemnly removed it. They settled down again.

'Action!'

I peered into the unfriendly black lens.

'I've come ten thousand miles with my family to live on this deserted island and you can read why I did it in tomorrow's *Daily Mirror*.'

'And again, and put the stress on WITH MY FAMILY.'

I did it again.

Then I did it again, saying 'desert island' instead of 'deserted island'. All three of the children were squatting on the ground, watching me. A chicken was pecking the ground behind the two men from the *Mirror*. They shifted out of the sun a bit.

'You don't look very cheerful,' said Harry Page, when I had recited the sentence at the lens for the eighth time.

'It's so unnatural,' I said, squirming. 'What do I want to say this for, I don't want to talk to millions of people.'

Harry Page sighed and said something about the meaning of life.

Harry Arnold said we'd got enough and thanked us very much.

Cath offered them a drink of coconut water back at the tent and I went to find Teré and Junior. I felt embarrassed; I wanted the Harrys to go. They made too many demands, they brought pressure with them, I thought. I would have explained this to Teré, but she had woken up and was setting out her afternoon tea, that is, three coconuts and two cans of corned beef. She had drunk the few litres of sweet water from inside her coconuts and was now busy opening the cans with a knife. Cupping her hand, she scooped some soft white flesh from inside a coconut, wrapped a thick slab of corned beef in it and tucked in, as you would with a sandwich. Teré and me sat together in the shade while the others gathered at the tent behind us.

In the far distance across the lagoon, away from Aitutaki, I could see shadows that were other islands. I had heard that tourist boats went from Aitutaki to One Foot Island.

'Why's One Foot Island called that?'

She swallowed a mouthful of corned beef and told a story she had told many times before.

'Once upon a time a man and his son landed there. But a hostile war party had followed them from another island. The man said to his son, "Walk quickly to that palm tree and climb right up to the top and stay there." The son obeyed him, and once he was safe and invisible up the tree the father followed. He placed his feet very carefully in the footprints the boy had left in the sand. Only he went right past the tree, so that his own prints continued; and when the war party arrived, they saw the prints and thought that there was only one person there. They followed the tracks and caught the man and killed him, but the boy up the tree they didn't find. That is why it's called One Foot Island.'

She munched steadily through her supplies while Junior slept a few feet away. Suddenly she said, 'Do you know why there're no dogs on Aitutaki?'

I hadn't noticed that there weren't any.

'No.'

'Because there used to be leprosy. Do you see the little *motu* this side of One Foot Island?' She pointed at a shadow across the water. 'That was once a leper colony. Until the 1960s it was. And people thought that dogs carried the disease, so we don't have any dogs to this day.'

I thought of being isolated as a leper, and the idea chilled my heart. It was one thing rejecting the world, but quite another to be rejected by it.

The Harrys were gathering up their cameras and slipping and sliding down the bank to the beach with them. Harry Page landed near us in a shower of sand.

'Most beautiful light I've ever had,' he said, adding sadly, 'We'll be back in London on Thursday.'

'D'you think you got what you wanted?'

'Oh, I think so. It'll make a great story.'

Harry Arnold came down with his video-camera. He was carrying a big piece of white coral. There was lots of it on the beach since the storm.

'You'd pay £50 in Harrods for a piece this size,' he said.

'Take some back. You could pay for your trip,' I said. He smiled.

'We'll come out again in a few months.'

'We won't be here then. We're moving on.'

'Yes, you said. We'll find you.'

'Don't be so sure of that,' said Teré, from under her big beach umbrella. 'Palmerston is a lot more remote than Aitutaki. The working boats don't go there and there's no airstrip. You might have to wait months for a boat that's visiting. That's what Tony and Cath are doing.'

'We can pay,' said Harry Arnold indulgently. 'Open a chequebook and people will do most things.'

Teré shook her head. Our eyes met and she grinned, white teeth in her brown face, and she threw her great shoulders up in a shrug.

'Islanders are not like that,' I said.

But I don't think the Harrys understood.

I woke up every morning for days feeling relieved that the men from the *Mirror* had been and gone; I hadn't realized how much the prospect of their visit had been weighing on my mind. But now that we had discharged our obligation, I was worried in case Cath's father took on at the sight of the pictures.

In fact, Maina was spoiled for me. Journalists could get out to it, light planes landed several times a day on Aitutaki and tour boats visited the other *motus* near by – knowing this made a mockery of what we were doing. I said so to Cath.

'I don't understand you,' she said. 'It's not as if we can *see* the planes. We're on our own. It's all in the mind, this problem you've got, Tony.'

But nothing helped. At some stage John James Marsters would turn up to take us to Primrose; and I felt that I wouldn't settle until he did.

We were still suffering physically. The blisters on my face and back were septic and oozing, and Cath and the children were covered in red bumps from mosquito bites. Craig's face especially was scarred and crusted from bites and old blisters that had suppurated and burst.

The tent seemed more like a hot coffin every time we had to get into it, yet the hut we had made was no protection against mosquitoes at night. So to put off zipping ourselves into the tent we talked and sang around the camp-fire for hours, after dark. Coconut husks smouldered like twisted vermilion tongues and cast a glow upwards on to our faces, accentuating the eye sockets. Crabs shuffled briskly through the undergrowth outside our circle of light, or shouldered their way up from the sand near the fire. Sometimes the baby-cry birds whimpered. Stacey spotted mosquitoes like a cat, and jumped up and smacked her hands together when she saw one, bursting the insect in a gobbet of blood.

Beyond our little group the sea lay black and so did the islands, uneven humps on the horizon. The sky was miles higher than in Wales. It was full of stars, great trails of glittering dust, and some that twinkled very big and white like the ones on a Christmas card.

Junior had told me that there are no street lights on Aitutaki at night. I thought of him stumbling home from the village by torchlight along the gravel road, no dogs barking, just the rustle of the surf and the wind through the palm tops.

Cath and the children had slowed down. I noticed especially how Craig had relaxed, having been so tense at school with all the homework. Sitting round the camp-fire, we heard about Craig's and Matthew's friends and schoolteachers in a way we had never done when we lived in Swansea. The boys would not normally have told us which teachers could keep order and which children bullied the others and who got punished for what. Especially since Craig started at senior school we had heard none of this, because although we could go to parents' evenings and find out how well he was doing in History or Maths, like other parents, we only saw the public face of school. Now, ten thousand miles from the spring term, we heard what it was really like. A tapestry of intrigue and politics, it was. And boyfriends and girlfriends. Children of ten going out with each other. Cath and I were careful not to laugh.

Matthew was scornful. He said girls were sissy. Craig did not seem so sure. He asked me whether I had had a girlfriend when I first went to the comprehensive. I hadn't. And I told him how my brother Alun must have been at a great disadvantage in that line because he had to go in on his first day in a pair of my mother's suede boots with chisel toes and Cuban heels. He was a big boy for eleven, and had grown out of everything else.

I had felt lonelier at the primary school with him gone. In summer I bunked off sometimes, to go and play on railway land beside the caravan site. There was a gate into a soggy field surrounded by bushes and when you pushed your way through the greenery to the railway embankment, it was as if nobody had been there for years and years; it was like a secret garden with wild flowers and mysterious bits of broken stone. I thought it had probably been part of a Roman city, with pediments and capitals, and the steep sides of the railway embankment had once been an amphitheatre.

It was very wet and smelled pleasantly earthy and I was sure that if I dug around the stones I would find relics of a bygone civilization. I got a spoon out of the drawer in the caravan and spent days down there, digging. I got some old pennies and bottles and finally, an entire doll's tea service. I had heard about pixies, little Celtic folk who were driven west when the Romans invaded, and I guessed at once who this tea service had belonged to. Reverently I washed it in the sluggish stream and set it out on the grass. It had a sense of mystery that was almost tangible: the tiny rosebuds on the cups and saucers, the perfect handles for the fingertips of fairies. The tea service was unknowable, from a past dimension, just as treasure islands came from a past that yet might survive into my own lifetime.

'D'you think there is treasure on this island, Dad?' Craig asked me one night. The flickering embers of the fire illuminated his elfin face and eyes agog with curiosity under his yellow fringe. I told him a strange fact that had occurred to me a lot lately.

'They say there is treasure on Suwarrow. Joey said that's why Tom Neale spent so much time there, because he was looking for it.'

'Last time we were here, William told us there used to be treasure on Palmerston,' Cath remembered. 'His grandfather said so because when he was a little boy, William Marsters the First used to buy things from traders who came to Palmerston where they lived.' Cath stopped to cough in the smoke from the camp-fire. 'And he paid with little heavy bags of gold coin that he took out of bottles that he kept buried in the ground.'

'How did he get those?'

'Nobody knows. But they were somewhere on Palmerston.'

'Where? When we get there, can we go and look?'

'No, Matthew. All the land's owned, they won't let you dig it up. Anyway it's their great-grandfather's, it's their treasure.'

A wail of disappointment. 'Bet it's not true.'

'We'll never know if it is or not. Nobody's found it yet, and there are still about fifty people living on Palmerston.'

'Will they let us look for it if we ask?'

'We'll have to see when we get there.'

In the next few days mysterious excavations appeared in lonely parts of Maina, but the bone-dry sand was difficult to move with Stacey's tiny plastic bucket and spade, and the craze for treasure-hunting soon faded.

Stacey was not motivated by greed or romance. She stayed near the waterline, happily filling half a coconut with damp sand and tipping it out again.

10

When Kauraka had led me and Cath round Rarotonga in 1989, he took us to meet some friends of his. They were a big family of islanders who had a rambling plot of land away from the coast; one of them had married a Filipino woman who spoke good English. I remembered her saying how the Cook Islanders didn't know how lucky they were, because her own country had been raped by western culture, but here in the Cooks they had a charmed life.

We were standing to one side of her yard when she told me this. There were chickens idling about in the sun, stabbing the ground occasionally for corn, and a dog chained up, and I was trying to ignore what was going on. One of the men was killing a pig. It squealed, the sort of squeal you would make if you were dumb and a big creature seized you with knife upraised. Its tiny feet scratched hopelessly in the dust. Cath went white and turned away towards me.

'You don't like it?' Kauraka said. 'Look. There are chickens on a lot of the islands, you may need to eat them. Watch me.'

He stepped forward, agile despite his weight, and grabbed a chicken. He tucked it under his arm. It clucked and looked surprised. He took its neck in one chubby hand.

'Look.'

His hand was firm as a vice. The neck twisted, hung down limp. The legs kicked a few times.

I wouldn't dream of killing things at home. At home if you buy a chicken in the supermarket you'd never know it had ever breathed or had senses, it's just a cold clammy lump that goes flaky when you cook it.

Yet here, I felt I had a right to take what I wanted and feed my family on it. I could kill fish or chickens and not feel guilty about it. And there were chickens on Maina, at least a hundred of them, so all I had to do was catch one.

I put it off at first. Then I felt somehow that I couldn't really show that I cared for my family unless I did it. I wasn't very confident about catching it and picking it up like Kauraka. The chickens here were wild, they were not used to people and they shied away if you got really close.

I therefore invented a trap made out of the fishing net. Craig and Matthew and I hacked our way through the bushes to a clearing. There we weighted one end of the oblong net with stones and stretched the other ends up over sticks so that the chicken would walk into it, like a goal mouth. We laid a trail of coconut fragments into it. Then we waited. We sat near by and played games with stones.

After a couple of hours a big brown hen came along, bobbing its head down all the time to pick at the bits of coconut. When it was well under we let the net fall. Craig and Matthew knelt on the sides and held them down taut over its feathers. I wanted to get this over with quick. The thing didn't move under the net. I grabbed the neck and twisted hard.

I gave silent thanks because I had done it right first time.

Cath plucked it and boiled it in coconut water, but it tasted rubbery and slimy with a whiff of crab.

The children tried to sleep in the palm hut one night, but within half an hour they were traipsing back to camp, complaining about mosquitoes. I told myself that when we got to Primrose, I would try to construct something stronger.

'I wish Gareth was here, we could do with a handyman,' I said. I had laid a mat of palm fronds well away from the camp, to kneel and meditate on, and now Cath and I were lying on it under the sun that bore down on us like a radiator. While the children rested in the afternoon we had some privacy here on the ocean side of the island.

'He'd need a bloody long extension for his Black & Decker. Anyway, what would he do for wood? I can't see Palmer being too happy about Gareth felling trees all over the island.'

'You wouldn't need to fell trees, you could build a hut out of driftwood. Like William Marsters the First did for his wives. We could have a school hut and a sleeping hut and a love hut.'

'A what hut?'

'A love hut.'

'You're going on again.'

'It's the coconut water, it makes you virile.'

'It's the tent you mean, it makes you frustrated.'

'Help me make a hut, then.'

We made a shelter under the palm trees. I thought

about Kauraka and what he had told me about island marriages before the missionaries came, how a young man and a girl held hands in the bushes, and they were married. It didn't take much longer than that to build a private place out of leaves, climb into it, and twine together in erotic passion, our skin smelling of the salt sea and coconut oil, our nakedness zebra-striped by the sun shining through the palm fronds.

'Eeech!' yelled Cath. 'I'm on a bloody trochus, geroff!'

The five of us evolved a pattern, like an elaborate dance: we spent time together, then drew apart and went our separate ways. In the mornings the children wrote or read or did sums from their schoolbooks in the hut; and as the sun went down they sat around the camp-fire and talked to us. Sometimes in the afternoon my hours of meditation would be interrupted by voices raised in the interior.

'No, you can't, it's Conan the Barbarian.'

'It's not if you let it go over the bridge, it'd be Superman, then it could have rescued Conan, look –'

'Get off, this is the bridge, here, look, he can't fly, Craig, gimme it, gimme it, here, Craig.'

Then there was a slap and a howl and I got up off the mat.

'What's going on in there? What you doing, you two?'

And Craig emerged red in the face.

'Matthew won't let me play with his figure-men.'

'He makes them all stupid, he wants them to fly and they can't, stupid, they can't fly. They're my figure-men and it's my game.'

Matthew puffed out his small bare chest and grabbed at the toy in Craig's hand. I had to hold my sons apart.

'I never quarrelled like this with my brother,' I said.

'Yeah, he never took things,' said Matthew, glaring.

'Yeah, he wasn't a big baby,' said Craig.

Cath came crashing through the bushes. She wore a sarong all the time these days, and flip-flops, and I suddenly saw how different she looked, how much browner and stronger.

'What's going on here? I could hear you two right over the beach there. Craig, give that back to Matthew. Go on, give it. Matthew, you know what I told you. You got to share your toys. Do you understand that, Matthew?'

'Yes,' said Matthew reluctantly.

'You can keep them, I don't want to play now anyway,' said Craig.

'Good.'

Matthew stuck out his tongue at Craig's retreating back. They set off in different directions and we stood and watched them.

'Where's Stacey?'

'She's by the tent, she's built a stage out of stones, the way Craig showed her. You've got to come and see it, she says, that's what I was coming over for.'

We skirted my meditation mat and started walking along the edge of the interior to the camp. A minute or two later we could see Stacey in the distance, squatting happily on the beach near the tent, absorbed in her game.

'It's a good thing we've got a lot of space,' Cath said. 'Wish we had a back garden this size at home.'

'It's really good for self-expression, isn't it?'

'I was thinking more of getting away from each other.'

'No, it's all the space you need, Cath, look, you can do what you want and there's nobody to say you shouldn't –' I was feeling very enthusiastic and as I talked to Cath I leaped over a log without looking. A red hot needle shot into my toe.

My scream brought the children running.

'Yeugh.'

'Oooh, look at that.'

'What is it?' I had sat on the ground with my leg out straight and Cath was looking at my toe.

'You're better off not knowing. Craig, give me your T-shirt. No, keep your leg still, Tony, I'm going to get it out.'

Craig wriggled out of his T-shirt and Cath used it to cover her hand. I felt a slight tug and squealed with pain.

'Stupid thing,' Cath said, peering at my toe. 'Half of it's still in there.'

'Half of what?'

'You landed on this.'

In the folds of the T-shirt was half of a shiny dark insect something like a scorpion, and something like a giant centipede.

'There's a long black bit under the skin.'

I hobbled back to camp supported on Cath's arm, and sat in the dust while the boys found fuel.

'Craig's getting good at climbing up for firelighters, isn't he?' Cath said conversationally, with her arm round my shoulder. Firelighters were the dusty ribbons of copra that hung below the crown of the coconut palm.

I was too far gone in pain to bother with this sort of talk. My toe was slowly inflating, the skin stretching taut around the nail. I lifted the foot gingerly towards my nose and looked again at the long black string beneath the surface.

'Do you think you can get it out, Cath?'

'Stop asking daft questions. Wait and see.'

When the fire was started she boiled a needle from her sewing kit in coconut water. I sat still, feeling my toe throbbing, and coughed slightly as gusts of smoke blew in my direction.

'You sit beside me with the limes, Stacey, there's a good girl. This might hurt, Tony.'

My wife approached the sole of my foot with a large needle. She poked it slowly into my toe and I winced. Craig and Matthew knelt beside me, watching.

'They used to have whisky,' Craig said.

'Who did?'

'In the Wild West. Cowboys when they had to have a foot off.'

'Tony, keep still! Craig, I'll murder you if you say one more thing.'

Matthew was giggling.

'There! All out. Give us some lime juice, Stace.'

Cath dabbed lime juice on to my toe as Teré had told us to if we got bitten. After that I sat and nursed my toe while Cath got some fish from the lagoon and boiled it. Matthew sat beside me and asked questions about amputees, which gave Craig an excuse to do his

182

Long John Silver impression. He caught my eye after a while and stopped.

Sometimes in the afternoons I used to hear Craig entertaining the other two. He was perfecting an American accent that he had learned playing Baby Face. It was ironic that he had this talent for acting. Cath's family said, 'You know where he gets that from, don't you?', and I knew what they were thinking.

But I thought they were wrong.

After my mother got the four of us down to the caravan in Swansea, my father stayed on in the grey house in the dead-end by himself. My mother took him to court for maintenance. He had just been made redundant from the mine and was still in his thirties, so now that he had no ties he could probably have found work. He never did. I could picture him with his smooth tongue and injured smile, persuading the court that he, Welsh miner, salt of the earth, redundant through no fault of his own, had made one mistake: a bad marriage to a flighty woman. And she had left him now, robbing him of his dear children.

It was early in the 1970s and a lot of educated people felt guilty about the miners. The judge must have been stricken by my father's performance because he awarded a penny a week maintenance against him.

As long as his income did not rise before the last of us reached the age of sixteen, ten years off, he would never have to pay any more than that. His income stayed the same. But he got himself an education. He went to evening classes and got O-levels. He had always won cups at eisteddfods as a boy – my grandmother had a cabinet full of them in her parlour, always polished they were – and now he started going in for them again, and winning £50 here and £20 there.

He was a man who would lock a six-year-old child away by itself because it had dropped something. Yet he could make his voice read poetry in great arcs and dips of sound, like the sea tumbling into a cave; he could express tenderness and compassion that would make you weep. He mugged up on Dylan Thomas and joined the industry, going from one Dylan Thomas Society to the next, giving readings.

So when people said, 'You know where he gets it from, don't you,' I knew what they meant. But I have always felt that Craig isn't even related to my father.

When I was about seven, I got a punchbag for Christmas. It was wrapped up, in the lounge, near the tree, but it had my name on and I could guess what it was. My father came in from work and there was a huge row. I was frightened.

I forgot the incident until, years later, my mother explained it. She said my real father was an amateur boxer, and that's why she'd bought me the punchbag. I didn't know what was going on, it was a coded message only my father could read.

I resented that – not being told. Not being told who I was, by my mother; not being given credit for who I had turned out to be, by the school or the council or anybody whose opinion might have made a difference. If you're dumped in a dead-end or a caravan site or on the street, you feel you've been robbed of your identity.

Of the identity you might have had, if things had been different.

I met a cousin of the boxer one night in Swansea, who looked as if he'd seen a ghost – because I look exactly like him. He had died young. He'd died before I knew he existed.

I don't look at all like Alun. But we are united for ever because of our childhood. When I was on Takutea and started writing, everything I put down turned into a diatribe against my father; once I got ten thousand miles away from him I could pour out all the resentment that had been there for years.

I heard on the radio how angry fathers can make their children into brutes. They can make them gentle too; he did that to us. In any case me and Alun always knew that our father and mother were not like other people's.

I used to go home with Gareth to his mam's after school when we were boys. She hadn't got a husband. She was on social security and lived in a tower-block. She was a lovely woman, used to keep the oven door open with the gas blasting to keep us all warm and get us a big mug of hot tea each and talk to us. I used to wish my mam was like that.

Then when I was seventeen I met Cath. She took me to her house and I felt like a person freezing in ice and snow who is brought indoors and cuddled in a warm blanket.

So I knew there was love; but I was still frightened. Our father had brought us up with a worm in the stomach that told you at any moment you might do the wrong thing and not know why, because what the wrong thing was changed from day to day; sometimes it was the way you looked or stood or breathed.

Later on I found the best way to survive at school and at work was to check everything with somebody in authority before you acted. A caretaker's job is not one in which initiative is appreciated. You are a servant of the county council.

I was dependent on County Hall for my job and my house. County Hall took the authority over me that my father had once had. When County Hall told me to go to work, I went; when County Hall said I was free, I knew they must know best. It was as if all the initiative I had suppressed for years had gone into my efforts to get us to the South Seas. I had escaped that father in the valleys; I had grown up; and, more than that, I had left the bleak unforgiving family of my blood and found William Richard and the Marsters clan who smiled a welcome to waifs and strays. I only wished I had met them when I was ten, instead of twenty years later.

'Here comes the King of the Island,' Craig said. He was lying on his stomach with his chin in his hands, gazing at the big cockerel. It was like a chicken in a picture-book, red and orange and yellow with a warty red crest and an imperious demeanour. It took one step towards us, hesitated and stepped back.

'That's Meg there. Look, give us the cabin bread, Matthew, give it here.'

Cath wet a piece of bread in warm coconut water and gently put it in front of Meg, who was a plain brown chicken and wife to the King. She stretched out a fat feathered leg gingerly, then another, then extended her neck down to peck at the bread.

'The lady hens are all dowdy.'

'Except for the little white one, she's a pretty chicken, look, she's all fluffy.'

'The Prince is after her, see.'

'He won't get her, the King won't let him.'

There was a hierarchy, you could see it. None of the chickens came scrabbling around after breakfast unless the King of the Island had been over first to take a look at us. And he never took any food, he considered it beneath him. He let his big sons and his womenfolk grub about for bits of coconut and then he rounded them up and led them all off into the bushes again.

Stacey had given Meg her name. She had six chicks, but she only fed and sheltered five of them. The other one was a weakling; it had something wrong with its eyes. Craig had caught it, held it tenderly and bathed the eyes with Dettol and water, and it wobbled off uncertainly after the others.

A little red chicken led her four young ones, scrappy things still shedding fluff, into the clearing. She looked self-conscious, like a young matron who had dressed up to go to the shops because she knew the whole neighbourhood would be talking. She was about to take a piece of coconut when the Prince took a big step towards her and pecked sharply at her neck. He chased her squawking into the bushes.

'He's always doing that to her.'

'She's his wife, he's jealous.'

'She's the one who wants to be jealous, he's after the

pretty white chicken, look, he's shameless. Bloody polygamist, he is.' Cath directed this at me, laughing.

Craig said, 'See that black one there, with the red crest. He reminds me of somebody.'

'It's the way he walks, see, he stays on the sidelines and he won't look at you. He doesn't want to be with the others.'

'Looks like he's looking for dog-ends in the gutter.'

'He's got a surly look, hasn't he? It's Gordon, that's who he's like. He's a punk. Imagine him with a couple of chains linking his legs up.'

'When can we have some more chicken to eat?' Stacey asked. She had been the only one of us who liked the boiled chicken. 'I want chicken and chips and sauce.'

'You'll be lucky.'

'I don't want to kill another one, Stace,' I said. 'We've got to know them now, it's different.'

'Well, then just a leg,' Stacey persisted. Meg was peaceably pecking at the dust, but, as Stacey marched over, she looked up and squawked and stepped away. 'Look, we could have one leg, she'd still be able to hop.'

'Yeugh.'

The chicken chuck-chucked and made her way indignantly into the undergrowth.

The hens were like characters in a soap opera. We had spent weeks watching how they looked after their babies, tucking them under their wings to sleep at night, and picking up bits of coconut that they disgorged tenderly into the mouths of the littlest ones.

Stacey felt no remorse about hunting dumb creatures and eating them. She particularly enjoyed pulling the fish out of the net by their heads. She sat on the sand, head down in concentration, pony-tail bobbing, her tiny fingers deftly tugging the fish through the drift of white net. Everybody else found this a fiddly job. At first she pulled them through the wrong way, by the tail, but that made the head and spine stay stuck in the net with most of the flesh.

I usually sat near her, taking the fish as she released them, gutting them with my fingers and throwing the waste into the lagoon for the crabs. Sometimes I ate a few fish raw as I worked. They had a pleasant chewy texture and tasted of the sea. With a bit of vinegar and pepper they would have been just like the cockles Cath and me used to get in Swansea market when we were first going out together.

After all these weeks I should have felt settled. Cath was happy and loving, Craig's sunburn had almost healed, Stacey liked the beach and Matthew seemed contented climbing for coconuts and playing ever more heavily plotted games with his figure-men. I meditated every afternoon. Yet I was the one who still fidgeted and talked about the future as a time when everything would miraculously be better than it was now.

It was as if any stress at all, any feeling that some important watershed was approaching, spoiled my peace of mind. I wanted to feel that time had stood still. I couldn't settle down because we were getting nearer now to seeing John James Marsters turn up.

We were on a desert island; yet we were not yet abandoned. It was that feeling of being on our own, of controlling our own destiny, that I was looking for.

I was sitting on the sand near the water's edge, cleaning the net of its last few fish. It was that quiet time in the late afternoon when all the living things except us seemed to be enjoying a siesta. There was no sound at all, only the lapping waters of the lagoon and the soft hiss of the breeze in the palm tops. Everyone except me was in the shade by the tent, helping to build the fire, but from here I could not even hear them talking. The net was white against white sand; I shut my eyes for a second and saw red netting against red sand. The heat bored into my shoulders.

'Hullo?' said a man.

My heart turned over. I jumped to my feet. He was a tall white man in a baseball cap, a T-shirt that said ADIDAS and shorts. He looked frightened when he saw my face. I suppose I looked a bit rough, with my growth of beard and sunburn scabs.

'Hullo, who are you?'

'I come in my boat,' he said in a German accent. 'Why are you here? How do you come here?'

'We live here.'

'There are others?'

'There's my wife and children up there,' I said proudly.

He looked where I pointed. I suppose it looked less than idyllic, the tent with the washing and the water container outside and the suitcases, but I didn't expect him to look quite so shocked.

'Have a bit of fish?' I said cheerfully, and bit into a piece and offered him another. He pulled a face and made a disgusted take-that-away sort of motion with his hand.

'Well, go up and meet the family, why don't you,' I said.

Cath had stood up now and so had all the children. They stood and stared at him. He looked from them to me and back again.

'We've got a fire up there, you can have some fresh cooked fish with us.'

He started walking hesitantly along the beach in the direction of the tent and I rinsed my hands in the lagoon and set off to follow him. As he drew level with the tent he didn't head for it, but started walking faster. Then unexpectedly, he broke into a run. He grabbed his hat from his head and sprinted along the damp sand at the water's edge, his figure growing ever smaller until he disappeared round the far end of the island.

Cath jumped down the bank to meet me on the beach and the children crowded round.

'He looked petrified, what did you say to him, Tony?'

'Nothing.'

'You do look a bit wild, your hair's all up and you've still got those scabs –'

'He said he'd got a boat.'

'I'll go and look,' said Craig, and set off after the man, with Matthew in pursuit.

'They won't catch him now.'

'Should hope not,' said Cath. 'He looked white as a sheet. I think he thought he might be dinner.'

I followed the boys and was in time to see the man clambering aboard a small boat that he had anchored about thirty feet off shore. He disappeared into the cabin and a motor started. Smoothly the vessel wheeled away from us in the direction of One Foot Island. We watched for a while and then walked on, round the island, the way he had first approached us.

'Look, he left prints in the sand, Dad.'

I stopped and looked where Matthew was pointing.

'It's a good thing we saw him.'

I wondered what I would have felt if I hadn't met the man face to face. Frightened maybe. I was feeling a bit vulnerable in any case. I had almost lulled myself into imagining we were living in seclusion, and we were not. We were a hundred and forty miles from Rarotonga, certainly, but our privacy was an illusion. We were still just across the lagoon from a tourist island.

'We need to get to Primrose as soon as we can,' I announced when we were back at camp.

'That's out of our hands, isn't it?' Cath said calmly. 'You're starting again, you are. You will hanker after what you can't have. You want to enjoy the moment.'

'Yes, but how can I when we're not on a desert island at all?' I said. 'First it's the *Daily Mirror*, then it's a German tourist. We'll have *Hello* magazine here next.'

'That'd be good,' said Cath, ladling the fish on to plates. 'Cath Williams talks to our reporter in her hi-tech kitchen with built-in barbecue. And patented waste-disposal unit,' she added, chucking a bit of coco-nut towards a large grey crab that was shifting lazily like a sleeper about to put a toe out of bed.

'Will we have our picture taken again?' Stacey asked.

'Oh, Lord,' I said, feeling a black depression descend.

That night I dreamed that I woke up because somebody was kicking my feet. I unzipped the tent and a microphone was shoved into my face. At the other end of it, grinning maniacally over a false beard, was a man in a trilby hat and a long raincoat.

'Hullo,' I said. Cath's father was sitting behind the man on a sofa, roaring with laughter.

The cockerel began to crow. I opened my eyes wide and stared at the orange canvas glowing with sunshine. We had as usual changed position in the night, all chasing each other round in a kind of circle so that Stacey was now curled into a corner and the rest of us were sprawled in a swastika with our feet kicking uncomfortably together. There was a crab just outside the zipper; that was what I had felt against my feet. I prodded gingerly and the canvas went flaccid again.

I struggled out of the tent, took a deep breath of cool air and slid down the bank to the beach. You had to be careful crossing it this early, because sometimes scores of hermit crabs were still about. They only went into their burrows as it got hotter. I always thought I might get one hanging on to my toe, like on a seaside postcard.

The lagoon water was tepid and refreshing, and I walked out until it was up to my chest. It would have been nice to just belly-flop into it and swim, but I had given up trying a long time ago. Cath tried to teach me at the Leisure when we got back to Swansea last time and I never managed it. You feel a bit of a fool trying to kick your legs out with your wife holding your hands and old-age pensioners gasping past in shoals, doing the breast-stroke. Their skin always looked like crêpe, as if they'd been in there all afternoon. And I had a horror of putting my head under water. Cath said I should be able to do that and I could start in the bath, but I prefer to have a shower at home. Matthew's the same, frightened of the water. Cath tried him with swimming lessons as soon as we got to Maina but he wasn't interested.

Craig lived in the water, like a porpoise. He used to go off and swim on his own and we had to make him promise not to do it without one of us knowing.

A few days after the German tourist came, it was Craig, in the lagoon, who spotted Teré's boat.

We were all pleased to see her. As she hoicked up her skirts and strode through the water on her sturdy brown legs, I waded out to help Junior pull the boat in and suddenly felt just like an islander. I really liked these people; they were so unhurried, so undemanding and kind. They didn't complicate matters with forward planning and worry, they just took life as they found it.

Teré had found a way to help us.

'A boat is in,' she explained, as she sat down and spread a picnic round her. 'Junior, get a coconut. There are some people from Rarotonga who are moving to Manihiki. They're over there now, fixing their engine.' She nodded towards Aitutaki and dug in her bag for tins.

'They're willing to take you to Primrose, if you'd like to go, but they leave at dawn tomorrow.'

'Oh, I don't think so,' Cath said. 'John James Marsters must be coming soon.'

I said, 'I think we should go, Cath. I want to get on to an island where we can settle. There's too much chance of people coming here.'

'Come on, one tourist.'

'And the Harrys.'

'Yes, but they won't be back.'

'Don't be so sure,' said Teré. 'They were telling me they might come back and see you on Christmas Day.'

'What, on Primrose?' I was horrified. 'Oh, no, Teré, tell them we changed our plans. Tell them you don't know where we are.'

She was grinning. 'Even if I tell them the truth they won't be able to get there. You know nobody sails that way except the supply ship from time to time.'

'I was settling in nicely here,' said Cath regretfully.

I looked at her in amazement. The past months held bad memories for me, with my burned flesh, the storm, and visitors popping over without so much as a by-your-leave. I had been sure she must secretly feel the same way. It would be typical of her to cheer me out of my depression even while she shared it. Yet now she was as good as telling me that she wanted to stay on Maina as long as possible.

'John James is sure to come to Aitutaki to look for you,' said Teré. 'I can tell him you've gone on ahead.'

'Let's move on, Cath,' I urged. 'This place is too much like a tourist island.'

'You've got some funny ideas about tourism,' she said sharply.

I fell silent. Cath sighed.

'If he wants to go,' she said to Teré, 'then there's no stopping him. But won't John James mind? He was going to show us round Palmerston. William Richard said your great-grandmother had a hut there, and it's still there, he was going to show us.'

I could see that Teré changed her mind when she heard this.

I watched Junior striding along the beach behind her, with Matthew trotting at his heels. Junior knelt, balanced the coconut he was holding in the sand and took the top off it with one decisive swipe of his machete. I envied Matthew; I wanted to be able to look up to somebody, to trust them and admire them without reserve; but I would never be able to do that again. It was always better to flee from people.

I knew we had to go to Primrose. Now.

'It'll be all right, Cath,' I said. 'We can explain. We can leave a note with Teré.'

'Well, I hope John James is as understanding as you think he is,' said Cath. 'Because if he isn't, we'll still be on Primrose for Craig's twenty-first.'

11

Craig was on the point of tears. He had just seen the littlest chicken, the wobbly one, scrambling weakly after the rest.

'Hey, cheer up, Craig.'

'Please can we take him? Dad, *please*.'

'We can't. I'm sorry.'

I pulled up the pegs that held the guy ropes and watched the tent subside on to the sand. Most of our things looked as battered and damaged as we did after the weeks on Maina. The cassette-recorder hadn't worked since it got wet in the storm, most of the batteries had grown a green mould, and some of the children's schoolbooks weren't worth taking with us.

Craig kicked a tree-trunk and muttered, 'It's not fair on him, Dad.'

He was red in the face with the effort of not crying.

'Life's not fair,' I said sadly. The way you do, you tell your children; but in the end they have to experience it for themselves.

Cath was pregnant with Craig when we had to move the first time. It was early in 1981; before Christmas we had been living in a flat that a friend of ours had off the council, but they found out it wasn't in our name and sent bailiffs round to evict us in the New Year. Cath's parents had no room, they had her brother and sister both still at home, so I had to go to the

Guildhall in Swansea to ask for accommodation and they said they'd put us on the list. It was years long but if you were in a hostel, you were an emergency case and you got put to the top.

They told us to go to Cwm Clwyd, which was well known, the way you knew the name of the football ground or the prison but had probably never been there.

Cath was seven months gone, and we left what we could of our stuff at her mam's and packed the rest into one of our suitcases and a carrier.

'You want to take the television,' her mother said. 'There won't be one up there.' I took her word for it. The portable TV from the flat was quite small and had a carrying strap on the top.

We got a bus out of the city to a place called Gypsy Cross, and started walking. There were no houses there. It was just a crossroads at the top of a lane out in the country, with high hedges at all four corners. We had been told which road to follow, and we set off between the hedgerows.

There was no pavement, and the lane was only wide enough for a cart. It had a steep camber to it, so we walked along the middle, listening for cars coming as dark gathered. The lane wound upwards into woods. We could have been going anywhere. Every time we turned a bend in the road I expected to see this hostel, but all we saw was another stretch of shady lane and another tantalizing bend ahead.

At last the lane flattened out and I saw a building behind trees in the far distance.

'That's not Cwm Clwyd,' said Cath. 'That's the asylum.'

She had been up there to visit one of her mother's friends when she was small. There had been people standing stock-still in the garden, she said, gibbering.

I hoped we wouldn't have to pass it. From here you couldn't see much that might stop the inmates running out in pursuit.

They say a television's portable when they mean it can be carried from room to room. That doesn't make it comfortable to take on a country walk when you've got a suitcase in the other hand. I kept stopping and putting the luggage down. Cath found the carrier was getting heavy.

No cars passed. Our footsteps shuffled along the road. The light was so dim now that we could barely see as far as the next bend. They had told us at the Guildhall that it would be a bit of a walk from the bus stop, but I hadn't expected this. There were no street lamps up here, we could walk right past the hostel in the dark.

'Tsch! Hey, you two!'

I put the television down. Cath stopped.

'Do you want to come to my TEA PARTY? Ha ha ha!'

It was a man's voice, and it came from behind a hedge.

Cath swore. I picked the TV up and we both started walking as fast as we could. Footsteps rustled along with us on the other side of the hedge.

'Have you got the KNIVES? Have you got the KNIVES look? Hurry up, then, hurry up! Ha ha ha!'

We were half running now, but I was struggling with the luggage.

'I think I might leave the telly,' I panted.

Just then we saw a house. We rounded a corner and saw a two-storey cottage right beside the road.

'Thank God for that,' Cath said.

We hobbled up to the door and rapped urgently at the brass knocker.

'Yes? Who is it?'

'We need help,' I said to the door-knocker. 'There's somebody following us.'

The door opened. A short young man, neatly dressed in twill trousers and a pale yellow windcheater with a shirt and tie underneath, looked at me with the television and Cath with her bump behind me.

'Yes?'

'Pardon, but there's an escaped maniac out here, he's following us, we can't shake him off.'

He stared, and suddenly shut the door.

We stood about outside helplessly. After a while we told each other that the crazy person had gone away. I thought, briefly, about walking back down to Gypsy Cross in the dark, about two bus changes and arrival at Cath's mam's . . . carrying all our things into their lounge with the four of them sitting there watching television.

'Come on,' said Cath, picking up her carrier. She tilted her heavy body towards me and kissed my cheek. 'Come on, it can't be far.'

Cwm Clwyd was only another quarter of a mile. We trailed up the drive towards a dim outline of dirty white Nissen huts. A cold-eyed warden in a hut marked RECEPTION took the chit I had been given at the Guildhall. We signed in a big book and he put the time beside our names.

'Right. You sign in here every night, same time.'

He led us in single file along a narrow line of paving slabs that ran past the huts. Every so often, four steps led up to a door. We could hear people inside, shouting at children. We squeezed to one side as a sullen woman passed us, carrying a bucket of anthracite.

The warden went up the last set of steps, opened the door with a jangling set of keys, took one off the ring and handed it down to me.

'There you are. Home Sweet Home. There's a bath in that hut by the trees, get the key from me when you want one,' he said, and came down the steps, leaving us room to go up.

We walked into a square room with a table and two chairs and a two-seater settee. No two of anything were the same; it all looked like furniture from a charity shop, which I suppose it was. There was a double hotplate on top of a low cupboard, and a dead black stove against the back wall, with a scuttle beside it containing a few lumps of fuel. The next room had a double bed with a pink plastic mattress-cover, glistening like wet salmon. There was a cupboard that hung open because the door catch had gone. Inside the cupboard were two blankets.

The bedroom was freezing. I struggled to shut the top flap of the window, but it was jammed open by rust. There were bits of yellowing sellotape all round the wall near it, where previous inmates had tried to block the draught with cardboard.

I sat on the bed with my head in my hands, wondering how long we would have to spend here, and noticing, as I glanced sideways into the front room, that a thin film of dust was blowing under the front door.

There was no alternative. If we stayed at Cath's mam's, me on the floor and Cath on the settee, we would not be classified homeless any more, and would have no chance of housing. I was still temporary as a caretaker, and until I was made permanent I couldn't get a job with a house. We had to stay on the homeless register, we had to get a council house, but how long were we going to have to stay here? The wind blew through the window.

We took the plastic cover off the mattress because it looked worse than the stains underneath. The blankets smelled, but we had to keep warm somehow. We itched a lot overnight, but it was a couple of days before another pregnant girl, one of four or five in the huts, told us there were bed-bugs.

You had to get out of the hostel in daytime. Cath walked down to the bus stop and went to her mother's, and I cycled over to work at Loginfach School.

At about six o'clock we were back in the hostel every night for the warden to check us off in the book that went to the Guildhall. The clerks in Housing had to be assured we were still there, and not skiving in some luxurious refuge like Cath's mam's lounge.

We had been in this place exactly a week when we went up to our front door one night and heard children's voices and a transistor radio. Inside there seemed to be a jumble of people and things and colours. The people turned round, and we all looked at each other. The muddle resolved itself into a huge fat woman and a little man, and two small children. The two-seater settee had gone and been replaced by three narrow camp-beds and a cot. They had a lot of stuff, mostly carrier-bags and laundry-bags with clothes spilling out, and a couple of buckets full of kitchen equipment.

They didn't want to share with us any more than we did with them, but they had been billeted here because the hostel was full up. I got Cath to come outside and led her down the path.

'I've got the school key,' I said. 'Let's do what I said.'

Last night, when neither of us had been able to sleep for the cold, I had suggested we'd be warmer in the school cupboard. Other people in Cwm Clwyd had told us that as long as we were in by six o'clock, the warden didn't check again, so if we got out without him seeing we could stop out overnight. Some people did that, and piled in with relatives rather than suffer this place.

'I can't,' she said. 'Suppose somebody comes? You'd lose your job.'

'Nobody'll come,' I said. 'There's only the Headmaster has got a key, and he's no reason to. Come on, Cath. At least we'll be on our own.'

She looked back at the chalet door. The older one of the two children came out, slammed it shut, and ran down to the lavatory we were going to have to share.

'All right.'

The nights were dark; you could get past the warden at the gate all right, he kept his radio on so he didn't hear you, but on nights when his wife was there to sign you in, it was harder. She was a watchful woman, and Cath was a big shape in the moonlight.

All the same we were very cosy, down at Loginfach.

We slipped into the school after dark and had it all to ourselves. We never put a light on, except in the cupboard, which had no windows. It was lined with deep shelves that held audiovisual equipment and there was a lengthways space between them just big enough for two people to lie down in.

We used to plug one of the school televisions in and huddle under Cath's coat and watch it. We had no blankets but it got quite warm in there, after a while, and I had an alarm clock so that Cath could get out early. All the same I couldn't help lying awake long after the television was off, listening; I was nervous in case kids off the estate broke in, to try and steal the video-recorder.

One morning we overslept and I had to bundle Cath out the back door while I could hear the Headmaster parking up in the playground in front. He was a nice man, Len Evans, but I don't think even he would have stood for people living in his school. He wouldn't have blamed us, he'd have said what a scandal it was that there was no housing.

Cath went into hospital for four days to have Craig, and when she came out we slept in the cupboard with him in a buggy for a week and then moved into Cath's mam's lounge. We still had to traipse up the hill and sign in at Butlin's every night of course.

Whenever you thought life was unfair, you usually came up with a way it could be made fairer, if only some self-satisfied person in authority would take action. But they weren't listening.

Teré and Junior brought us back to Aitutaki for half a

day. It seemed like a bustling metropolis after what we had been used to. Six people wandering along the road looked like a crowd to me now.

Cath said if we were going to Primrose she was going to buy some groceries to take with us, just to break the monotony of fish and coconuts.

'And before you say anything, Tony, I don't care if it is cheating, I'm getting it anyway.'

I didn't mind, I could see that the prospect of a bit more variety might console her for leaving Maina. We all trooped into a low dark shop, like somebody's front room, that smelled of dusty grains and oil, and started ordering big quantities of rice and flour from the young girl behind the counter. She laughed when she found out where we were going, she said she wouldn't go there for any money, what she wanted to do was go to America or New Zealand. She thought we were mad.

So did Junior's young sister. She was the girl who had met us off the boat from Rarotonga; she was still at school. But while we ate our dinner I talked to her. She had such a longing for the bright lights, it was sad. You could see she would leave the island in the end, so many young people do.

'They have television now on Rarotonga,' she said to me, her eyes shining.

I knew: I had seen it at the Edgewater. Five or six hours of broadcasting a night: *Sesame Street*, *Doogie Howser MD* and the news in Maori. There was nothing there that might corrupt anybody. Yet most of it was foreign, and was irrelevant to the island culture that Kauraka had told me about, the stories of maidens and

warriors and magic fish at the bottom of the sea.
These synthetic American pictures invading the minds
of people who had sunshine and sea and all the bounty
of nature – it seemed wrong to me; it seemed designed
to make them discontented.

Junior's little sister wasn't unhappy, but even without the influence of television, she was longing for a
faster life. I said so to Teré's next-door neighbour, a
stern fellow who was a minister. I wished I hadn't,
when he pulled out a pen and a notebook and started
jotting down what I was saying.

With religious people here, you never knew if you
were dealing with a strict observer or a fanatic. There
was a woman on Rarotonga who marched around with
a cross, saying she was Jesus Christ. They had all
kinds in the Cook Islands: Jehovah's Witnesses who
said television was an abomination; Baha'i followers;
Seventh Day Adventists; even a few Roman Catholics,
like Tukaki Williams, who lived on Rarotonga and had
got his surname from a British ancestor who deserted
his island wife and sailed off home years ago. Tukaki
Williams had made a lot of money out of pearl farms
on Manihiki, and because he was rich I think people
wondered if his outlandish religion had anything to do
with it.

'Do you remember Kauraka's tree?' I asked Cath
suddenly, as we walked back to Teré's house after we
had ordered our supplies.

'Don't remind me,' she said. 'I never embarrassed
myself so much in my life.'

Kauraka wasn't one for anything to do with Christi-
anity. When he was born they buried the placenta in

the ground, in the old island style, and planted a tree on top. On our first visit he had taken us to see the tree, which was supposed to progress in a way representative of Kauraka's personality. We stared. It was a lovely tree, graceful and twisted.

'This tree represents my life.'

Cath squinted up at it. 'All that tree says about you is that you're crooked,' she said, and realizing how rude she had been she blushed red to the roots of her hair. Kauraka was shaking with laughter; his shoulders were heaving up and down.

The missionaries had never stamped out the old ways completely. *Bligh and the Bounty* had dried out since the storm and I still had it with me. It was written years before the missionaries came and was not disapproving, the way they had been. Captain Bligh came to the South Seas on a business trip, to collect plants, and the islanders' religious preferences were no business of his. All he wanted to do was trade and be friends. He called Aitutaki 'Wytootackee', and the *Bounty* anchored off the coast about two weeks before the mutiny. The islanders rowed out and exchanged gifts.

It was funny how things stuck in your mind and didn't make sense until years later. Alun and me used to go into Swansea Public Library to keep warm after school; you had to sit quiet, under the high ceilings at the worn mahogany tables, or the librarians threw you out; and *Bligh and the Bounty* was my favourite then. I never expected to see Wytootackee in real life.

'What you want to get these for?'

Aitutaki was a speck in the distance. We were on deck, with the ship's engine throbbing ceaselessly as it transported us to Primrose in the first light of dawn, and I was poking about in our cardboard boxes full of supplies.

'What?'

'All these packets of soup.'

'They're very tasty, they are. You just get us where we're going, Tony, leave the cooking to me.'

I was in no position to get us anywhere, I could no more have navigated this boat than I could have jumped off the deck and flown, but I knew what she meant. I looked at the list the shop girl had tucked into the side of one of the boxes:

20 lb rice
2 pks salt
15 pks soup
8 cans corned beef
10 lb flour
cabin bread
curry powder
12 toilet rolls
3 soaps
cooking oil
3 bottles shampoo
5 gallons water
2 plastic tubs

It didn't seem a lot to keep five people for the next four or five months. Or did it? I didn't know how much rice we would eat at a sitting, I had no idea. I have never cooked, I never needed to; if Cath got ill at home I could always get something from the chippy or take the children down to her mam's. Once when she was pregnant with Craig and in that first flat, before we were made homeless, she was ill in bed and I did my best. I brought her a glass of milk and she took a swallow. Then she choked.

'What was that?' she gasped. I was thumping her on the back. I explained I'd put a raw egg in it, it was good for you. Her face went green and she said she'd never let me in the kitchen again.

Palmer had looked worried when I told him how bad we had been on Maina with the sunburn. He was a caring person, like William and Teré; he always wanted to help; he saw us as babies really, which we were in these circumstances. He said we ought to have a canoe to get us off Primrose and over to Palmerston in case of emergencies, and he had a spare one he would lend us. He found a white boat, seven or eight feet long, with frets at right angles and a fish-shaped float, like a modern miniature of the big old hollowed-out log in William's outhouse. It was very kind of him and I accepted it. It was loaded on board the ship, but I was a bit nervous of getting into it because I've never paddled one. Also, he lent us a trowel. We should have something for digging, he said.

We were in an oily, battered green and white boat crewed and occupied by a family of seven: three young-ish men, an elderly couple who occupied the cabins below deck, and two boys about Craig's age. The man who seemed to be in charge was about forty, and he said his name was Ricky. He was stocky and smiling, with a head of tightly curled black hair, and spoke English well. The older couple were his parents and the two boys, who also spoke English, were his children. They were off with Craig, Matthew and Stacey most of the day, exploring the boat.

I knelt and meditated, and Cath sunbathed, and from time to time the children whooped down the steps from the bridge or charged past in the middle of a chasing game. It was a choppy journey, and when the others had something to eat I couldn't face it.

The sea stretched to the horizon on all sides, the only shade was alongside the rowing boat they kept slung on deck, and the noise of the engine made it difficult to speak without shouting. The day wore on.

'Only one hour more,' Ricky said, coming to join me as I gazed out to sea. It must be nearly evening now, and I was far away in my mind. I said, 'I wanted to go to Suwarrow at first. I've always wanted to go there.'

'To be caretaker?'

'Pardon?'

I was baffled; I hadn't told him I was a caretaker.

'You could take your family. People live there to report the pearl smugglers.'

'What, on Suwarrow?'

'Yes. They have radio contact with Manihiki.'

I was dazed. Cath came up behind us.

'Cath! Did you hear that? There's a job I could do on Suwarrow.'

Ricky explained about the pearl smugglers.

'But the lagoon is very wide and deep,' he said doubtfully. 'You would have to be a good sailor to cross to the *motus* if you thought something was wrong. For instance, you might see a yacht coming in.'

'He can't even swim,' said Cath fondly, clinging to my arm. 'But you can practise paddling Palmer's canoe now, can't you, Tony?'

I thought whether or not I could swim was an irrelevance. People didn't think you could live on any desert island if you couldn't swim, and I'd managed, so I thought there would be no greater problem with Suwarrow than with anywhere else.

I was quickly distracted from these thoughts.

'Look.' Ricky pointed. 'There's your new home.'

Far away on the horizon was a tiny dark stain. We churned across the ocean towards it.

This was to be what I had been aiming for all this time: a *motu* of our own. We would be left truly alone, outside the rest of humanity at last.

I watched avidly through every second of our approach. Primrose looked a lot like Maina, although perhaps the interior was closer to sea-level and less dense. Above the white beach, scrubby grass started, and low trees; and, rising from the middle, some very tall coconut palms that soared erect above the surrounding foliage like tall young warriors in feathered headgear. I wondered if they were the last of the ones planted by William Marsters's men in the 1860s.

Ricky waved an arm to the right and said, 'See over there? There's Bird Island.' I could see a blur of green.

'William Richard said Tom's and Cook's were bigger than Primrose, they'd have more food on them,' Cath said. 'Where are they?'

I didn't like the sound of this.

'They're over there.' Ricky pointed to the left but we could see nothing. 'And Palmerston itself is on the other side of Primrose, across the lagoon.'

'John James is expecting us to be on Primrose,' I reminded Cath, hoping that she wasn't thinking of changing her mind at this stage and getting Ricky to drop us off somewhere different. 'We should go where he said we could.'

She just smiled, but I knew I had forestalled her. When you have been living with somebody for a very long time you usually think you can read their mind, and although she had not said so, I felt Cath was hostile to Primrose. She had not really wanted to leave Maina. Maina was the island we shared; we were going to Primrose because I, alone, wanted to.

'I won't be able to go in close, it isn't deep enough for the boat,' said Ricky, starting back up the rusty steps to the bridge to join his brothers. 'I must get on before dark.'

Craig, Matthew and Stacey were watching from further along the deck. I asked Cath quietly, 'You happy?'

''Course I am.'

'How do you think we'll get ashore?'

'I hope he's going to take us. I don't fancy my chances in that canoe.'

Ricky came clattering down the steps. 'We'll lower the boat and I'll take Cath and your supplies on to the island,' he said, to my relief. 'You can take the children in your canoe.'

I had to confess that if I paddled the canoe now, it

would be my first try; and of me and the children, only Craig could swim. Ricky didn't make fun of me, but simply made new arrangements. The canoe was lowered into the water and Ricky's two boys jumped in, followed by Craig and Matthew and Stacey. The two island children started paddling at once, skilfully and evenly, in unison.

We followed in the rowing boat with Ricky and one of his brothers. I felt ashamed that I did not know how to row. Even nowadays, islanders learn these skills at a young age. I tried to make some comparison with what living in Swansea teaches you: how to use a remote control, perhaps, or how to get a credit card. Passive pleasures. About as useful here as knowing how to climb for coconuts in West Cross.

The children got to shore before we did. Craig and the two island boys seemed to be discussing something. They were still talking, a hundred yards away along the beach, when we jumped out of the boat and started loading our packages on to the sand. When we were finished Ricky clasped our hands in goodbye, then handed out a huge bunch of bananas, a present from his family. He called his children. He had explained that they wouldn't be able to stay, as he needed to get well clear of the lagoon before nightfall.

His children ran up, shouting in Maori; the older one was proudly clutching something in one hand as he climbed into the rowing boat.

'I gave him my Bank-raid watch,' Craig explained. He had a computer game on a wristwatch.

'I'd forgotten you had that till I saw you playing with it on the boat.'

'Yeah. Well, he liked it.'

We waved until they were out of sight, the pearl fishermen bravely sailing across hundreds of miles of empty water as generations had done before them – while their children were engrossed in a Japanese computer game.

Then we left our stuff piled on the beach against the up-turned canoe and set out to look for a place to pitch the tent. Cath followed slowly behind us.

12

'We made it, Cath! This is it! We've got our own island!'

I stretched my arms in the air and ran. I raced Craig and Matthew a little way along the shore and the sweet warmth caught in my throat like champagne.

Primrose was not as round as Maina; it was more like a triangle, and we had landed at the point that stuck out into the ocean. The beach was tiny white shells and bits of bone and plant and sea creature dried to brittle sticks, a gritty plain dimpled by the dips and bumps that crabs lived under. Cath caught up with me when I stopped to stare into the lagoon. There were as many shoals of little fish here as there were on Maina.

I hoisted Stacey on to my shoulders for a piggy-back, and Craig and Matthew cut away near a bend in the coast and ran through the undergrowth to the other side before us. When we got there they were kicking water at each other. The joy of having my family here, on this beautiful beach with all we could ever want in the world, took my breath away; I put Stacey down and just stood and stared at the tall trees against the sky.

'You can see Palmerston over there, look,' Cath said.

It was true; from this side of the island you could see a low dark streak across the lagoon. William had told us Palmerston was barely raised from the waves, no more than six feet above sea-level at any point.

'It looks close, doesn't it?' It was the single unexpected reminder of the rest of the world, and I was almost disappointed to see it. I had said the wrong thing.

'Close? You call that close? With a motorboat or a helicopter it would be. It might as well be the moon as far as we're concerned.'

'What's the matter, Cath?'

'Nothing's the matter! I just think we ought to take this seriously, that's all.' I was dumbfounded. Cath had never been as irritable as this on Maina. 'Craig! Matthew! Stop messing about, you two.'

She walked quickly ahead of me along the beach with her arms folded in front of her, then stopped and turned to me. 'Well, you've got us here. Is this it, then?'

'Pardon?'

'Is this all there is? We just exist? Here with the crabs? We don't do anything to change anything? Is this how we're going to spend the rest of our lives?'

'What's got into you, Cath?'

She sat heavily on the sand, hugging her knees and staring towards Palmerston.

'It's just – oh, never mind.' She scrambled to her feet.

We trod along the sand together in silence. The children seemed suddenly subdued. I didn't know what to say. She gets moods; you're better off ignoring them. It was like that now, because as we walked she seemed to lose her anger.

'There's a good place to put the tent,' she said at last, nodding towards a clearing between the trees.

She had picked a narrow strip of sand from which our tent would face Palmerston. I would rather it didn't, but since Palmerston was four miles off and she might get into a funny mood again I preferred not to make an issue of it.

We spent our first evening carrying our possessions from the sea side to the lagoon side of the island, and setting up home.

Weeks passed. Cath felt trapped, she said.

Now it was my turn to say it was all in the mind. She said we were helpless, and I said we were independent. She said what if something happened to one of us and I said if you worried, you'd never do anything. In the end she seemed to settle, or at least she stopped complaining.

As for me, I had found paradise at last. Even the tent seemed cooler, with a breeze going in because of the way we had set it up. We had months of freedom to look forward to. No visitors, no stress; I could do anything I wanted to.

Getting this far had been like fighting through a thicket of demands and counter-demands. I was used to asking permission for things, all my working life I had had to say please and beg pardon, even for an hour off to go to the dentist's, and just to get here we had had to present ourselves to be assessed and judged at every turn – and now, none of it mattered. I could try and build, or fish, or paddle a canoe, and if I failed, nobody was going to judge me or refuse me anything.

We collected palm fronds and laid them criss-cross

to make my meditation mat on the ocean side of the island, where I knelt with my back straight and my eyes shut in the *seiza* position every afternoon. Cath tried to meditate beside me, but giggled and gave up and left. Craig and Stacey were not interested but Matthew came and knelt on the mat.

'Show me the abominable breathing, Dad.'

I tried to teach him abdominal breathing. He was silent, breathing deeply and trying to centre his consciousness.

The mat wasn't woven, it was just a thick carpet of branches laid on top of each other. Sometimes when Matthew had had enough and gone off to play, I meditated for so many hours that I simply keeled over sideways and lay on it with my eyes shut. It was cool and it slid like silk against the skin.

'Craig's winning! Craig, come on, Craig!' Stacey's shrieks woke me up.

'Come on, Matthew!'

The others were having a crab race on the beach fifty yards away. I sat up.

'Have you got one for me?'

'Nah, you get your own crab, Tony,' Cath called. 'We're into the semi-finals now.'

We started again. You found a champion crab, what Craig called a good scuttler, and carried him dangling between your finger and thumb and put him in the ring with the rest, in a heap. Then you tried to entice him out with a bit of coconut on a string. The one that got out first was the winner. Usually it was one that just shuffled out in its own sweet time, ignoring the coconut; crabs are stupid creatures.

There was a lot of shouting with this game. It was funny how you felt you should tell the children to calm down and then you realized it didn't matter, there was nobody else to hear them for miles. Exhilarating it was; we all yelled and clapped and roared for our own crabs, and when the races were over we felt energized and would get up and chase each other off to look for coconuts or firewood or to pull some fish in.

Cath and I sneaked away for an hour on our own together sometimes. I wanted her more than ever here.

'You're really happy, aren't you?' she said softly. She was tickling my eyelids with the tip of a palm frond.

'Mm,' I said.

'It makes you sexier.'

'That's the coconuts.'

'You what?'

'It's the coconut water. I reckon I could market it. All these men who have problems – I'd have a slogan. Three coconuts a day – the well-balanced way.'

'Oh, yeah?'

'Keeps you satisfied, though, doesn't it, Cath?'

I thought about Julie sometimes. She was a girl who came and sat down with me in the coffee shop at Paddington Station that night when I was sixteen, and Gareth had got the train back to Swansea. Resilient, she was; she had had problems but she fought back. She had a pretty face and dark hair coiled up, and a slim figure. She had a child that was with her mother in Liverpool, and she had to send money home, so she made a living in London the best she could.

She took me back to a room she had and we stayed

together. She was twenty. She went out earning and most nights she brought a meal home from the take-away. She was always happy at night and her mouth tasted of Bacardi and cigarettes. I didn't need to do anything, I was just there, in the room in the Cromwell Road, a place for her to come back to. You could see the tops of red double-deckers going past under the windows. Julie looked after me.

One day she said she was going back to her baby, she couldn't take it with these men any more. So we packed our things and kissed goodbye at the bus stop. I got a train to Swansea. On the way home I thought how much courage she had, to earn her living like that. It was odd how she thought of her customers as brutes, yet she was so tender with me.

'I don't want you going out in it on your own, you can't swim.'

Cath stood on the beach, looking doubtfully at the canoe. It lay up-ended where the children had dumped it when we came, on the ocean side of the island, and none of us had moved it since. We pulled it over, the right way up, and dragged it down to the water's edge, and that was when Cath started getting nervous.

'I'll go, Mam. I can swim.'

'No, you're not going out on your own, Craig.'

'I'll go too,' said Matthew.

'No. This is hopeless,' said Cath. 'I'll go with you, Tony.'

'What, and leave the children on their own?'

'What if it leaks? I can save you, but I can't save Matthew and Stacey as well.'

'All right, then. Just a little way out.'

We dragged the canoe out a little way and climbed in with difficulty; the thing seemed to want to capsize before you were in it. I sat on one of the board seats with Cath in front of me.

'Ooh – I've dropped the paddle.'

I reached into the water and watched it sink out of sight too fast for me to catch it. As one end touched the bottom, the other languidly rose into my searching hand, and I grasped it.

Craig and Matthew, up to their waists in the water, gave us a shove. On the beach Stacey began to cry. I took no notice and tried to remember how Ricky's sons had done this.

'You go that side, then I go this side.'

'No, we both do it together, we're turning round, look.'

'Ow, look what you're doing with that thing, Cath.'

'Sorry. It's all right, Stacey' – this was at the top of her voice, across the few yards of lagoon to the beach. 'Craig, tell her we're all right.'

We did our best. The paddles were very much heavier, when they were wet, than you'd think, and we did not seem to be making much progress. Stacey was keeping up a long wail that was very irritating.

Cath had clearly told me, on the boat on the way from Aitutaki, that she knew how to row, although she might be a bit rusty at it. I felt cheated and spoke sharply to her straining back. 'You done this before, have you, Cath?'

'Only in the park. Like I said.'

'You never said it was in the park. What, the boating lake?'

'Mm. We shouldn't have started this side, we could drift out.'

On this ocean side there were sharks. Not far out either.

'When?'

'When did I go on the boating lake? Um – when I was about fourteen. There were three of us, we went round and round.'

I was quiet for a minute. It was hard work. Cath said, 'We should try and keep in close. The sharks can smell sweat.'

'We've got a lot of choice, haven't we? Look, if we both go together and I count, look start now, you got your paddle that side? Right you are. *One*, two, *One* two.'

'Oh, bloody hell.'

We were both silent for a while, and there was a lot of splashing but we did move along the beach a few yards. The canoe didn't leak. That was heartening. The sun was hot on my skin and I was enjoying myself. We kept going, in the direction of the camp, and, as we mastered the paddles, we slowly steered back to the beach, near to our tent. It was a moment of triumph when Craig pulled us to shore and I climbed back into the water. Matthew was waiting on the beach.

'Hey, Dad, can we go to Palmerston?'

'What for?'

Matthew opened his mouth and shut it again. He looked discouraged and I realized I had said something wrong.

'We can go anywhere now that we've got the canoe,' I said.

'When can we go, then, Dad?'

'But we don't need to go anywhere. It's just in case we did. If we wanted to get supplies.'

'You don't want to go anywhere, do you, Matthew?' Cath asked. He shook his head. She was standing at the water's edge, tying her sarong more tightly round herself. 'You don't want to think just because we paddled a hundred yards we can really go anywhere like your dad said.'

'We could try, though,' I said. 'Look at William Marsters, eight hundred miles – we could go to Suwarrow, Cath.'

'Tscha,' she said. 'Take no notice of him, Matthew. He's trying to wind me up.'

There was no cockerel here to wake us up in the morning, and fewer birds. The ground and the low tree-trunks were constantly twitching and moving with creeping things, lizards and beetles as well as crabs. Most of the reptiles were small, no longer than your hand, and quite tame, although one day at breakfast the others fell silent while I was talking and I saw they were watching a big yellow lizard. It was as if you'd parked County Hall in the middle of our estate of little houses; it was out of scale. Beside the other lizards, it looked like a crocodile. Its wrinkles looked dry and sandy. Its eyes slowly opened, and you didn't see its head move, but suddenly its teeth had snapped shut on one of the small lizards. A greenish tail and splayed legs were flailing hopelessly between its tight jaws. We watched horrified as the beast seemed to digest the front end of its prey before the rest shifted a little way further in.

'That's horrible,' I said. Without meaning to I found I was clutching my own throat. 'It makes me claustrophobic.'

'It's natural, though. You're always going on about things being natural, Tony.'

'So what's that got to do with it?'

'I'm just pointing out that because all this is natural it isn't necessarily harmless.'

'All what?'

'You know what. This island. Primrose. This place we're trapped in along with a load of man-eating lizards.'

I dumped my plastic plate on to the sand. The children looked at each other and got up, and went down to the beach to play with stones.

'Give it a rest, Cath. You've been moody for long enough. Months. Ever since we left Maina.'

'I'm not moody! It's being stuck here, Tony.'

'We were stuck in Swansea.'

'We were never stuck at home, there are trains –'

'I feel trapped in Swansea,' I said. 'You know I do. Everybody putting on pressure, judging what you do.'

'But that's not consistent,' she said. 'You're trapped here. You can't get away, there's no freedom in being here.'

'No, you're wrong. We've got the sky and the sea, we've got each other's company when we need it and there's plenty of space to walk off in when we don't. That's the whole point. We've got lots of room, we're not shut in.'

She started stacking the breakfast things together, ready to wash up in the lagoon.

'Yes, I can see you feel like that, Tony. But I don't. It's not like it was before.'

'It's better.'

'No, it bloody isn't! There was somebody coming out eventually, before. But there isn't now. There's nobody coming. When we want to go home how are we going to know when six months are up? How are we going to get to Palmerston?'

'We've got the canoe.'

'Oh, yeah. Bloody useful that'll be. And then when we get there we could wait months for a boat to Rarotonga, what are we going to live on?'

'Same as we do here, fish and coconuts.'

'It's not the same over there, where there's people. They *own* the coconuts.'

I couldn't say anything. I felt angry and disappointed. I felt like somebody who has been saving up to buy his wife the diamond ring she always wanted, only to find when he brings it home that she was hankering after a fur coat. Why hadn't she said so before?

'Tony.' Cath took my hand. 'I'm sorry. I just find it hard to get used to, that's all. We're really cut off here.'

'I thought you wanted to be on a desert island as much as I did.'

'I did, I did. It's just that this is – more of a desert island than I was looking for, that's all. I'll be fine.' She kissed me and said again that she was sorry, but by now I was worried for her. They are all rooted in Swansea, Cath's family. Her gran used to live in a long terrace up a hill in Dyfatti, all the neighbours were

225

cousins and everybody married friends. When her gran was seventy the council moved her out to a tower-block two miles away and demolished the houses; and she died of it, she was so unhappy. We cuddled and I asked Cath, 'Will you? Will you be all right?'

'I've got to be, haven't I?'

Sometimes while I meditated I thought about the hut we would have. At first I pictured it like a little Swiss chalet, made of coconut logs. Then I thought that was silly, I could never chop down that many trees, I would have to do it with driftwood. As it happened I hadn't seen very much driftwood, at any rate not planks, just twisted twigs that we used for burning. I went back in my mind to my first plan, coconut logs. Cath came along in the late afternoon and asked me what I was thinking about.

'I could build a proper hut with two rooms.'

'We haven't even got the new school hut started yet.'

'No, but eventually. We've got plenty of time.'

'It's hard work, weaving those palms, Tony, it'd take months and I still can't do it like the islanders.'

'No, with wood. I could build a hut with wood.'

'What, with that machete? Every time you husk a coconut you nearly take your fingers off.'

'I could get a saw from Palmerston.'

'If we could row to Palmerston.'

'We could rig up a hose out of the rain barrels and have running water.'

'Tt. You stay here long enough, you'll invent the wheel, you will.'

I ignored her.

She said, 'There is one thing you could do for me, Tony.'

'What?'

'You know by the camp where I keep the cooking things.'

'Yeah.'

'There's beetles crawling out of the sand. I need a shelf. I've seen a good place. Will you try and put a shelf on the coconut tree?'

I said I would. Without a hammer and nails, it would be difficult, of course. I would have to think of a way; but then it takes a person with vision to start things off. I looked forward to my retreat to the meditation mat every afternoon; it was an opportunity to kneel alone with my eyes shut and plan the shelf, and the way our accommodation would look.

The two rain barrels we had brought collected only a saucerful of fresh water for the first month or so. Then one night I woke up and heard rain, not the lashing kind the cyclone had brought on Maina, but a steady downpour. I groped for the torch and switched it on. Cath was stirring in her sleep.

'I'm going out, you coming?'

She whispered agreement and we tried to sneak out quietly but Stacey woke up and wanted to come too, and then the boys, so we all crawled out, sleepily kicking saucepans and tripping over suitcases. I stroked the torch's beam back and forth along the beach, but all the crabs had disappeared. The rain splashed cool on to our faces and shoulders, and we licked it from our lips. Craig made a war-whoop like a

Red Indian brave and started hopping around in a circle and we all took up his lead, leaping and hollering in a rain dance. We were exhilarated by the soft sand, the warm air and the cool water like a blessing.

Cath and me joined in the children's games. We marked out two kinds of hopscotch on the sand with shells, and hopped heavily along the grid on demand. I got quite good at London London, the game where one person stands with his back to the others and turns round suddenly, hoping that he can catch one of them moving towards him. It was an eerie game to play on Primrose, because you have to listen for every rustle, every bare footfall on sand, and you become aware of the silence. You hear the just perceptible breathing of the sea and the palms in the heat of the day.

Cath and I had agreed not to mention birthdays. We no longer had any idea what month we were in, and in any case, birthdays would remind the children of presents, parties, and their nan and grandad, Cath's mam and dad. There would be tears. It followed that we were drawn to birthdays, the way a woman who's slimming is drawn to a shop window full of cream cakes. I found it impossible to tell a story at the campfire without recalling some event that had happened on somebody's birthday. Cath would have a tune stick in her mind all morning while she was tidying the camp or washing clothes in the lagoon, and she started humming 'Happy Birthday' over and over again. In the end one afternoon when she flopped down beside me on the meditation mat I said, 'Let's have a birthday party.'

228

'Good idea,' said Cath. 'I'll send out the invitations, you blow up the balloons. Whose birthday is it?'

'It's for all the children.'

Once we had worked out what to do it was easy. We would have a treasure-hunt, with clues that they all had to follow as a team. All the children were such different ages that we couldn't have winners and losers. Instead we made a trail of clues from the tent. At each point Cath made a number out of shells on the sand.

It took the children most of the morning to follow the whole thing, and when they got to the last number, at the meditation mat, there was real treasure buried for them. There were Cook Islands coins, exotic and foreign as doubloons and pieces of eight. Some were round with wavy edges and engraved with the figure of Tangaroa, and others were triangular, like a secret sign to show the shape of Primrose Island itself.

We sang 'Happy Birthday' to them when they found the treasure, and played games; it was a party.

We were resigned to sleeping in the tent by now, but we started building a school hut anyway and told the children they could sleep in it if they wanted. We were slow. Even with the Cook Islands summer nearly over, the temperatures were quite warm, and I felt like sitting down all the time. It took the five of us three afternoons just to get a space clear of crabs and stones and *pod*, and sweep it with palm fronds. We had started laying the mat for the floor, to get the shape right, when I realized what had been bothering me all day. I had a raging sore throat.

Once I started thinking about it I felt worse. Cath put the back of her hand to my forehead.

'You've got a temperature.'

Eating seemed like a horrible idea. I just lay around after I'd got the fish for tea, and drank from coconuts. Talking was getting difficult, so while the others had dinner I dozed under a coconut palm. Their voices murmured across the sand, uninterrupted by birdsong or any breeze.

'What d'you miss, Mam?' I heard Craig ask.

'Breakfast at Tesco's,' Cath said. 'When you're at school on Fridays and we do the big shopping, we can get breakfast in the café after, for £1.59. You can get coffee and toast with it for £2.50. What d'you miss?'

'Um – chips I think. And David. I wish David was here.' David was Craig's best friend at school.

'I want Nan and Granddad here.'

'Ah, don't get sad, Matthew,' Cath said.

I looked up and she was cuddling Stacey and Matthew both at once.

'I'm bored, Mam.' This was Matthew.

Lying there with my throat throbbing I felt depressed. It seemed none of them was as happy as I was. When they were with me they all said what a good time they were having, but secretly they were all homesick in different ways. I began to feel suspicious. I fell asleep and dreamed that Cath approached me. She bent over; I could see where the skin on her chest stopped being brown and went white. Her hair flopped across her face.

'He's asleep.'

'Shall we go, then?'

'Yes, you put the things in the canoe. I'll stay with him in case he wakes up. If he says anything we're just off for a ride round the island, see?'

I opened my eyes. Cath was alone, sitting on the ground with her back to me, looking out to sea. We could both see the children in the canoe, bobbing far away on the blue water, and as I watched she waved to them, got to her feet and ran down the sand. She started to swim out, with strong strokes that quickly took her out of reach. They were all leaving me and I couldn't shout after them. My voice had gone.

'Tony!'

She was leaning over me again. It was too dark to see her face.

'Come on, Tony, you've got to get in the tent, you'll get eaten alive out here.'

'I'm coming with you.'

'That's right, come on. Come on, the children are ready for bed.'

When I stumbled into the tent the children were all there, asleep. I knew I had been dreaming but I had a horrible fearful feeling that wouldn't go away, as if I had lifted a stone and found something primeval and unpleasant underneath.

I lay near the camp for the next two days, feeling nauseous and taking very little part in what was going on. Cath looked down my throat and said it looked yellow.

The others seemed to be getting on all right without me, and that made me depressed. The children played London London on the sand every afternoon as usual. But I sensed an impatience in Cath. She was doing everything, even husking the coconuts with the machete. I was afraid that she might have an accident.

'Cath,' I croaked. I wanted her to promise to stay with me whatever happened.

'What is it, love? D'you want another drink?'

'No.'

It wasn't the right time for what I had wanted to say.

She came and sat down beside me and put her hand on my forehead again.

'You'll survive. What's the matter?'

'I had a funny dream,' I began.

'Did you? So did I, it was really weird, Tony, I flew over the clouds back to our mam's and in through the door and I was in her kitchen.'

I looked at her expectantly. My throat made it hard to talk.

'I was standing there, opening all her cupboards and I turned round and I said, "You haven't got much in, have you?" And she said, "We're going down our Stephen's. Since you been gone, we've been eating out a lot."'

'Strange. Then what?'

'Then I got back here through the clouds.'

I lay with my eyes shut. She added thoughtfully, 'That's the trouble with dreams.'

'What?'

'They never go anywhere. They sort of tail off. It's like this dream of yours. All this is your dream, this paradise island. What are we going to do, Tony? I mean what happens when it's time to go home? What are we going to do when we get back? You'll never settle in Swansea again.'

This was a bucket of cold water. I hated this kind of thinking, this fretting your way through life. I groaned. She was silent for a while, then she gave an impatient little sigh, got up and went off to get some fish in.

A few days passed and I was all right. But the food seemed not to taste of anything. I was sick of fish. Cath made a flour-and-water batter and fried it sometimes, but it still didn't appeal. She was putting the pan on to boil some coconut water one night when I started complaining about the food, and she said, 'I've got that soup.'

'Yah, I don't like packet soup. I don't know what you got that for.'

She just coughed. It was hard to see her through the smoke. I told her, 'You want to move over this side, you always sit over there and the wind takes the smoke right in your face.'

She dumped the pan heavily on the fire and scrambled to her feet.

'Oh, bloody hell. I've done my best for a bloody week while you lay there like a dead prawn. You bloody cook, then, if you're so clever.'

I got up and walked off. I wasn't going to cook; I never had. I knew she wouldn't leave the pan with the children on their own, so I made myself scarce and went without supper.

I sat on the meditation mat as the sun went down. There was a breeze now, and I wished I was wearing a T-shirt. When the very last flush of orange still showed in the sky, Cath came round the island and walked up to me. I had my eyes shut.

'You coming back?'

'I'm meditating.'

'What for?'

'You know what for. To centre myself.'

'Tsch.'

'You don't understand.'

'How should I understand? You never argue, you just walk off and sulk.'

I didn't say anything.

'If all this finding yourself did any good you'd answer back, wouldn't you? You'd have centred yourself enough to say what you want, Tony. Instead of just going like a lump of wood.'

She started to cry. I tried to comfort her, but I had no idea what she was talking about.

'It was only the food, Cath.'

'It wasn't about the food, that had nothing to bloody do with it!'

I was mystified. I thought we had quarrelled about the packet soup. But she kept snivelling so I thought it best to keep quiet.

The next night, when we were both on our knees by the fire, I refused fish again.

'Don't be offended, I'm just not hungry.'

The night's catch was bubbling in coconut water over a fresh fire. She slammed the pan deep into the burning twigs and coconut husks, scrambled to her feet and stomped off, her face scarlet. I looked after her in amazement.

'I've had enough. I've had it up to here. Paradise! Bloody fool's paradise. I'm off.'

The children looked dismayed. Cath strode out of sight towards where we had left the canoe. On the fire, the pan had tipped a bit, and flames were licking up it.

She would get over this in a minute. I would leave the cooking for her to do when she got back. I was no good at it, I had never tried so I would probably make a mess of it, and it was better if I left it to her. Matthew ambled off after Cath. Craig and Stacey got up and went too.

All the same I had better take the pan off; the water was seething. I grabbed the pan-handle and let go, cursing. Cath always picked it up with a cloth wrapped round her hand. She should at least have left the cloth somewhere where I could see it. I felt resentment building in me. It was really stupid and inconsiderate of her to have gone off leaving a pan of boiling fish on the stove. I was staring round, looking for the cloth, when Matthew came back.

'Dad.'

'Where's your mam keep that cloth she uses?'

'Dunno. She's gone off, Dad.'

'I know. Tell her to get back here, I can't get the pan off the fire.'

'She's gone in the canoe.' He looked as if he wanted to cry.

'Well, I'll come and look in a minute but I can't leave the fire.'

Craig ran up to me. 'Mam's gone off in the canoe.'

'Where's that cloth for taking the pan off the fire with?'

'What?'

'The handle's too hot.'

Craig ran and got a T-shirt from the line and folded it. He gave it to me and I lifted the scalding pot on to the ground beside the fire.

'All right, I'll come and get her.'

I followed them along the beach.

'She's gone!'

235

There was no sign of Cath or the canoe. She must have paddled around to the ocean side of the island. Matthew screamed, 'Dad! Dad! That's her! Look! Save her, Dad! She's waving in the water!'

Something whitish was sticking up from the waves. I began to wade out and he ran with me, but not far, because he was starting to sob and he couldn't swim. Nor could I. We had stopped and I was wondering if the white smudge was a bit of coral or a hand, when Craig yelled, 'There she is!'

Cath was a few hundred yards out in the lagoon, in the opposite direction from where we were looking. She was paddling the canoe round and round so that it progressed like a leaf drifting lazily down a river. As I watched, she got up off the board she was sitting on, hauled the paddle in, leaned forward gingerly and crawled along on her knees to one of the pointed ends. There she sat, higher up, though the distant end of the boat rose alarmingly out of the water. Then she seemed to take both paddles and try to row. The canoe obstinately turned round, so she was facing the shore. She propelled it rapidly for a few yards towards Palmerston, swerved, stopped, and made a kind of three-point turn in the water before apparently heading sideways towards the ocean.

It was interesting, watching her. She was making a lot of noise and shouting at the canoe and then she stood up and banged herself down crossly on the board in the middle of the boat again. After about ten minutes she seemed to be drawing closer to the shore so I went out to meet her. I was nearly up to my neck in the water before I could grab the side of the canoe, and then I couldn't pull it to shore without drowning myself. I clung on while she kept paddling a few more yards, into shallower water. She jumped over the far side and swam off in her sarong. My side shot up spitefully, just missing my chin. Craig helped me pull the canoe back on to the beach.

Matthew ran along to where Cath was striding out of the water. She tightened her sarong, wrung out her dripping hair and took Matthew by the hand. She walked back to where I stood with Craig and looked at me boldly. There was water running down her face and shoulders and legs.

'Just testing.'

She marched back to the camp-fire. We all followed. The fish pan sat on the sand with a sprinkling of small dead flies floating in the water.

The next day when we were alone I asked her, 'Are you sorry you came?'

'No. I'm just frightened, that's all.'

'What of? You were never frightened before.'

'But I keep telling you, we were never like this before. There were people coming. If we can't paddle that thing to Palmerston at the end of six months, nobody's ever going to come and fetch us. Don't you see?'

'Six months. You keep going on about time. Time is irrelevant here, Cath.'

'But it's passing.'

'Not here it isn't.'

'Of course it bloody is. You saw Ron Powell and his wife, they've been on the islands since the first time we came, d'you think time hasn't passed for them?'

Ron was a man we had met on Rarotonga the first time; a dignified man who loved the islands and entertained everybody with stories. But now, four years later, he had had a stroke and could hardly speak and his wife had Alzheimer's. The change in both of them filled me with dismay and pity. Rationally, I could see Cath's point, but if I thought rationally I wouldn't be here.

'Anyway, I'll run out of tablets for my epilepsy before Christmas.'

It was the only way we had of counting the days: Cath remembering to take her tablets every morning. Sometimes she forgot. Nothing much happened, except that her eyes went funny and she seemed a bit vacant for five minutes. I said, 'Would you feel happier if you practised in the canoe a bit?'

'I suppose so.'

We lay side by side with our eyes shut. After a while I felt for her hand and held it. She said, 'You know Ruby?'

Didn't I. Ruby had been Cath's best friend when we met. When Cath started going with me, Ruby was dating a market stallholder who had a Jaguar. She would come round Cath's mam's and show off.

'Lovely dress, Ruby.'

'It is, isn't it? Must have cost £800, this, I saw one like it in Cardiff, he just came over with it in a box. All packed nice in tissue, it was. And this ring, see? Garnets and diamonds.'

She had once said she didn't know how Cath could go out with a boy on a pushbike, disgusting it was. She used to call in at Plasmarl in the Jaguar and gloat

over the peeling walls and ask if I still got a lot of
punctures. We hadn't seen her for a long time.

'She hasn't been round for years,' I said to Cath as
she lay beside me, with the palms waving above and
the hot sun toasting our toes.

'She came over before Christmas.'

'You never said.'

'You were over Alun's. I said after, but you didn't
take any notice. Her voice has gone posh. She came in
the kitchen when I was making the coffee and she
turned round and said, "You don't really want to go,
do you?" But I did.'

She tucked her head comfily into the curve of my
arm. She went on, 'I did, I thought she was stupid to
say that. But I didn't really know how cut off we
would be.'

I said, 'We could get some different food from Palmerston.'

She made no reply; she seemed to fall asleep.

I tried to understand the way Cath felt, but something
in me was optimistic; I thought we might stay on
Primrose for years. Time seemed to stand still here; it
was a delicious existence and I planned to ask John
James if we could stay longer.

I thought about my past and was convinced that it
had always been my destiny to join the list of British
men who loved these islands. I read and reread the
passage about the mutiny in Captain Bligh's book. In
1789, two weeks after the *Bounty* left Aitutaki, Fletcher
Christian and his friends cast Bligh adrift with some of
the crew. When Bligh tried to work out why the

mutiny had happened, he concluded that it was because so many of the men had fallen in love with women on Tahiti and had been welcomed by the islanders:

> Under these, and many other attendant circumstances, equally desirable, it is now perhaps not so much to be wondered at ... that a set of sailors, most of them void of connections, should be led away; especially when, in addition to such powerful inducements, they imagined it in their power to fix themselves in the midst of plenty, on one of the finest islands in the world, where they need not labour, and where the allurements of dissipation are beyond anything that can be conceived.

This passage supported the arguments I had started to have in my own mind. I was 'without connections'. I had everything to live for here, and nothing in Swansea. Here was family, warmth, freedom; everything that Wales had failed to offer me. It was natural to want to bring up my children here.

'We could live here. Set up a business. Be partners with William Richard.'

'What business?'

'I dunno yet. Or there's that job on Suwarrow.'

'You have to be able to get from one island to another, Tony. Suwarrow's lots of little islands, you know what Ricky said. There's sharks in the lagoon at Suwarrow. It's deep, like the open sea.'

Four years ago, when I first wanted to go to the South Seas, she said I had to get it out of my system, but now that it was even more in my system, and part of my future, she seemed worried.

'You're always discouraging my ideas these days, Cath.'

'Sorry. I don't mean to. It just sounds like a dream to me.'

'Getting here in the first place sounded like a dream.'

'Yes.'

'We could sell the house. That money would go a long way on Rarotonga, Cath.'

She stayed quiet and I knew she was hoping I would get over it.

'I feel sick,' Matthew said.

The children had been sleeping in the school hut at night. The mosquitoes seemed to bother them less than before. The hut was nearly finished; it had a slippery floor of palm fronds, walls made of more palm fronds stuck upright in the sand, and a leafy roof that was supported on tent twine that I had interlaced between two posts and two trees. It was much bigger than the shelter we had made on Maina and was shady even at the hottest part of the day.

Matthew was lying on a beach towel on the floor. Usually he was up by now, splashing in the lagoon or climbing for coconuts with Craig. I felt his forehead the way I had seen Cath do it, but it meant nothing. It was hot, but my own forehead was hot.

'Maybe you've got what I had,' I said.

'Your throat was all horrible inside,' he said.

'How do you know?'

'Mam told us. She said it was all yellow and yuk.'

'You coming over for breakfast?'

'Nah. Will you read to me, Dad?'

'After breakfast.'

The camp-fire smoke smelled pungently of coconut husks and fibre. This morning we needed more of the long blackish dangly tongues of copra that we called firelighters, and Craig was already high up in one of the palms, throwing down strips from the very top, while Stacey ran around underneath picking them up. I bent to take a bundle off her and walked along the beach to Cath at the camp.

'Matthew's got tonsillitis or something.'

Cath went to see him and announced that it wasn't tonsillitis. I took the top off a coconut for him on the sandy ground outside the hut. As I crashed the machete down, I suddenly felt fearful. What if I hurt myself? Chopped my fingers off? I missed, of course, but the machete was rusty so you had to be decisive with it and I bungled it. Cath had to do it.

'What's the matter with you?' Expertly she sliced the top off the coconut and widened the hole to make it easy to drink from.

'I don't know. It's Matthew being sick. Have you given him anything?'

'Lime juice and paracetamol. He's got a temperature.'

Matthew didn't want the coconut. His figure-men lay neglected on the shady silken floor in a yellow carrier-bag marked SWEETMAN'S BAKERY, SWANSEA.

We took turns to stay in the hut with him most of the day, reading aloud. Later I walked along the beach with Stacey on my shoulders, thinking how much less separated by age we were here. We shared all our experiences. At home Craig and Matthew were at different schools and one seemed much older than the other, but that distinction had vanished here.

When Stacey and I got back from our circuit of the island, Cath was kneeling at the water's edge in her sarong, her hair wet and sticky with shampoo, sluicing it off with rainwater from the plastic barrels.

'How is he, Cath?'

'He's worse. You know how you were, not eating and not talking. He'll get over it.'

Matthew was curled up in a corner of the palm frond hut when I went to see him. He looked ill.

'I'm sorry, Dad,' he said. I was mystified.

'Sorry? What for?'

'I can't help get the coconuts down.'

'Don't you worry about that.'

We were all a team here, and he felt it. He'd never have apologized at home. He'd have just lain there taking our care as a right, which it would have been, but that remark of his showed me how grown-up and responsible he'd got. Just from helping collect food every day.

I sat with him. I remembered being ill in the caravan when our mam had gone away for a few days, and I knew it was important to have somebody there.

'Tony, he's delirious.'

Cath was shaking my shoulder. I sat up and saw that she was shining the torch on to the canvas above us, and Craig's anxious little face was peering into the tent from the zipper end.

'He keeps talking and crying in his sleep, Dad.'

I followed them out of the tent. The torchbeam danced in front; there was hardly any moon tonight, just a vast twinkling sky like diamonds suspended in black jelly. The sea scraped at the beach and big grey coconut crabs heaved themselves towards it.

Cath was in the hut first. I followed, and looked down at her as she knelt over the little white form on the ground.

'He's got a hell of a temperature.'

'Did you give him some paracetamol?'

'Yes. Oh, God, what'll we do?'

Her eye-sockets looked white in the light that reflected up into her face. Matthew was covered in perspiration and seemed to be unconscious. Then he opened his eyes and gave me a blank look. The only time I had seen a look like that before was on Cath, when she was having one of her attacks.

She stood up and walked outside with me, under the stars.

'He'll be all right,' I said.

'What if he isn't? How long are we going to wait to find out?' Cath said to me. I knew what was coming. 'We shouldn't be here, Tony.'

'What d'you want to do?'

'We'll have to get him to Palmerston.'

'There isn't a doctor there.'

'No, but there's other people. We can't take the responsibility for him when he's like this, Tony. He's got to have help.'

It was the middle of the night. I thought of the canoe, which I had never tried to paddle by myself, and the four miles of deep lagoon between us and Palmerston.

'Will you take him, Cath?'

'What, and leave you here with Craig and Stacey? You'd never manage. What if anything went wrong with us two?'

'I'll go, then.'

'No. You can't swim.'

'I'll be all right.'

'We'll all have to go. As soon as it's light.'

I kept quiet. I hoped that Matthew would get better by morning so there would be no need for any of us to go. But the hours passed and he seemed to get hotter and more disturbed. Cath went back to the tent to pack.

It was dawn. The canoe was up-ended on the sand. I tugged it the right way up, with Craig's help. It looked tiny.

'It'll never take all of us.'

Cath didn't answer. She was tucking the children's little rucksacks under the seats.

'Will you get the suitcases?'

'We don't need all that. Matthew'll be all right, Cath, we'll get him to a doctor and –'

'What doctor? You know there probably isn't one. There's only fifty people on the whole island. If he needs a doctor we're going to have to radio to Aitutaki. God knows what'll happen. What if we have to pay for a doctor to come over to Palmerston? Have you thought of that, Tony?'

'Calm down, Cath.'

She stood up, pushing hair out of her eyes. In this half-light she looked grey and tired.

'Craig. Go back to Stacey and Matthew, we'll be over in a minute.'

Our son ran off.

'I'm trying to tell you, Tony. We need to get off this island and stay off till he gets better.'

'Yes, but what makes you think it'll take so long? We could be back by this afternoon.'

She bent to pick up a rucksack and muttered something I didn't catch. Then she said to me, slowly, 'Well, that's all right then. Maybe we will be. But if we're not we'll need our things. All right?'

I could see it was futile to argue. I went to get the suitcases. She had put some clothes into both cases and fastened them. They looked prepared, tidy, waiting for a human decision, like obedient puppies. I carried them down the beach.

Cath bumped and shoved the luggage along the bottom of the canoe with a couple of spaces for feet, but I couldn't see how we were going to get in.

'It's easy, Tony. Stacey tucks her feet under that end and we'll put Matthew lying down at the other end. Then Craig can sit back to back with Stacey, with his feet under my seat.'

'You've got it all worked out.'

'No, I haven't. It's obvious.'

I fell silent.

'You're so bloody suspicious, you are. You think I arranged for Matthew to be sick on purpose?'

'No. But now that he is – oh, never mind.'

'What d'you expect? D'you want to sit here and watch him go delirious?'

She was right. I wasn't being fair. But my feelings

were a maelstrom. I wanted to get Matthew to a doctor, but I wanted to stay on Primrose. She said, 'You want me to leave you here, is that it? Take the children and leave you?'

'No. Of course not.'

'Because if you do I will.'

'Don't be stupid. I'm coming. I'll go and get him.'

I was terrified. We had struggled at first, the canoe turning gently in every direction other than where we wanted to go. At last Cath and me seemed to be paddling in unison in the direction of Palmerston, but now that we were out on the lagoon, the canoe was much too low in the water. The surface lay around us like a mirror, reflecting an indigo sky turning to blue as the sun came up. There was very little wind this morning, and no birdsong; as we dipped the paddles rhythmically they made a soft plashing sound. Matthew was in front of Cath.

'How is he?'

'He's gone to sleep. He's still very hot.'

She was silent for a moment. 'Tony.'

'Yes?'

'We'll go back, won't we?'

To the side and behind me, the lagoon side of Primrose had so receded that we could see all of it stretched out: the place where, behind the trees, the school hut was; my morning route to the meditation mat; our camp, the saucepans and plastic rainwater-containers still beside the fire. The crabs would be investigating the tent now.

Craig's knees were poking into my back and mine

into Cath's back. She went on, slowly paddling as she talked, and it was hard to hear her sometimes because she was talking to the air in front and I was behind her.

'I know you don't think I want to stay. But that's not it. I do. I want to live there with you. But I can't stand the worry. You know Harry Arnold said about a radio? Couldn't we take one for times like this?'

I sighed. 'I suppose so.' To my mind, radio contact was like contact with the twentieth century.

We kept paddling. Sometimes we seemed to zigzag. We were getting further away from Primrose, but no closer to Palmerston.

'My arms are tired, Tony. Let's stop a minute.'

We stopped and drifted. I could feel Craig's forehead resting against my back. The sun was up now.

'Mammy, I'm squashed.' Stacey was struggling past Craig. I turned and caught her little hand. She was on the very edge, close to the water, and if she fell in, she couldn't swim a stroke.

'Stacey, keep still. Keep still!'

Craig lifted his head. 'I'm squashed as well. I'll get out and swim, shall I?'

There seemed no other way; we were cramped, and our legs were aching; we needed the space he left. He slipped over the side and swam on his back with his eyes shut.

'Hold on to the float, you can steer us.'

We began to paddle again. He kicked out and kept up the momentum of the boat.

Matthew dozed uncomfortably, curled up in front of Cath. We had nothing to protect him from the sun.

'It isn't getting any nearer.'

'It must be.'

'Looks just the same to me.'

Palmerston was the same thick grey stroke along the horizon that it had been before. Perhaps a bit greener; I could not be sure. The lagoon stretched around us and Primrose was now distant, its few tall palms nodding over the interior and the beach.

If you can't swim and are bobbing about in deep water in a boat about eight feet long with your entire family, you start to imagine difficulties. I was frightened that we might sail past Palmerston altogether, paddle hard but be carried on through the lagoon and out into the open sea.

Craig kept kicking out as he held on to the float. I could hardly bear to watch. I was terrified he might lose hold, swallow water and we would not be able to circle round and get him. Cath and I had mastered paddling so long as we were going in a straight line, but we relied on Craig to steer us.

Hours passed. The sun was hot. William had told us it was a four-mile journey from Primrose to Palmerston, but that was meaningless. In the canoe it was like an endurance test.

All the same, Palmerston was definitely close now. We could see how exactly it looked like Primrose, only bigger; the same flatness, the same tall palms sticking up like spikes. Ahead of us and to the left was a smattering of white dots that signified habitation, a few bungalows and a jetty with what looked like a small ship tied up. All these things stuck up above the skyline, because Palmerston was not much higher than a sandbank.

'Is that a big boat?'

Craig was clinging to the float and barely kicking at all. He was tired, and a drag on our progress but he was alert. Cath said, 'What d'you think, Tony?'

It was hard to tell, but it must be a sea-going boat as big as the one that had brought us to Primrose if we could see it from this far out. If it was still in port when we got to the little town we might have a lifeline to Aitutaki or Manihiki, where there would be a doctor.

Matthew was drowsy, pale and thirsty. We kept giving him drinks from the coconuts we had wedged between the rucksacks.

We had made it. A hundred yards out, and figures stood on the beach, one of them apart from the rest. Silently they waited for us. Big people, men and women in plain brown and red clothes: staring.

We paddled in close. The boat was smaller than any of the inter-island boats we had been on and when we passed it we could see nobody on board.

Craig got his feet on to the sand and pulled us to shore. We climbed out stiffly. I carried Matthew. The figures were silent and drew back.

'We need a doctor,' Cath said. One of the women pointed to the boat. They muttered in Maori among themselves.

The solitary figure was John James Marsters. Carrying Matthew slumped in my arms, I approached him.

That was when I knew that we had offended him.

He was courteous. He told us there was no doctor but the boat we could see was going to be in Rarotonga by tomorrow evening. We should take it, he said, and we would be able to return in a supply ship later this week.

But I knew from his body language, his slight coolness, that we had done something for which he would not easily forgive us. It was as if, by taking up his invitation to Primrose before he arrived to escort us there, we had camped in his back garden without calling at the house first. If we had come as he planned, the islanders would have wanted to welcome us, arrange a feast perhaps and show us the hut where the third great-grandmother had lived. Islanders usually beam and welcome you literally with open arms. This subdued politeness indicated that we had offended them deeply.

Cath was standing in the water, talking to a man on the boat's deck. She waded back to tell me that she could get a passage for all of us.

Slowly, and in silence, we took our rucksacks and suitcases from the canoe, and carried them through the water. The crew reached down and heaved them on to the boat.

There seemed nothing much to say. The few people on shore drifted away. We clambered aboard. John James followed us on to the deck. He was polite, and told us to come back to Palmerston at the end of the week with Tom Marsters. But I could see how Cath was relaxing despite herself, stretching herself like a cat in anticipation of going back to civilization, and I wondered whether she would really want to return so soon.

Matthew was sitting on the bare deck, looking over the side of the boat. I remembered how he had started to get bored recently and talk about his nan. When he got sick, I thought back to this boredom of his and put it down to his illness.

If they got to Rarotonga and didn't want to come back here, I would have broken faith.

All those months ago, in the Parliament House in Rarotonga, I had told John James that I would be different; I would not be one of the foreigners who live on a desert island and take the best of the experience and hurry away.

Now John James shook my hand and climbed down from the boat and all I could do was stand dumbstruck. We would cast off in an hour, the captain had said.

Should I stay? Leave the rest of them to go to Rarotonga and paddle back to Primrose?

I looked at Matthew. He was conscious again, it was true, but he did look ill. I would never forgive myself if there was anything seriously wrong with him . . . I had to go. I told myself we would be back almost at once.

All the same, I had a terrible fear that no one but me would want to return.

We did not go back to Primrose.

Our tent is still there, and most of our things.

On Rarotonga, Matthew received medical attention and was well within days.

We picked up letters which had lain unanswered for months. There were people in Balham and Braintree and Bootle who had read about us in the *Daily Mirror*. They wanted to come and join us. 'Four pairs of hands are better than two,' said one man, who wanted to bring his girlfriend, and claimed to have spent six months alone on an islet in Micronesia.

The last letter I opened was from the solicitor in Cardiff. The council had paid some money into court. I could either accept it or turn it down and insist that the case should continue. She wanted a decision; I didn't know what to do. I asked Cath.

'You can't decide from over here,' she said. 'We should get back home.'

We took a vote on it. I lost.

We were back at Gatwick before the end of the week. There were football hooligans at Paddington. The noise and dirt were terrible. At Cardiff I bought a paper. Nothing had changed ... A man, I read, had fallen and impaled himself on an eight-foot pole. When rescuers arrived he was still conscious. 'Will you call my wife,' he murmured, 'and tell her I'm fine. Tell her to remember to record *Brookside*.' To me that said everything about how you could waste your life in Britain.

We are returning to the Cook Islands in the summer of 1994 and hope to emigrate permanently as soon as possible.

SIGNET

Published or forthcoming

THE VANISHING

Tim Krabbé

Obsession is the ultimate weapon ...

On a driving holiday in France a young couple stop at a motorway service station. As the man fills their car up with petrol, his lover, Saskia, disappears. Who is her abductor? And where has she gone?

Eight years later – still haunted by the nightmare of the vanishing – the man receives tantalizing clues about Saskia's fate. Someone knows what happened that day: *now they are ready to use their power.*

Is Saskia alive or dead? To find out he must submit to the evil will of his tormentor – the only one who can end the agony of not knowing ...

SIGNET

Published or forthcoming

THE DEVIL TO PAY

Mark Daniel

Riding his father's horse in the Cheltenham Gold Cup should have been the highlight of Nick Storr's career as a jockey. Instead he was relegated to the sidelines on the morning of the race and the hotly fancied favourite failed to win by a nose. What went wrong?

When the racing authorities fail to take any action, Nick decides to do some investigating of his own, beginning with the father he'd worshipped all his life. Now it seems the respectable trainer is up to his neck in a very dangerous game. Too late, Nick stumbles on the devastating truth ...

If you start out as a gambler, you always pay to win. No matter whose life is at stake ...

SIGNET

Published or forthcoming

THE SAS AT WAR
1941–1945
Anthony Kemp

The SAS are the most feared and respected élite fighting force in the modern military world. But what about the 'Originals', the valiant soldiers who turned an outlaw unit into one of the most effective strike forces of the Second World War?

First activated in 1941, Lieutenant David Stirling's 'L' detachment, Special Air Service, were the forerunners of today's SAS – taking part in more than 100 daring secret operations before being temporarily disbanded in 1945.

Until now, their story has never been definitively told.

Compiled with the help of previously unpublished military records and the accounts of the surviving Originals, *The SAS at War* reveals the truth about the early days of the Special Air Service, and shows how this unique fighting force overcame the disapproval of the military authorities to win glory and fame in North Africa, Italy and north-west Europe.

SIGNET

Published or forthcoming

Dead Reckoning

Sam Llewellyn

Charlie Agutter's livelihood depends on his revolutionary new rudder. So do the lives of the ocean racers who use it, and too many of them are dead. Including Charlie's brother. If there's nothing wrong with Charlie's design, someone must have designs on Charlie. And the only way to find out is to win the Captain's Cup, or the saboteur will leave him dead in the water . . .

'A drum-tight plot . . . formidable . . . Llewellyn does for boats what Dick Francis does for horses' – *Literary Review*

'Slick, readable, racy and punchy – an outstanding thriller' – *Sunday Express*

SIGNET

Published or forthcoming

THE FEATHER MEN

Ranulph Fiennes

In the years between 1977 and 1990, a group of hired assassins known as the Clinic tracked down and killed four British soldiers, one at a time. Two of the victims were ex-SAS. All four had fought in the Arabian desert.

The Feather Men were recruited to hunt the Clinic. Without their intervention more soldiers would have died. At the end of their operation they asked Ranulph Fiennes, one of the world's best-known explorers and himself a former SAS officer, to tell their extraordinary story . . .

The Feather Men is the first account of a secret group with SAS connections – still unacknowledged by the Establishment – who set out to achieve their own form of justice. And how, in September 1990, they finally got their result . . .

SIGNET

Published or forthcoming

THE GREY HORSE

Richard Burridge

The true story of Desert Orchid

Richard Burridge was an impoverished writer when he bought a half-share in a promising grey known only as Fred in 1982. Yet for the next nine years he watched in amazement and admiration as the horse they renamed Desert Orchid galloped and jumped his way into racing legend . . .

After an early fall at Kempton Park, Desert Orchid went on to become a champion hurdler and a record four-time winner of the National Hunt Horse of the Year Award. Right up until his retirement in 1991, 'Dessie' captured the hearts of the British public with his jumping, his enthusiasm and his courage.

The story of Desert Orchid is a fairy tale come true. *The Grey Horse* is that story. The full dramatic account of the life and times of Britain's favourite racehorse, as told by one of the people who knew and loved him best.